BOOKS BY SHANNON K. BUTCHER
(NOW ALSO WRITING AS ANNA ARGENT)

THE SENTINEL WARS
Burning Alive
Finding the Lost
Running Scared
The Collector (in On the Hunt)
Living Nightmare
Blood Hunt
Bound by Vengeance
Dying Wish
Falling Blind
Willing Sacrifice
Binding Ties
Shadow of Truth (in The Secret She Keeps)
Blood Bond

THE EDGE
Living on the Edge
Razor's Edge
Edge of sanity
Edge of Betrayal
Rough Edges

DELTA FORCE TRILOGY
No Regrets
No Control
No Escape

Saving Daylight

by

Shannon K. Butcher

Saving Daylight
The Sentinel Wars, Book Eleven
By: Shannon K. Butcher
Published by Silver Linings Media, LLC
Copyright © 2019 by Silver Linings Media, LLC
ISBN: 978-1-945292-25-5

Cover art: Dar Albert
Editing: Julie Finley

CHAPTER ONE

Texas, January 23

Morgan Valens had been assigned countless dangerous missions over the centuries, but this one was definitely going to end up in the top five, assuming it didn't simply kill him.

Serena Brinn was as deadly as she was beautiful. More than one Theronai warrior had returned home bearing the scars she'd given them as a warning not to seek her out again. Now it was Morgan's turn to convince the stunning, violent woman to come home, where she belonged—where her people could protect her.

Not that she seemed to need much help in the protection department.

After two weeks of searching, Morgan had finally found her a few miles outside Austin, Texas, out in the middle of nowhere, standing at the maw of a giant system of caves known to house Synestryn demons. Her sword danced through the night air, the blade wet with dark red blood, and glinting, tiny reflections of the stars overhead.

Her lean body was completely encased in dark leather that clung to her like a second skin. Her long, flaming red hair had been cut off at her shoulders recently. She wore no coat to protect her from the cold—or to give the demons she fought something to grab hold of. She was a streamlined, practical killing machine, all wrapped up in a sleek, curvy package.

Morgan stood mesmerized for a moment. He was so stunned to see a woman fight like her—using a sword rather than magic—that even the crushing pain he carried around seemed distant and muted.

He was completely entranced by the efficient beauty of her movements. Each one seemed choreographed, as if it had been designed to accompany an epic, sweeping soundtrack. The slash of her sword was too fast to see, leaving behind only arcs of silver starlight. While she lacked the strength he had, every blow was both powerful and clean, severing limbs or heads with each strike.

A pile of demon bodies lay all around as proof of her skill.

From his position a dozen yards away, he could see her breath glisten in the cold night air, mingling with that of the monsters she fought. Their animal stench was on the breeze, as well as the scent of wood smoke from a nearby farmhouse.

Several of the demons were still alive—all eerily humanoid—wielding rough, rusty metal blades that were more clubs than swords. Unlike their furry cousins Morgan was used to fighting, these Synestryn were nearly hairless, with only small patches of fur dotting their shiny, grayish skin. They were almost seven feet tall, dwarfing Serena, with huge hands, thick limbs, and heads too wide for their bodies.

Round, black eyes bulged from their sockets, gleaming with a feral light. Each beast that fell by her sword served only to embolden those left standing—more of her blood left for them.

Only a second or two had passed, but it was too long to stand by and let her defend herself. As skilled as she was, a lucky blow could kill her just as dead.

Morgan shook off his surprise at finding her in the midst of battle, drew his sword and charged.

Before he'd taken three steps toward her, he realized his two-second pause had been too long. He was going to be one second too late to save her.

Her sword arm extended for a heavy thrust into the guts of one demon, but in doing so, she'd left herself exposed. The creature on her right flank saw the opening and moved fast to take advantage of it.

The heavy, rusty weapon it wielded swooped down hard. There was no way she could escape the blow—nowhere she could move to save her sword arm from amputation. Once she was weaponless and bleeding, it wouldn't take long for the Synestryn to finish her off.

And if these creatures didn't, the scent of her blood would draw more from miles around.

Morgan sprinted as he pulled in a breath, but before he could shout a warning, her body blurred, moving faster than he could believe.

The air around them shimmered, and a strange, dull pop emanated from the center of combat. As that odd vibration washed over him in his mad dash toward combat, he felt a moment of vertigo and a rolling swell of nausea.

Before the sensation vanished a split second later, Serena and her overextended arm were gone, leaving the demon swinging through nothing but air.

With nothing to slow the momentum of the blow, the creature pitched forward in a clumsy fall.

Serena stepped out from behind the demon and lopped off its head before it could recover its balance. Then she shifted her stance to avoid a heavy, lumbering blow from another one of the enemy coming from her left.

"Behind you!" Morgan shouted as he ran toward her.

Her gaze flicked to him, and then she spun around and launched into a series of slashes that were an impossibly fast blur of motion.

"They're mine!" she shouted as he raced through the surrounding brush. Before the words even reached his ears, another of those bulbous heads was severed by her wicked blade. "Stand down!"

If she thought he was going to simply watch her fight and wait for one of those creatures to get in a killing blow, she was even more off her rocker than reported.

Rather than waste oxygen arguing with her, Morgan

entered the fray, lifted his blade and went to work.

The first demon was so intent on reaching Serena's tender flesh that it didn't even see Morgan coming. He sliced it in half with one powerful blow through its midsection that both killed fast and left a hell of a mess in its wake.

The smell of rotting flesh and filth hit him hard. He had to hold his breath to keep the fetid stench from reaching inside of him. Better to fight without air than to breathe in something so noxious.

He shifted his stance to engage one of the two demons left standing, and hoped for a nice, brisk breeze to carry away the smell of death.

Even with all the gruesome trappings, Morgan loved combat. His muscles sang with familiar exertion. His pain eased enough that he could see through his entire field of vision. His mind cleared of all but the singular focus of taking out the enemy. He'd never fought shoulder-to-shoulder with a woman armed with a sword before, but there was a first time for everything—even for a man who had lived as long as he had.

He was used to fighting beside his brothers, guarding each other's flanks, and tracking minute shifts of movement that signaled their intent. But fighting with Serena was different.

Female Theronai were rare. They were to be protected at all costs, not cast into the front lines of combat—at least not without the ability to sling around some serious magical firepower.

She wasn't bound to a male. She didn't have access to the stores of energy they carried. As deadly as she might be, she had no business facing so many enemies in melee.

He was so worried for her safety that his blows were off by a fraction of a second.

That fraction cost him.

Rather than lopping off the sword arm of the nearest demon, Morgan's blade lodged in the thing's hip bone and stuck fast.

The monster screamed in rage. Its eyes bulged in pain as

it flailed around, twisting him off balance. He tried to rip his sword free, but there wasn't time. The demon's weapon was speeding toward his head, and there was no way Morgan could stop it in time.

A split second later, he saw a flashing arch of light, and the hand holding the crude sword spun off to his left in a twirling arc. The rusty blade hit his shoulder, but there was no force behind the blow anymore.

Morgan shoved his boot against the demon's thigh and jerked his sword free. Before he was done, there was another arcing gleam of light, and the creature's head flew off in the same direction as its hand.

The giant demon body toppled over next to the rest of its kind, spewing a pulsing ribbon of oily, dark red blood from its neck.

The night fell quiet, except for the sound of dripping blood.

Now that the demons were dispatched, Serena whirled on him, glaring. "I told you they were mine. You had no right to interfere."

Morgan scanned the area for more threats. "You looked like you needed help."

The second the words left his mouth he knew that had been the exact wrong thing to say.

The temperature around him dropped in the face of her icy stare. "I've been on my own a long time, Theronai. If I'd wanted help, I would have requested it."

"Morgan," he said.

Her perfect brow wrinkled in confusion. "What?"

"My name is Morgan, not Theronai."

Convinced that there were no immediate threats lurking in the shadows, he turned his gaze to her.

As soon as he did, he forgot how to breathe.

Serena was even more beautiful than he'd thought. He'd seen her from a distance once or twice at Dabyr before she'd gone out on her own, but he'd never been this close to her before.

There was a powerful presence around her that sucked him in and refused to let go. He knew he was staring, but he couldn't help it. She was so damn pretty, so enticing, he couldn't even blink.

Loose red curls framed her face, which was an artistic composition of dainty and bold features. Her eyes were huge, almost doll-like, the same rich, deep blue as a summer twilight. Her lips were a sweet ruby pink, full and completely kissable. She had a few freckles scattered across her narrow nose, but her skin was otherwise flawless. Not that he saw those freckles as flaws. He found them the only cute thing about her in the midst of sheer elegant beauty. They somehow made her seem more real, almost touchable.

Not that he would make *that* mistake. She was too fast with her blade for him to take any chances. He liked all of his parts firmly attached to his body, right where they belonged.

Besides, the warnings of the other men who'd come back with scars she'd caused were enough for him to proceed with caution.

"I'm aware of your name, Theronai." Her gaze dipped to his throat where the iridescent ribbon of his luceria lay close to his dark skin. Infinite colors swirled in the band, matching perfectly with those moving within the ring on his left hand.

He'd been born wearing the trappings of his kind, and the fact that he still wore the necklace told the world he had yet to find his mate.

It had been so long since he'd been in the presence of an unbonded female, he'd forgotten how intimate it could be to have a woman lay eyes on the necklace.

But rather than seeing longing for what he could offer her in her twilight blue eyes, all Morgan saw was a cold, empty chill.

The rumors were true. Serena Brinn was no longer the happy, carefree girl she'd been before her ordeal. She was hard, relentless, angry.

Deadly.

She bent to wipe the blood from her sword—blood that

was more red than black, which made it somehow even more disturbing.

Demon blood was supposed to be black. It had always been black. That it was changing to become more human in color was deeply unsettling.

All Theronai warriors had taken oaths to protect humans. If the demons the Theronai fought became too much like those they were sworn to protect...

Morgan refused to dwell on that thought for long. He had a job to do, and one that demanded his full attention.

"I saw your car parked out at the road," he said. "Will you promise to follow me back to Dabyr, or do I need to make you ride with me?"

"Neither. If you'll excuse me, Mr. Valens, I'll be on my way."

So, she did know his name. It made him wonder what else she knew about him.

Or what she thought she knew.

Everyone thought he was a player, with women three deep wherever he went. They thought he hopped from bed to bed whenever the whim struck him. He'd gone to great pains to cultivate that persona, because it was the only way to keep his fellow warriors from learning the truth—a truth he barely even allowed himself to think about.

"No mister. Just Morgan," he said. "And I can't let you wander off alone again, especially after seeing the kind of risks you're willing to take. I think you know that."

She sheathed her sword, and instantly, it disappeared. He could see the slight tug of its weight at the waistband of her clinging black leather pants, but that was the only visible sign, thanks to some ancient hocus pocus.

His kind had learned long ago that walking around wearing a visible weapon was a good way to draw unwanted attention among humans. So, invisible swords were born to solve the problem, because going without was too dangerous. Until the recent surge of these too-human demons, the only way to kill a Synestryn had been through fire or decapitation, and beheading was definitely faster.

The only thing worse than a demon coming at you to eat your face was one coming at you that was also on fire.

Serena let out a longsuffering sigh. "Please don't make me hurt you, Mr. Valens. I'm far too busy to spare the time."

Morgan cleaned and sheathed his own weapon in a series of movements as familiar as breathing.

"I suppose you could try," he said, his tone light, almost teasing. "I might even like it."

Her deep blue gaze hit his like a brick made of ice. "I promise you would not."

Morgan nodded. He knew this wasn't going to be easy, but he'd hoped that she'd found some sense of reason since the last man had tried to bring her home. "Joseph's orders were clear, Serena."

She flinched slightly at the use of her given name. She'd only been free from her prison for a few months now, and clearly, she wasn't used to the current lack of formality in society. In her time, the use of first names was an intimacy saved for close friends and family, not men she barely knew.

"I'm aware of his orders," she said. "I simply don't care for them. I've sworn him no oath of obedience."

"You're worried about oaths? The walls of Dabyr have fallen. What's left of our home is under attack almost daily. The first Theronai baby in two-hundred years has been born and there are more on the way. Demons want them. Our fighters are spread out among shelters, trying to protect both them and the humans who managed to make it out of the attack alive. We need every sword arm we can get, and from what I've seen, yours is formidable."

Serena hadn't been at Dabyr when the walls fell. She hadn't seen the carnage and devastation left behind after the attack. As much as Morgan wanted to spare her the pain of seeing their home destroyed, seeing the graves of the dead, her feelings were a luxury their people couldn't afford.

She started walking away, back toward the nearest road where she'd parked her ride.

Morgan followed.

This time of year, the brush was crunchy and dry, scratching at them as they passed. "I heard you were a charmer. Please know that flattery will get you nowhere."

"Why don't you want to go back?" he asked. "What possible reason could you have to abandon your people when they need you most?"

"My reasons are my own. Please respect them."

"I'm sorry, Serena. I can't do that. If you're not going to play nice, you at least have to tell me why."

She whirled on him. "I'll tell you why. I spent two centuries cut off from the world by an overprotective mother so that no harm could befall me. I had no contact with people, no interaction. I rarely even caught glimpses of the world moving on around me as I floated inside the void that was my prison. And when I did see others, no matter how loudly I screamed, they never heard me. Never saw me. I was utterly and completely alone. But I was safe, just as Mother had intended." She pulled in a shaky breath. "I understand Joseph's desire to protect me, but I refuse to spend even one more minute being caged or coddled. I'm going out in the world to live, to fight as I was born to do, and there is not a force on this earth powerful enough to compel me or trick me into changing my mind."

She stalked off, leaving Morgan reeling.

Two hundred years alone? No one to talk to? No one to touch? It was a wonder she hadn't gone mad.

Then again, he'd seen the way she fought, throwing caution to the wind, taking chances. She hadn't been careful. In fact, she'd bordered on reckless.

Maybe she was a little crazy, after all.

Serena ducked under a loose strand of barbed wire to cross some grazing land. As she bent, he saw a slice through the leather covering her calf. Blood coated her skin and dripped from her heel.

"You're hurt," he said.

"It's nothing."

"You're bleeding. You know the demons in the area will smell that and come running, right?"

"I'm counting on it. The night is young, and I'm bored." She glanced at him as she said it, making him wonder if it wasn't a jab meant to wound his pride.

"What if you got their blood on your cut? It's hard to fight when you're poisoned."

"I'm fine. Those demons aren't poisonous like the ones from my youth."

"How do you know?" he asked. "We haven't been fighting their kind for long."

"Experience. As I said, I've been out alone in the big, cruel world for a while now. I'm no novice."

The idea that she'd been injured before with no one around to care for her grated on his sense of duty. Sure, she was independent, and yes, his upbringing was a bit antiquated, but so was hers. She wasn't as old as he was, but she'd been raised in a time when women were protected and cherished, not left to fend for themselves. Besides, he couldn't just unlearn centuries of teaching. Male Theronai protected their women. Period. They didn't let them roam around alone, fighting demons without any kind of backup.

Even the idea was insane.

The female of their species was definitely the deadliest of the sexes, but only when she was properly bound to a man who could supply her with the energy her magic needed to function. Men stored magical power and women wielded it. It had always been that way, and no matter how independent she wanted to be, they were each born to play a specific role.

Serena was unbound. She had no access to a man's energy, no way to care for herself if she was seriously injured, and no one to drag her lovely ass out of a fight if things went sideways.

Which they would. They always did, eventually.

Morgan couldn't allow that to happen. There weren't enough female Theronai left to save his brothers from the pain their slow deaths caused. Without the outlet of power she would provide one lucky man, another of his kind would fall to the crushing agony caused by carrying around such vast stores of energy.

His own pain reared its ugly head now that the rush of combat was fading. He could feel it crushing him from the inside, always searching for a way out, as if it longed to be free.

Morgan wasn't as bad off as many of his fellow warriors. The living image of a tree covering his chest—his lifemark— still held leaves. He felt the strain of the growing power he carried, but he was tough. He could handle the pain.

What choice did he have?

If she could save one of their men, then it was her duty to do so—whether or not she liked it.

The other men that Joseph had sent to bring Serena home had failed, but Morgan would not. One of his brothers' lives depended on it, even if he didn't know which one.

He lengthened his stride so that she was within arm's reach. "Play time is over, Serena. It's time to come home. Do your duty."

"No, thank you, Mr. Valens. I'm content to continue on as I have been."

"You appear to be under the impression that you have a choice. I'm here to tell you that the only choice you have is to either come home with me willingly, or I will fling you over my shoulder and haul you home against your will."

Her entire body went tense. He almost expected her to run, but she wasn't going to get far with that injury.

And she knew it.

"I'm sorry you feel that way," she said with a resigned sigh. "I was hoping it wouldn't come to this."

"Come to what?"

"Good bye, Mr. Valens."

A strange pressure closed in around him, making his ears pop. He suffered through a fleeting moment of vertigo like he had when she'd fought the demons. When it was over, he was standing alone under the starry Texas sky, queasy, with nothing around but cattle and scrub brush.

Serena was gone, and he hadn't even seen her go.

***

Serena hated using her gift, but there was no other choice. She couldn't go back to Dabyr. She *wouldn't* go.

She choked down the wave of nausea shifting the flow of time caused, and drove away from the big, white truck parked next to her little sedan.

She had no idea how these men kept finding her, but she was beginning to think it had something to do with technology, rather than magic. She'd been out of her prison and part of this time for almost a year, but that wasn't nearly long enough to catch up on two hundred years of human advancement. She was barely used to wearing pants.

She'd tried to watch TV so she could learn current customs, but the jarring flutter of bright, frenetic advertisements made her head hurt. Every hour she watched only served to highlight just how much she'd missed, thanks to her mother's overprotective streak.

Never again. That was the vow she'd given herself when she'd finally learned to function in this time. She didn't understand what lay beneath the hood of her car, but she knew how to make it move forward. She didn't understand how a rectangle of plastic could serve as coin, but she knew how to swipe and sign like the rest of the world. She didn't understand how the man she'd loved for two centuries could have believed her dead, but she knew he was lost to her forever.

No one could force her to go back to his home and watch as he and his lovely wife brought their first child into this world—a child that should have been hers.

A life that should have been hers.

Let her people think she was cold, lazy or uncaring. Let them believe that she refused to defend their home because of some petulant display of independence. She didn't care what they thought of her, so long as she kept her secret safe.

No one could ever know that she was still deeply in love with a man who now belonged—irrevocably—to another.

CHAPTER TWO

It took Morgan all the next day to catch up with Serena again, but this time, it wasn't Synestryn she was fighting off, but a giant throng of human men.

The dance club was filled with gyrating, sweaty bodies flailing to a loud, frantic drum beat. He couldn't exactly call it music, since there was no discernable skill involved in creating the noise.

He knew his age was showing, but he didn't care. He detested modern music and had since the nineteen seventies had killed all he held dear.

Except Lindsey Stirling. She was a keeper.

Next, he was going to be screaming at kids to get off his lawn and lamenting over how easy the lives of today's youth had things.

Sheesh.

He headed straight upstairs to the second level and took up a position at the edge of the balcony. From here, he had a clear view of the dance floor and the swarm of flailing bodies covering it.

Serena was right in the middle of a testosterone donut, completely ignoring the men surrounding her.

She wore a vivid purple dress with a short, flouncy skirt and a pile of glittering crystals winking under the light show. Her arms were bare, raised high over her head in abandon as she moved to the music. Sweat glistened on her skin and plastered loose curls to the sides of her face.

The only visible flaw she had was a glaring, white bandage covering the cut on her leg. If any of the men were put off by the wound, they didn't show it.

The music shifted downward, its beat slowing and growing sultry. As it did, the men around her crept closer and reached out to pull her into their arms.

Serena evaded them all and simply danced with herself, swaying in a hypnotic display of pure feminine perfection.

Morgan couldn't look away. All he could do was stare and soak her in. He wasn't even mad at her for making him chase her around. All sins were forgiven so long as she kept dancing.

That was art.

His cock tingled, shocking the hell out of him.

He ripped his eyes away from her long enough to figure out what was wrong.

He didn't get aroused. At least not without thinking about his wife. She'd been gone a long time, but he'd never once strayed. Never even wanted to. He flirted with women and tried to charm them, but never anything more. He hadn't even kissed a woman in well over two-hundred years. Not since Femi's last night on earth.

But now, his libido seemed to be waking up and stretching, preparing for a new day. No coffee necessary.

What the hell was wrong with him?

A young woman in a slinky, black dress sidled up to him and pressed her breasts against his arm.

She was lovely, with long, blonde hair and all the right curves to make a man lose his head. And she knew it.

"Want to dance?" she asked.

All the tingles in his groin drained away as if they'd never been.

He gave her a charming smile to ease the sting of his rejection. "No thanks, sugar. I don't dance."

She slid a glittering red fingernail down his chest and looked up at him from under sinfully long eyelashes. "That's okay. You can just watch me."

As lovely as she was, there was nothing here for him. And he had nothing to offer her. She was human. His job was to kill the things that went bump in the night so she never even had to know they existed. There was nothing more between them than that, and there never would be.

"Thanks, but no thanks," he said.

She gave him a full pout that had probably worked on more men than not. "You're no fun at all. And here I was, willing to go home with you and give you a solo show. Ever had a woman dance naked for you before?"

Morgan frowned at her, shocked. He'd been so busy out in the field, fighting, that he hadn't spent any time in places like these for several decades. He'd heard his brothers talk about how easy it was to pick up women and relieve some of their pain through enthusiastic, casual sex, but until now, he hadn't realized exactly what they meant.

It wasn't just easy. Morgan hadn't even had to ask and already this girl was ready to jump in bed with him.

"You're not my type, honey. Sorry."

She laughed, like he'd made a joke. "I'm every man's type."

Morgan glanced down at Serena and was instantly trapped by the rhythmic sway of her body. That long-lost tingle of sexual arousal swept through his groin, and this time, he knew it was no coincidence—no fleeting memory of the woman he loved.

Serena turned him on, and she wasn't even trying.

A little voice in the back of his mind told him that his attraction to her was more than merely physical. He'd have to touch her to test his theory, but if he was right, then she had the power to save his life.

But first, he had to catch her.

Morgan didn't even glance at the blonde as she spoke. His whole world had shifted in the last few seconds, and he was struggling to catch up.

"Not this man," he told her. "I prefer my women to be a challenge."

***

Serena was being hunted.

She'd felt eyes on her since leaving the night club, and they weren't just any eyes.

Morgan Valens was on her trail.

He'd followed her back to her motel room, though she hadn't seen him behind her, hadn't seen him lurking in the shadows of the small parking lot.

She'd checked every corner of her small, utilitarian motel room, sword in hand. She'd looked behind the stiff curtains covering the single, wide window, though she had no idea how a man his size could possibly be lurking there. She'd bent low to peer under the wide bed in the center of the room, finding only a solid platform filling the space. She'd even searched behind the shower curtain in the tiny bathroom before she was certain she was alone. At least for now.

Even as she showered, she could feel his presence, so different from the other men who had sought her out. There was something about him that left her feeling unsettled. Excited.

Morgan Valens was not going to be an easy man to deter.

Her first instinct was to run—shower off the sweat and glitter of the club, dress and flee. Her belongings were packed, and in her car, even though she hadn't yet checked out of her motel room. She liked the freedom of knowing she could leave town whenever she wanted.

Over the past few months, the habit of staying mobile had come in handy more than once as she'd evaded a constant string of male Theronai, eager to please their leader by dragging her back to Dabyr. But she was tired of running. No matter how far she went, or how fast she got there, Joseph's men always found her.

It was time to make a stand. Confront the enemy and make it clear to all who would pursue her that she would go back to help rebuild their broken compound when, and if, she wanted.

No sooner.

After two centuries of captivity, that was the least she deserved.

She only wished that her freedom made her happy. Instead, all it did was ease the constant gnawing heartache she endured every time she thought about Iain and his wife.

She didn't want to love him anymore, but she didn't know how to stop. How was she ever going to fill the gaping void in her chest if she couldn't stop loving him?

He wasn't even the man he'd once been—the man she'd fallen in love with two hundred years ago. Time had taken its toll on him, and it had cost him his soul. He was no longer the sweet, kind man she knew. He was hard and cold, wrapped in flesh that looked like her Iain, but wasn't him. Not even close.

Jackie, his wife, had saved his life. She'd even opened herself up to him so wide that she shared her soul with him— like some sort of bizarre organ transplant.

Everything Serena had loved about Iain—his wicked sense of humor, his easy laugh, his deep kindness and tender heart—was gone. All of those things, all of who he was, had died along with his soul. She knew that. She'd tried to think of him as dead and buried so she could mourn him and move on, but with his body walking around, alive and well, she didn't know how.

She didn't know how to not miss the man he'd once been, even though there was no sign of him left in the man he'd become.

At least out here, beyond the broken walls her people called home, she was free to grieve as she liked, without judgment or blame.

Iain had thought her dead for two centuries. He'd had a long time to grieve for her. She'd had only a short time to adjust to the loss of the man she'd always loved—the man who'd consumed her thoughts for two hundred years. A man now gone.

Even in the face of such tragedy and loss, everyone was so happy for the expectant couple. They all cheered and celebrated the rare union of male and female Theronai and the precious, new life to come.

None of them stopped to think that they were also celebrating Serena's crushing heartache as well. Without realizing it, they cheered for her pain and gloried in her suffering.

How could any of them expect her to stay and face that?

No, she was better out here, away from all the happiness, where she could kill and scream and rail at the universe for all its unfairness.

Maybe one day she'd be able to go back and look into the eyes of the child that should have been hers and smile, but not today.

Serena let the hot water flood over her head as she braced herself against the cool, tile wall. She was exhausted from clearing out a Synestryn nest earlier tonight, exhausted from two hours of fending off the advances of a dozen men at the night club. All she wanted was to dance in peace, to revel in the feeling of being free from her cage, able to breathe, to move. The deafening blast of music and the anonymity of the crowd had always buoyed her spirits, but tonight had been different. There was no joy in the pulsing beat, no escape in the crush of bodies thrashing to the music.

Mr. Valens had been watching her.

She hadn't been able to see him in the dark, crowded space—hadn't known where he was—but she'd *felt* him. His presence shimmered around her, more palpable than the pounding, drumbeat thrum in her chest.

He hadn't come for her in the club, much to her surprise, but he *would* come. Soon.

Serena couldn't find the energy to run again tonight. She was too weary from her physical exertion, too heartsick from life's unfairness. But if she didn't run, she would have to fight, because the man hunting her would give her no rest.

Serena decided that her hotel room was as good a place as any to make her final stand against the men Joseph continued to send. The message she issued had to be clear, unmistakable, and loud enough that she wouldn't have to send it again.

She thought about Mr. Valens as she showered, how she might best prove to him that she wasn't going back with him. But every time her mind settled on him her thoughts seemed to scatter. She wondered about the magic he housed, what it must feel like to carry around something so powerful and alive—something so massive that it would one day kill him if he couldn't set it free.

She wondered why these men hadn't yet given up their quest to bring her back, and how much she would have to injure Mr. Valens in order to make her wishes clear.

Even the idea of slicing through his dark, smooth skin was sickening. She'd already shed too much blood and it hadn't done her much good. More men kept coming, her violent warnings unheeded. Perhaps she needed a new approach.

As she pondered this, she grinned.

Diplomacy had never been her strong suit.

When she stepped out of the bathroom, steamy and pink from her shower, wrapped in a towel, Morgan Valens was in her room, lounging on her bed.

His big body ate up the space, making the room feel suddenly smaller, warmer. The air around him practically shimmered with power, like waves of heat rising from sundrenched rocks.

She hadn't gotten a good look at him in the dark outside that cave tonight—just a vague impression of size and strength—but she could see him well now, under the golden lamplight bathing his skin.

He was a large, broad man, with thickly muscled limbs and impressively wide shoulders. He had brown skin and matching eyes that never left her body. His black hair was cropped short and his features reminded her of Egyptian pharos, steeped in power and mystery.

His pose was relaxed, regal. There was no hint of threat in his expression, though she could see from the dip in the waistband of his jeans that he was armed with the sword their kind always carried. It wasn't visible now, but the evidence that he knew how to wield it was obvious.

Even from across the room she could see thick pads of callused skin on his palms where the hilt had left its mark from centuries of use. The short sleeves of his gray T-shirt revealed muscles in his forearms that were created only from wielding a heavy weapon.

The branches of his lifemark snaked out from under his sleeve. She imagined the living image of the tree all Theronai men wore spanning across his chest, the roots slipping low under his belt, toward his groin.

Heat suffused her cheeks as she realized she was staring, but she couldn't stop herself. She wondered how many leaves his lifemark still held—how much time he had left until his soul began to decay the way Iain's had.

The urge to help Mr. Valens, to save him, was strong. She'd been raised knowing her role as a female of their kind. She was born to be powerful, deadly. But that power came with a price. She had to tie herself a to man who could offer her protection and allow her to tap into a reservoir of energy she could only imagine. Only when she was bound to such a man would she realize her true potential.

The idea chafed as much as it intrigued her and she wondered if Mr. Valens could see that in her eyes—if he knew how much she craved that strength.

If he knew her weakness.

She clutched the damp towel tighter and lifted her chin as she moved toward her small suitcase.

He followed her with his dark eyes, tracking her movement. He stayed still where he lounged on her bed, seemingly no threat.

Serena knew better.

If she bolted for the door, she couldn't say who would reach it first. Even with her gift.

She was too tired for wielding more magic today. She'd used every meager ounce of power she had tonight to clean out that nest. She was completely tapped out, and somehow, she was sure Mr. Valens knew it.

The hotel towel was soft, but far too thin for her peace of mind. She was acutely aware of her nudity, and based on the flare of Mr. Valens' nostrils as he stared, so was he.

"How did you get in?" she asked.

She wanted to reach for her clothing, but worried that if she loosened her grip on the towel, it would fall.

"Charm," he said. "You should try it sometime."

She wrinkled her nose. "Not my style. I prefer honesty."

He lifted a brow at that. "Are you calling me a liar?" His voice lilted more with amusement than accusation.

"Should I, Mr. Valens?"

He stared at her so long, she started to shiver, though whether it was from the chill of the cooling towel or the heat of his gaze, she couldn't tell.

"It's time to come home, Serena," he said as he sat upright. "Tell me what I can do to convince you."

That surprised her. None of the other men who'd come for her had asked her such a question. They'd all spewed speeches about honor and duty, never once stopping to ask her what she wanted.

Was it a trick?

Serena studied his face for signs of treachery, but found none. "Why do you care? If Joseph is calling in his warriors, then the Sentinels will have all the protection they need to watch over both the humans they protect as well as the new Theronai babies. I'm not necessary."

He rose from the bed, and she was shocked again by the size of him. He stole her breath, like a splash of icy water across her skin.

The human men of her time weren't so large. Some of the Theronai were, but she hadn't been around many of them, thanks to her overprotective mother. Only men who could further their family's station were allowed near Serena. She was a tool, her beauty and youth a bargaining chip her mother used well and often.

Other than at their local church, which was all but mandatory attendance back in the day, Serena was rarely allowed to mingle with the locals—human or Theronai—and never with Slayers whose savage ways were to be mistrusted.

She was definitely mingling now. Alone, after dark, in a private room with her wearing only a towel.... Her mother would have been scandalized. Furious.

Serena grinned at the image.

She knew that times were different now. Men and women often disrobed in front of each other within moments of meeting. Sex was spoken about openly, displayed everywhere, and people dressed so provocatively, it was a wonder anyone ever got any work done at all.

Still, modern clothes were wonderous creations of lace and sparkle. She could barely stop herself from spending all her allowed funds on colorful, flirty gowns that would have gotten her flogged for wearing in her time.

Now they simply gained her more male attention than she liked, which she could handle. The inconvenience was well worth such beauty gracing her skin.

Even the underthings women wore now were delicious. Soft, silken and beautiful, coming in vivid colors and an array of adornments she could have only imagined in her time.

She had such garments only inches away from her, but dared not reach for them. What if Mr. Valens saw what she wore beneath her clothing? Would he be shocked, disgusted? Or would he continue to give her that hungry look that made her body shimmer and tremble?

He moved slowly across the space. The closer he came, the bigger he got, until he was all but blocking out the light behind him.

A yellow glow from the bathroom lit his features and made his dark eyes glitter. Shadows caressed the hollows beneath his cheekbones and filled the space beneath his wide jaw. Her gaze slid to the base of his throat where the luminescent colors of his luceria swirled deep within the surface of the magical band. The dance of those colorful ribbons caught her attention and held it, almost hypnotically. She ached to run her finger along the smooth surface and see if it carried the heat of his body, or if it was cool to the touch like metal.

That necklace wasn't his. He was only a caretaker, holding it for the woman to whom it would one day belong. Like the matching ring on his left hand, the luceria was a magical conduit for the power he housed—the way the female Theronai siphoned off the energy the male stored.

Serena lifted her arm to reach toward him, but the towel slipped a scant inch, shocking her back to attention.

He tipped his head down and spoke in a low, quiet voice, as one would to a skittish animal. It was a nice voice, smooth and deep. Like the rest of him, there was no frantic rush to his words, only easy patience and absolute control.

"Bringing you home is as much for your protection as ours. You need to be with your people and we need your help to rebuild Dabyr." His gaze dipped to her mouth, then back to her eyes. "Please, Serena, just tell me what I can do to keep from chasing you down again. This doesn't have to be a fight."

She lifted her chin with an air of confidence she didn't feel. This man put her off balance and made her shake, though not with fear.

The reason she trembled was far more dangerous than mere emotion—a reason she couldn't bring herself to acknowledge, even within the private confines of her own mind.

"Do you think I'm afraid of you?" she asked, her voice weaker than she'd intended.

"I don't think you're afraid of anything. That's part of the problem."

He was wrong. She was afraid. Terrified.

She held his gaze and forced her voice to come out as smooth and even as his, without the slightest tremor. "Courage is an asset."

"Right up until the point that it gets you killed."

"Why do you care?" she asked. "You don't know me. We share no past or kin. Why don't you just go home and leave me in peace?"

Something was about to happen. She felt it in the very air,

saw it in the slight tension of his body and the way his pupils flared. Something was about to happen, and it was going to change everything.

"Because of this," he said, slowly, with absolute confidence. Certainty.

Mr. Valens wrapped his big hands around her bare shoulders and held her in a firm grasp.

Serena's world shifted in an instant. Everything inside of her began to shimmer. Hot summer sun, sweat-slick bodies gliding together, soft fur rugs, and the endless moment of tension before orgasm—all those feelings mingled together under his touch and radiated out along her skin.

The sensation was amazing. Consuming. She closed her eyes, basked in the glow of it, and let her head fall back on a groan of delight.

Reality altered to reshape itself into something new and exciting. Endless possibility and hope wrapped around her, filling her mind with the purest form of temptation.

Morgan Valens was raw power walking around on two legs—power that belonged solely to her.

As soon as she realized what this feeling was—what it meant—her mind turned cold as her heart rejected the idea outright.

"We're compatible?" she asked, her words breathless and filled with apprehension.

He didn't answer. He didn't have to. She knew the truth.

Morgan Valens could be her mate. He could offer her everything she'd been promised as a girl—boundless power and the strength to fight their enemy. Beside him, she would be a formidable force of nature. Unstoppable.

She looked up to find him staring down at her with raw desire tightening his features. His fingers slid down to shackle her upper arms. Those long fingers of his wrapped all the way around her biceps, proving just how scrawny she was compared to a physical powerhouse like him. As he held her, her towel loosened from where she had it pinned around her torso and slipped to her feet, leaving her damp, shaken and completely naked.

She didn't care. She knew she should, but there were too many sensations winging through her for her to worry about modesty.

Serena had far larger problems.

She'd been touched twice before by men who were compatible with her—men whose vast stores of power she could wield—but never before had it felt like this.

Iain's touch had been sweet and warm—fuzzy puppies and spring breezes. With Mr. Tolland, it had been sharp and stinging, like lightning storms and static electricity in the dead of winter.

With the man touching her now, their connection was like liquid intensity flowing through her veins, heating her skin and making her want. Desire.

Need.

Her body softened against his, heated. She couldn't help her reaction, or how she swayed on her feet, tilting toward his massive gravitational pull on her.

His fingers tightened around her biceps to hold her up. His arms flexed slightly, and without effort, he drew her toward him until her naked breasts were pressed against his soft, gray shirt.

She had never wished for the feel of a man's bare skin on her flesh more than she did in this moment. If she'd had any control over her limbs at all, she would have ripped the offending garment from his wide shoulders and taken what she wanted.

Hot skin on hot skin. Her aching breasts against the taut, muscular planes of his chest. His power flowing into her, her hungry body lapping up every spark he had to offer.

"I suspected it was true when I saw you dancing," he said, his tone strained and uneven for the first time since they'd met. "But I never realized it would be like this."

There was a sense of wonder weaving through his words, a sigh of relief with every breath he took.

"It's never been like this for me before," she said.

Why had she said that? Why had she revealed such a truth to a virtual stranger?

He opened his eyes and looked at her. Into her. Satisfied. Pleased. "That's good."

Her knees quivered, threatening to buckle. Heat suffused her and left goosebumps dancing along her skin. Her nipples hardened against his chest, and based on the clenching of his wide jaw, he'd felt it too.

"Let me claim you," he said. "Protect you."

Everything in her went cold. This was what she'd feared. This was what she had to avoid at all costs.

Like all men, Mr. Valens wanted to chain her, cage her, steal her meager freedom.

She shoved herself away from his body and his embrace, and all the physical temptation he offered.

As she stumbled back, he doubled over in pain. A rough, pitiful moan erupted from his chest, and he fell to his knees. Harsh, painful gagging sounds came out of him, like he was struggling not to vomit.

Her heart felt a moment of sympathy, of regret, but it passed quickly as her self-preservation instincts shooed all that away.

Serena had heard that all the unbound male Theronai still alive today bore hideous pain. The energy they housed was designed to grow and replenish every day, but without a female of their kind to siphon off some of that power, it grew until it was nearly impossible to bear. Many of her kind had killed themselves to escape it, and even more had succumbed to the strain it placed on their lifemark—the visible indicator of their magical health. Once a man's lifemark was bare of leaves, his soul would die and he would become twisted and evil.

Just as Iain had.

Serena hadn't been able to save him, but she was capable of saving the man kneeling in front of her, trembling like a child.

But could she? Could she give up her freedom and allow

herself to be claimed, as he said? Could she willingly place herself in this man's care and allow him to protect her?

What if he caged her, as her mother had? What if he coddled her and took away her freedom?

She couldn't live like that again. She'd already given up too much of her life. She had nothing left to give and not lose her sanity as well.

"No," she said, forcing her wavering voice to harden into solid, unquestionable resolve. "I'd rather die free than live caged."

No matter how alluring the prison he offered might be.

He looked up at her, his face a tense mask of pain. He was incredibly handsome, and suffering deeply, but she couldn't let either of those facts sway her. Many men were handsome. Many men suffered. She couldn't let him hold sway over her simply because of his nearness.

"I'd never cage you, Serena." His gaze dipped to her naked breasts, then lower, to her sex. Hunger drove back some of the agony in his expression, softening the lines between his brows, as if merely looking at her eased some of his pain.

Her towel was at his knees. If she got close enough to pick it up, she'd be close enough for him to touch her again. And if he did that, she wasn't sure she could remember why she shouldn't accept his offer and give into the liquid intensity he sent winging through her veins.

So instead, she remained uncovered and forced herself to not to squirm.

"Easy to say," she said. "But I'm not like these new women who were raised as human. I know the true nature of our kind, of men like you. Your intentions would be honorable, but as time went on, you'd find ways to justify taking away my freedom, little by little. It would all be for my own good—or at least it would be in your mind—but the end result would be the same. I'd be bound to a man who sought to control me and tuck me away in a comfortable cage meant for my own protection." She shook her head slowly. "I won't live like that ever again."

He pushed to his feet on powerful legs that strained the denim of his faded jeans. Even shaken as he was, he radiated strength.

Serena envied him for that even as she admired him.

She had to tilt her head back to keep looking him in the eye as he rose. She didn't dare look away—not when it would be too easy for him to physically overpower her. As tired as she was, it wouldn't take much to bind her against her will, stuff her in his truck, and drive her back to the last place on earth she wanted to go—Dabyr.

While the idea of his big hands on her naked flesh again held a certain appeal, she wasn't about to sacrifice her entire future for a few moments of pleasure.

To his credit, his dark gaze stayed fixed on her face, rather than straying lower again. "What if I gave you my vow?"

Serena hadn't considered that. Any promise he gave her would be binding. The magic behind a vow one of her kind made could not be broken—not unless she allowed it. And that, she would never do.

"What kind of vow?" she asked, calling herself a fool for even entertaining the idea.

He picked up her towel and held it out to her. "Cover yourself so I can think straight. No man can be expected to negotiate with a woman as beautiful as you standing in front of him, naked."

She took the towel and held it over her breasts. "Negotiate?"

"Isn't that what this is?" he asked. "We each have something the other wants."

"I understand that you want me to come home and help rebuild, but what do you think you have that *I* want?"

A slow, languid smile lifted the corners of his mouth. "Freedom, and the power to make it stick. Bound to me, you'll have access to my power. No one would be able to force you to go where you don't want go or do things you don't want to do. Taking my luceria and tapping into that power is the only way you'll ever truly be free."

Serena went still. Her mind was the only part of her that moved, and it was spinning at a blurring speed.

Was he right? Was power the only way to freedom?

If she bonded with this man, no other men could claim her, so none would bother her. With his power at her command, no others could stop her from doing as she willed. She'd finally be able to stop running and live her life by her rules.

But there was a catch, and it was huge. Mr. Valens would always be able to find her. As their bond strengthened, she'd be able to wield more of his power, but he'd also be able to read her thoughts and feel her emotions. He'd become part of her. He'd know her deepest fears and highest hopes. She'd be able to hide nothing from him.

Two hundred years ago—before Synestryn had attacked and killed most of the female Theronai—things had been different for her people. Male and female Theronai who were compatible often bonded for short periods to see if their personalities were well suited. It was a kind of courtship, though not always a romantic one. After a pre-determined period of time, some couples would carefully end their tentative bond and seek out new mates, because there were plenty to go around.

Since the slaughter of most females, things had changed. Without a mate, the power male Theronai stored grew with no outlet, causing extreme, endless pain. Men became desperate. There had been no children born to them for two centuries— no new girls to bond with the remaining men and siphon off their power. A few Theronai women had been found recently, living among humans without knowledge of who or what they were.

Iain's wife had been one of these women.

Because of the scarcity of mates, pain drove men to demand permanent bonds that tied a woman to them for life. It was the only way they'd never again have to endure such torment.

There was no doubt in Serena's mind that Mr. Valens would want the same permanence.

She didn't know him. She didn't even know if she liked him. And, she was still in love with Iain. It would be wrong of her to commit her life to another man, even if it meant gaining access to the power she craved. But on the other hand, she didn't think she'd get another offer as good as Mr. Valens'. She owed it to herself to at least consider her options.

What harm could there be in a simple discussion? Or negotiation, as he called it.

If Serena was going to negotiate with this man, she was going to have to do so carefully, because there was no way to know if he was giving her the key to her future, or locking her in a cage of her own making.

"Let me dress," she said. "Then we'll negotiate."

CHAPTER THREE

Morgan had done a lot of difficult things in his long life. He'd battled demons and borne witness to the death and devastation they left behind. He'd endured tremendous pain on a daily basis for decades with no escape in sight. He'd buried more loved ones than he could count. But keeping his eyes off of Serena's stunning, naked body had been one of the hardest things he'd ever done. Literally. His cock was still stiff and throbbing from the sight of her smooth flesh, bared for his pleasure.

The woman was beyond merely beautiful. She'd locked herself away in the bathroom to dress, but he could still see the shape of her burned into his retinas. Perfect, feminine curves covered in smooth, flawless skin. Her nipples were the same ruby pink as her lips, and just as tempting to kiss. Flaming red hair shielded her mound, but all it did was make him think about what lay beneath. Would she part those long legs for him and let him have a taste? Or would he have to spend the rest of his life wondering how sweet she was?

As soon as the wayward thoughts crossed his mind, he felt like an ass. A cheater.

Femi had been gone a long time, but that didn't mean he should tarnish her memory by lusting for another woman. He'd promised himself after her death that he'd never love again—the pain of loss was too much to bear. Since then, he'd barely more than glanced at a pretty woman.

But with Serena, it was different. *She* was different.

Maybe it was simply a trick his luceria was playing on him—trying to get him to bond to her. He'd always believed that the matching ring and necklace were more than some magical artifact he'd been born wearing. He'd heard rumors that some people thought the luceria was sentient, working its will in the lives of those it touched.

What if they were right? What if he was being played by some fucking magic jewelry?

He looked down at the band on his finger and watched the iridescent colors swirling beneath the surface. Plumes of fiery orange and dark pink danced in a frenetic display, reminding him all too keenly of Serena's beauty.

"I'm on to you," he whispered to the ring. "Don't think you're going to get your way. Serena and I will make our own decisions."

She came out of the bathroom, frowning. The delicious scent of lavender followed her. "Who are you talking to?"

His cheeks warmed with embarrassment. "No one. Just entertaining myself."

She'd put on a frilly dress that looked more suited to a high school prom than a negotiation. Cobalt blue and metallic silver ruffles frothed around her thighs in a skirt that showed off far too much of her sexy legs for his peace of mind. Glittering sequins and beads coated the bodice, which lifted her breasts in prominent display.

His mouth watered for a taste, and his fingers tingled with the need to touch.

"Nice dress," he said.

She beamed and twirled in a circle. He noticed that the wound on her leg had already closed. Like him, she healed quickly.

Thank heavens.

Her smile brightened as she looked down at herself. "The gowns today are so fine. So sparkling. I know there are better ways to spend my allotted coin, but I just can't help myself. I want to own them all. I've discovered something called a thrift store, where apparently, women send their cast-off clothing." She shook her head. "I can't believe someone would ever part with this dress."

She was so pleased with herself, he didn't have the heart to tell her how there were few places she could wear a dress like that and not be gawked at.

Then again, she was so beautiful that she could wear a Hefty bag and still make men stare and drool.

The image of her naked body blazed in his mind again, clear and perfect. His traitorous body reacted to even the memory of her, and suddenly, the fly of his jeans was too tight across his welling cock.

Morgan took a seat in the only chair in the room so she wouldn't see the effect she had on him. The only place left for her to sit was the bed.

"Have a seat," he said.

Was his voice usually this rough or was lust playing havoc with his vocal cords as well?

She eyed the bed with apprehension, as if there was something wrong with it. It was then he realized that even sitting on a bed in the presence of a man would grate on her antiquated sense of propriety.

"It's okay," he said. "Times have changed. You have to adapt so you don't draw attention to yourself."

"I have been trying, Mr. Valens. Some habits are harder to break than others."

"Case in point. Call me Morgan."

She blushed, and the color reminded him all too easily of her tight, little nipples.

He could almost imagine them pressing into his palms as he covered her with his hands, memorizing the feel of her, the weight of her breasts. The need to learn every little detail of her body was so strong, his hands began to tremble. He had to clench his fingers into tight fists to keep the secret of how deeply she affected him.

"Okay, Morgan," she said. "What are your terms?"

His mind was already wandering down the lovely path her nude body had provided, so it took him a second to figure out what she was talking about.

Right. The negotiation.

He had to get his head back in the game. Fast. This chance to claim her as his mate was too rare for him to risk screwing it up.

He focused on a scuff mark on the wall behind her to keep his mind off sex and on track. "I think we should start by listing what we each want."

"Very well. You go first," she said.

He paused to collect his thoughts.

What would sway her? What was he willing to reveal? Like any negotiation, this one would all hinge on the starting point. It was important that he chose his wisely.

"I want to no longer live in pain," he said. "Touching you made all my suffering end, but when you stopped touching me, I thought the returning pain would kill me." He said it evenly, factually, giving no color or life to the extreme depth of his suffering.

Even thinking about that moment of crashing pain was enough to drive a man mad, so he shoved it down deep, where all painful things lived.

Sympathy lined the space between her brows. "For that I am truly sorry, Mr.—Morgan. I want to help, but we can't exactly go around touching all the time."

Morgan struggled not to think about just how much fun a life spent touching her body would be before guilt left him cold.

What would Femi think if she could see him now, lusting for a woman he barely knew?

"That's not what I'm proposing, and you know it" he said. "The men who've bonded with a female Theronai are no longer in pain. Once you tap into my power and reduce the burden I carry, I won't hurt anymore."

He could tell by her expression that the idea of binding herself to him made her uncomfortable, so he changed the subject. "Your turn. What do you want?"

"Freedom, as I've said all along. I fear that tying myself to you would destroy that freedom—if not now, then down the road."

"I told you I'd give you my vow not to do that."

"And what vow could you give me that wouldn't interfere with those you've already given to protect humans and obey your leader?"

"He's your leader, too."

"I've sworn no oath to him."

"You will. Eventually. But that's not the point. You want guarantees. I'm willing to work with you on that." He leaned back in his chair, considering. "What if I promised to never stop you from leaving Dabyr when you wanted?"

"Even if it meant I was walking into danger?"

He hesitated.

"That's what I'm talking about," she said. "If we were to bond, you'd promise to protect me with your life, as all of our men promise their women. If you knew that me leaving Dabyr was dangerous, how could you willingly let me leave?"

"I would come with you."

She shook her fiery curls. They danced around her bare shoulders. Soft against soft, silky against silky.

In that moment, he would have given his sword arm to be caught between those two, lovely surfaces.

"I'm not looking for a partner—or a warden," she said. "I don't want to be forced to be with you all of the time. I want to go where I want, when I want, with whom I want. Or alone."

"That's reckless," he spat.

"That's freedom," she countered. "*That's* what I want. I will consider no offers for less."

He opened his mouth to respond, but a knock on the door stopped him.

"Are you expecting someone?" he asked.

Serena shook her head and rose to answer the door.

"Let me."

She rolled her eyes. "This is what I'm talking about.

Synestryn don't knock. There's no threat at all here, and yet you can't stand to let me answer my own door."

She was wrong about there being no threat. While it was unlikely that demons would come knocking on her door, the humans they controlled would. Dorjan were everywhere, and for all he knew, there was one at her door right now.

Morgan opened the door with his hand on his sword, just in case.

A man he didn't know stood in the hall, dressed in jeans and a button-down shirt. He was about six feet tall and gaunt, with deep grooves under his cheek bones. He was handsome in an aristocratic kind of way with refined features and deep air of confidence. His eyes were gray-blue, his hair sandy blonde, worn in a cut that probably cost more than Morgan's entire outfit. At the base of his throat, inside the open collar of his pristine white shirt, sat a shimmering luceria as proof that this man was a Theronai.

Morgan tensed. While this man should be his ally, there were no guarantees that was the case. He didn't know him. He'd never seen him before. But he had seen men who wore the luceria turn on their own kind, once all the leaves on their lifemark had fallen and their souls decayed into rotted filth.

Whoever this man was, he wasn't getting anywhere near Serena.

"Can I help you?" Morgan asked, voice neither cold nor welcoming.

The man extended his hand and smiled in greeting. It was a warm smile, but one that didn't quite reach his eyes. A slight British accent lilted through his words. "I'm Link Tolland, from the European settlement."

Behind Morgan, Serena pulled in a shocked breath.

"Morgan Valens." He shook the man's hand, gauging his strength.

The man had it in spades, gripping tight enough it could have been either a display of worthiness or a warning.

Whoever he was, he was no stranger to combat. Morgan could tell that much by the position of the calluses on his hands and the way his eyes watched Morgan's every move.

"What brings you here, Link?"

Link leaned to peer past Morgan's shoulder to where Serena stood behind him. As soon as Link saw her, his face lit up with eagerness. "There you are, darling." To Morgan, he said, "I'm here to collect my belongings."

"Belongings?" Morgan asked.

Link nodded. "Serena's parents gave her to me two hundred years ago. I recently learned she was still alive, so I've come all this way to claim her."

CHAPTER FOUR

Joseph surveyed the battlefield. The area had once been lush, rolling hills, kept manicured by the loving hand of several human gardeners. The trees were kept pruned, the lawn mowed in a crisscross pattern that looked like verdant green plaid. The stone walls around the compound gleamed under the sun and kept out all the nasty creatures who wanted to feast on the flesh and blood of those inside the walls of Dabyr.

Now everything was different. Two weeks ago, the walls had been breached. Since then, the place they called home had been under almost constant attack.

The gleaming walls were now toppled in places, with giant chunks of stone laying like shattered bone on the frozen ground. The once lush grass, now winter brown and blood-soaked, was rutted and gouged, leaving deep furrows of dirt visible like dark, diseased tissue inside open wounds. The smell of rotting flesh and burning bodies filled the air, mixed with the fetid stench of demons. Screams of pain, bellows of fury and the clang of sword on steel rang out through the night.

From the top of a low hill, Joseph took in the devastation.

Another wave of Synestryn demons had just been pushed back. His warriors were finishing off the few remaining demons in the hopes that they'd have a few minutes to rest before the next wave arrived.

They couldn't keep going like this much longer. Even the

sunlight gave them no rest.

For as long as his kind had existed, Synestryn were bound by the dark. They couldn't venture out during the day, much less attack. But now things were different. A new breed of demon had risen—one that could walk in the light.

The dark, demonic creatures who ruled over the Synestryn had been working toward this achievement for years. Possibly centuries. They'd been stealing human children, feeding them blood and caging them in the dark so that one day, they could create offspring without the inherent weaknesses the Synestryn possessed.

Joseph had been seeing signs of what was to come for a while—more human-looking demons—but he hadn't realized what their end game was until now.

But now, looking over the war-torn field that had once been a safe haven for Sentinels and humans alike, he knew how foolish he'd been.

He should have seen this coming. He should have prepared better. He should have protected those who relied on him for their lives.

He'd failed. Utterly.

"You couldn't have known," came a soft, sweet voice that clashed harshly with the noise of combat.

Lyka. His wife, his soulmate. His everything.

She came up behind him, as silent as a cat. He'd felt her presence, of course, but he'd been so engrossed in surveying the situation so he could move men around to prepare for the next wave of attack, that he hadn't realized she'd found him.

Lyka was a glowing, golden vision in the night. She was tall and athletically built, with sunny hair and a body that made Joseph pant with longing, even as exhausted as he was. She was a strong, solid partner—something he'd never truly believed existed for him, much less that he'd find. But here she was, in the flesh, bringing him reassurance and support when he needed it most.

There was a warm, animal smell hovering around her, one that told him she'd shifted into her tiger form recently to patrol the perimeter.

"How bad is it?" he asked.

"There's a new crack in the southern wall. They'll be able to break through in a few more hours."

"I'll send some men to defend the area. Lexi can't mend any more holes right now. She's doing all she can."

Lyka touched Joseph's arm. He couldn't tell if it was a warning or a bid for comfort.

"She hasn't slept in more than a week. Zach is feeding her all the power he can gather, but the demons are tearing the walls down faster than she can rebuild them."

"I know," he said, hearing the sound of defeat echo in his tone.

Lexi had a gift that none of the other female Theronai did. She was able to imbue stone and mortar or timber and nails with the power to repel invasion. She could weave her magic around a building or a wall and create a kind of barrier that kept out dark magic and kept those inside safe and hidden.

Without her, they would have had to abandon Dabyr completely. There would have been no hope of repair.

But she was only one woman and the warrior who fueled her magic was only one man. There was a limit to what they could do and Joseph was afraid that the couple had now reached that limit.

She needed rest. So did Zach. Even now, as he watched the man standing over his wife, he was pushing so much power into her he was weaving on his feet.

Around them was a ring of warriors armed with swords, defending Lexi with their life.

Without her there would be no hope and every man down there knew it.

Every man down there was willing to give his life to save her.

"It's not as bad as all that, is it?" Lyka asked.

She'd heard his thoughts. He didn't have the energy to filter them anymore. Like Zach, he'd been fueling his wife's magic, allowing her to transform at will. She hunted along the perimeter, taking out stray demons and keeping watch for larger groups bent on invasion.

Joseph didn't like her out there alone, but he wasn't fast enough to keep up with her and she didn't stay out for long.

He fought beside his men, falling back only to reassess the situation so he could move warriors to shore up breaks in their defenses, or to remove from combat those too stubborn to fall back for the healing they needed.

At least during the night they had the aid of the Sanguinar on the battlefield.

Logan and Hope had done as much to keep Dabyr from falling as any of those who wielded a sword against their enemy.

Joseph still wasn't sure how it worked, but somehow, Logan drew strength from Hope, who drew strength from the sun, allowing him to heal when other Sanguinar would have been too exhausted to lift their heads. That he'd found her was one of the few bright spots their people had experienced recently.

And now Ronan had found Justice, a woman like Hope, who helped fuel his power. Joseph had assigned Ronan to the shelters where most of the humans who had been at Dabyr now resided.

For reasons Joseph didn't understand, Justice had seemed to know the attack on Dabyr was coming. She'd set up shelters around the country, filling them with food, water, beds and supplies. And while not as protected as Dabyr's walls had once been, they were warded and able to protect humans to some extent.

They were certainly safer than this place was right now.

So now, Justice and Ronan traveled between those shelters, taking care of the hundreds of souls that needed protection, healing and comfort.

They also were watching over the Theronai women who were currently pregnant—a rare, amazing gift that no one had expected, since there hadn't been a single child born to a male Theronai in over two hundred years. Now there were three.

Nika and Madoc were also being held in one of the shelters because their newborn was far too fragile and precious to risk. Madoc served as the protector of a shelter, the same way the other two expectant fathers did at other locations.

Everyone was doing their part to keep people safe, but in the end, Joseph was responsible for all of them.

"You're putting too much of a burden on your shoulders," Lyka said, as she wrapped her arm around him and leaned in close.

There were only a handful of demons left alive on the field now, and those were quickly being dispatched.

To his right, Joseph saw two men helping carry one of the wounded back to where Logan worked healing the injured. With luck, his work would soon be over.

There were no reports of more incoming Synestryn. But they would come. Dabyr was too rich a target not to draw demons from miles away. The warriors here, while exhausted and battle-scarred, were still the demons' favorite food. They were still huge sources of power.

More demons would definitely come.

"What we're doing isn't working," Joseph told his wife. "We have to get the walls back up. We can't fight off every demon on the continent—not with our dwindling numbers."

"Lexi needs help," Lyka said.

"None of the other women can do what she does. They'll just exhaust themselves."

He knew what Lexi needed, but couldn't bring himself to issue the order.

Lyka, as always, was in his thoughts, connected to him on a level so deep, it was if they shared one mind. Because of that, she knew what he meant.

"Andra will come," Lyka said.

"Of course, she will. But what about her baby? I can't risk her unborn child."

"You don't think that the collapse of Dabyr is just as much of a risk? If this place falls, there will be no safe place for her to raise the baby."

Lyka was right. She usually was.

"My kind fight when they're pregnant," she said. "And what you're asking of Andra would be far less hands-on. She'll be perfectly safe."

"I'm not sure Paul would agree."

But again, Lyka was right. Andra's ability to erect a forcefield that could protect those inside was amazing—as good as any warded walls could be. If she was standing inside her own shield...

"You have no choice," Lyka said. "Let her convince Paul. She'll know how to make him see the truth. We need her."

Joseph shook his head. "I don't like it."

The last of the demons fell. The warriors who weren't injured spread out to watch for the next wave of attack.

Sunrise was coming soon. There would be fewer demons to fight. They would rest as much as possible, heal and regroup. Because darkness would fall again tomorrow night and more Synestryn would come for their blood.

Lyka sent him a wave of reassurance. It hummed through his mind, as warm and soft as the woman who sent it. And just like her, it was powerful and determined.

Joseph lapped up that reassurance like a man dying of thirst. He grasped onto it and let it strengthen his resolve.

He didn't know what he'd do without the woman he loved.

He prayed he'd never have to find out.

CHAPTER FIVE

Andra was going crazy. Batshit, loony-bin, nut-balls insane.

"I can't stay here, cooped up like this," she told her husband.

In her opinion, Paul was quite possibly the most handsome man on the planet. Sure, he wasn't as pretty-boy perfect as the Sanguinar, but he was way hotter. With his dark blond hair, his chiseled, angular features, his kind, brown eyes, and a tall, lean body that made her drool, there was no one who could compete.

And he was all hers.

Her heart could not have been fuller. She had a husband who adored her, whom she loved with every bit of her soul, and a healthy baby boy thumping around in her belly. The child never seemed to sleep—something he had in common with his father. While she loved having the movement as a constant reminder that he was alive and well, all that internal commotion made it hard for her to rest. She had very little sleep to help her pass the time.

There was nothing to do here in this shelter—no battles to fight, no demons to kill, no lost children to find. They were housed in a defunct warehouse that Justice had purchased and stocked with enough supplies to support almost two hundred people. The space was wide open, with metal pallet racks the only feature in an otherwise bleak landscape. The floors were concrete. The walls and ceiling were held up with steel trusses and beams that made sound echo through the space almost constantly.

It was always loud in here. Even whispers seemed to grow in volume after they were spoken. People were agitated and afraid, making it hard for anyone to sleep. Couple that with the fact that there had to be people constantly on watch for attack, and the whole place seemed to constantly buzz with movement, noise and nervous energy.

At least Andra's little sister was here, where she could keep an eye on her. Nika's new baby, named Celine after their late mother, was thriving. She didn't seem to know that the world she'd been born into was collapsing around them. She didn't seem to care about the constant hum of voices echoing off the walls, or the smell of too many bodies trapped in too small a space. She appeared to have not a care in the world, content to sleep and eat in silence, with only the occasional birdlike, squawking cry to exercise her lungs.

That silence was probably due to Madoc—her father who doted on her, anticipating every need before Celine had it. He held her most of the time, cradling her tiny body in one burly arm, scowling at anyone who dared come close to his precious baby girl. Even when she had to nurse, he seemed to begrudge having to let her go.

Then again, his whole family had almost died the night of the attack on Dabyr. That kind of thing would leave a mark on a man—even one as hard as Madoc.

They'd been trapped here for almost two weeks now, and there was no sign that anyone was leaving anytime soon.

In the spirit of acceptance, the residents—mostly human—had used spare sheets or empty pallets to erect flimsy walls in an effort to give them a little more privacy.

Sibyl, an unbound female Theronai who had rarely left her room at Dabyr, was also here. She'd made herself a home in the darkest corner of the warehouse. She'd managed to move empty cardboard shipping containers the size of small walk-in closets around a square of concrete she claimed as her own.

Humans seemed to avoid her and the area she lived in. Andra wasn't quite sure why the woman repelled people, but she guessed it had something to do with the fact that she could see how people were going to die.

More than once, Andra had debated going back there and asking Sibyl if they were all going to die here, in this hollow, echoing shell of a building. She hadn't, because she truly wasn't sure if she wanted to know.

Her hand went to her softly rounded belly. She still had about four more months to go and she desperately wanted to watch her son grow up. The idea of something happening to him before she could see his face made her sick with fear.

Whatever Sibyl knew about Andra's death, she could keep to herself. It was better that way.

"Why don't you take a walk," Paul suggested.

She knew he could feel her agitation, her sense of captivity grating on her nerves. They were linked by a luceria, which meant that there were no secrets between them. She could read his thoughts as clearly as he could read hers.

Right now, he was worried that she'd crack under the strain of being here and bolt from this place.

He was right to worry.

"I'm tired of doing laps inside. Besides, people have spread out enough now that there's no clear path like there was a few days ago. I'd have to navigate through people's homes to take a lap around the inside of the building."

It was almost dawn. Maybe then she could go outside and walk around.

"You know that's not a good idea," Paul said. "The warding here is flimsy. I'm glad to have it, but the less we go out, the less likely it is that any Synestryn will find us."

She covered her face with her hands to stifle a groan. "I'd almost welcome a fight at this point. I'm going stir-crazy."

Paul moved behind her, skirting around the flimsy folding chairs that served as her living room furniture. He put his big hands on her shoulders and began to knead the knots of tension from them.

Maybe they needed to find a quiet, secluded spot and make a little cardboard house of their own. It had been too long since they'd made love. A long, hot, sweaty round or three of sex would do wonders to blow off a little steam.

She heard the smile in his voice. "I'd love nothing more. Let me see what I can do. There's got to be a shadowy corner we can use for a while—one where we won't be interrupted."

Before he could go make good on his plans, Iain walked up to them.

The look on his face was serious, but that was nothing new. The man had a kind of intensity about him that left Andra a little unsettled.

She'd heard he had no soul—that he had to share his wife's to remember how to walk the straight-and-narrow. As far as she was concerned, that made him a bit of a ticking timebomb.

Paul walked around in front of Andra before Iain could get too close. He noticed the move for what it was—a blatant act of defending his wife—and held back.

She watched Iain glance around the area.

There were people everywhere. Paul had claimed two narrow cots and two flimsy folding chairs as their own, but just inches beyond that scant bit of furniture, there were other similar setups filled with people.

Like many people here, she needed some damn privacy so badly, she wanted to scream.

"Can we step outside?" Iain asked. His voice was calm and even, but his eyes were anything but.

The man was worried. Maybe even scared.

Andra didn't know what could scare a hard-core badass like him, but whatever it was, she wanted to thank it for the godsend it was.

Finally, some action. Or at the very least she was going to get to go outside and breathe in some fresh air.

"You should stay here," Paul said.

"Like hell," Andra said. "I'm going with you."

She used the conduit of the luceria to make it clear she

wasn't going to back down on this. He knew how stubborn she could be, but in this, she was immovable. She was going outside. Period.

He let out a low, quiet sigh, but motioned toward the door.

As soon as they left the warehouse, Andra breathed in the cold, night air and let it clean out the metallic tang of rust, coffee and sweat from her nostrils.

The men flanked her. Their eyes were on the tree line a few yards away. Their hands were on their swords.

"What's up?" Paul asked.

"It's Jackie."

Andra, who'd been busy basking in the openness of the night sky and the lack of humanity around her, was snapped back into the here-and-now. Her hand went to her stomach. "Is something wrong with the baby?"

Iain looked at her and shook his head. "I don't think so."

He was as tall as Paul, but much wider. There was something about him she found odd—something she couldn't quite put her finger on. Maybe it was his soulless state that left her unsettled, or maybe it was his watchful, black eyes that seemed to miss nothing.

"Then what's wrong?" Paul asked.

"Ever since we came here, Jackie has been struggling. She sees things," Iain began.

Paul nodded. "I heard about that. Joseph said she can see the location of other female Theronai—ones we haven't yet found."

"That's what we believe it is. Ronan has been working with her to clarify what she sees. Until recently, it hasn't been a problem to turn it off. But now…she can't sleep. She can hardly eat. She can't focus on anything else. Half the time she's blinded by the visions. I'm worried the strain will be too much for her. With the baby due any day now…."

"Maybe Rory could help," Andra suggested.

Rory was another female Theronai who had visions. She'd been blinded recently, but was still able to see through the eyes of those around her well enough to navigate the world as if she'd never lost her sight.

"She's at Dabyr, fighting with Cain," Paul said, "Like all of the female Theronai who aren't pregnant."

"Must be nice," Andra grumbled.

Paul shot her a pointed look. "We're safe here. The baby is safe. That's all that matters. You have no business in combat right now."

Andra wasn't so sure, but she kept her mouth shut. They were discussing Jackie's problems, not hers.

"I don't think Rory can help. I think this is something bigger." Iain glanced around as if he was worried that someone would pop out of the shadows at them.

"What?" Paul asked.

Iain looked at Andra now. "Have you had any side-effects of your pregnancy?"

"I puked for a while and now I either sleep like the dead or not at all."

Iain shook his head. "No, I mean magical side-effects."

Andra blinked. *Magical* side-effects?

Paul went still. "Like what?"

"Like have your powers changed, strengthened? Have you been able to do things you weren't able to do before you got pregnant?"

"No," Andra said. "Is that's what's happening to Jackie?"

"I don't know. Maybe. Or maybe now that we're outside of the protective walls of Dabyr, Jackie is more connected to these women."

Andra felt a chord strike in her mind and nodded. "That makes sense. Whenever I was searching for a lost child, I could always feel them more keenly when I wasn't inside a warded building."

"But this one *is* warded," Paul reminded them.

"Not as strongly as Dabyr was." Iain said.

"Do you want me to see if I can help?" Andra asked.

"How?" Iain asked.

"Let me erect a forcefield around her and see if it dampens the visions."

"It's worth a shot," Paul said.

Iain nodded. "I don't want to upset the humans. They need to think we're able to protect them if the shit hits the fan here."

For an instant, Andra wished it would. Then, an instant later, she felt like an ass for wishing such a thing. As much as she missed combat and the thrill of the hunt, she would never willingly put anyone at risk just so she could stop being bored out of her mind.

Paul settled his hand at the small of her back in an effort to calm or comfort. Perhaps both.

"We'll find a quiet spot," Andra said. "No one has to know."

CHAPTER SIX

Serena went numb, then queasy. Shock radiated through her like a blast, leaving her swaying slightly on her feet.

It had been so long since she'd seen Mr. Tolland that she hadn't even considered that he might still be alive. Or that he'd still want her.

"Serena doesn't *belong* to you," Morgan said, his tone on the edge of anger.

"I'm afraid she does." He reached into his pocket and pulled out a paper, brittle and yellowed with age. He handed it to Morgan. "It's a bit hard to read, but you'll get the gist."

He shoved past Morgan and entered her room. As soon as he saw her, he came to a stop and eyed her up and down, like she was something tasty. "Serena. What a...festive dress. You always did enjoy a bit of sparkle. No matter. I've purchased you some appropriate clothing for our travels."

Morgan shut the door and turned to face her. Anger tightened his jaw and clenched his fist around the contract.

And it was a contract. Serena had seen it before, two centuries ago.

She didn't think she'd ever forget her mother's betrayal written down in black and white.

"What the hell is this?" Morgan demanded of her.

"My mother's idea of a sick joke," Serena replied.

Mr. Tolland frowned. "There is no joke. This document is

as legally binding as it was the day it was written. I paid handsomely for your bond, and I intend to get what I paid for."

"Not going to happen," Morgan said.

"My mother is dead," Serena said. "And even if she wasn't, she had no right to sell me like livestock."

"How much did you pay?" Morgan asked. "I'll repay you and you can go on your way."

"If memory serves, it was two bars of gold and a sword that had been in my family for generations."

"*I'll* repay you," Serena said. "I don't need anyone else cleaning up after my mother but me."

Mr. Tolland laughed. "With interest, that would be a small fortune. And even if you did have it, I refuse. All I want is you."

He stepped forward and held out his hand, expectant, as if there were no question as to whether or not she'd take it.

Serena remembered what it was like to touch him—the sharp, electric current he sent streaking through her like a static shock.

She hadn't liked it then and she wouldn't like it now that the power he carried had doubtlessly grown.

She kept her hands by her sides, tucking them in the ruffles of her skirt to hide the way they shook. Even she couldn't tell if she was angrier at her mother for signing the contract or at Mr. Tolland for asking for it in the first place. "I'm sorry, but I'm not interested. If you have a problem with that, then you'll have to take it up with the person you contracted with."

"But she's dead," said Tolland.

"Exactly."

Tolland's mouth scrunched into a tight ring of distaste. "As her sole living heir, it's your duty to uphold her promises."

Was it? Serena didn't know. She'd been out of the world so long she had no idea how things were done now.

Morgan came to her rescue. "Serena's only duty is to herself. I'm sorry you came all this way, but you're out of luck."

Mr. Tolland turned his gaunt face toward Morgan, and though he was shorter, seemed to peer down his aristocratic nose. His voice was filled with casual dismissal, as one would speak to a servant. "This is none of your affair. Please leave."

"Stay," Serena countered. "It *is* his business."

"How is that?" Mr. Tolland asked.

"Because I say so," she practically shouted. "I'm tired of everyone pushing me around and making decisions for me. I'm a grown fucking woman!"

Mr. Tolland sucked in a startled breath at her language.

Morgan grinned.

"Now, get out, both of you!" she bellowed.

"This isn't like you at all, Serena," Mr. Tolland said.

All her frustration whirled around in her gut and came spewing out of her mouth. "We spent all of three hours together two hundred years ago. You don't know what I'm like at all."

"You used to be a well-mannered, genteel lady."

"Well, I'm not anymore. My fucking mother locked me away in a fucking cage, alone for two fucking centuries. If you think I give a fuck about her or her fucking contracts, you can go fuck yourself." Her gaze went from Mr. Tolland to Morgan. "That goes for you, too. Out!"

"This isn't over, Serena," Tolland said. "We'll discuss our arrangement further, after you calm down from your hysterics."

Serena jerked the alarm clock from the bedside table, yanked the cord from the plug, and flung it at his head.

He dodged all but the trailing end of the cord, which bit into his cheek, leaving a faint, red mark. Plastic shattered against the door behind him.

"Get out!" she screamed.

Morgan's smile never broke as he opened the door, ushered the Brit out and closed it behind him.

Serena engaged the locks and leaned heavily against the cool wood.

She had no clue what she was going to do now, but she

needed to figure out something fast.

Neither of those men would stop pursuing her until they got what they wanted. Her only options were to keep running for the rest of her life, or tie herself to one of them.

She knew which of those things she was willing to do.

It took her less than three minutes to pack her bag.

For now, running was the only choice she was prepared to make. Maybe that made her a coward, but at least she'd be a free one.

***

Sibyl sat in the dim confines of her makeshift bedroom, hugging her knees. Anxious energy flitted around her like stinging insects, taking tiny bites out of her.

It was nearly her turn again—nearly her turn to see what the future held for her people.

Maura, her twin sister, was still out there, fooling herself into thinking that she was soulless, like the demons they fought. Sibyl knew better. She knew that Maura was wrong. Troubled.

As she did every day, she reached out for the thread that tied them together, hoping to feel some answer, some warmth. Instead, all she felt was an empty chill.

Maura was still alive. If she wasn't, then Sibyl would no longer have to wait for her turn to use her gift of sight. The toy they shared would be all hers.

As much as she hated waiting for insight that would help her people turn the tide of war, the wait reassured her, proving to her that her sister still lived.

Sibyl had spent years searching for a way to save her sister. She'd even used her gift of sight to seek knowledge, but had been barred from that future vision. Still, she'd been trapped inside a child's body until recently—a last gift from her dead mother who'd cursed her to live as an eight-year-old for centuries. But now that she was an adult, there were more options at her disposal.

She was a female Theronai, as well as a seer. She could tap into the tremendous stores of power a male of her kind would hold, if only she could find one with whom she was compatible.

Until now, she hadn't been ready for that kind of bond. But until now, she'd thought there would be time—time to get used to her adult body, time to get used to no longer having Cain around to protect her, time to grieve for the loss of her parents.

Time to find and save her sister.

It was clear now that time was not a luxury any of their kind possessed. The war was not going well. Their people were standing precariously balanced on the edge of defeat. All it would take was one little push to send them careening into the jaws of the demons who fed on their blood.

Sibyl was out of time. She needed a mate, which she would not find trapped inside this shelter with no unbound males of her kind to test.

She had to get out of here, which meant that she needed to be careful in her choice once it was her turn to see the future.

She would have only one chance, only be able to ask one question, before her gift was once again swept away by her sister—a sister who loved to hold it hostage for as long as possible, making Sibyl twist with impatience.

But her turn would come soon. Maura was as curious as a cat. She wouldn't be able to hold out for long.

As soon as the thought passed through Sibyl's mind, she felt a rush of power flood her body. It shimmered through her skin and bones until it became part of her. The whole space inside her cardboard lair lit up as her flesh began to glow and heat poured from her body.

Her gift was back.

Sibyl didn't know what her sister had seen. She didn't even know what she'd asked the future to reveal. All she knew was that whatever Maura saw, she'd used it against her own people. A traitor.

Regret dampened Sibyl's excitement. She should have

found a way to convince Maura to come home, to rejoin her family. She should have slipped out into the world and gathered up her twin in her arms and refused to let go until Maura saw the truth.

She wasn't beyond redemption. No one was.

Even with all the harm she'd done, all the evil she'd allowed to grow and swell, there was still part of her worth saving. And no matter what it took, Sibyl was going to find that part and rip it from her sister, kicking and screaming.

But first, she was going to need power—more of it than she'd ever had before.

Sibyl formed her question in her mind. She built it, framing it carefully, then covering it with an impervious shell so that her will could not wander and muddy her vision.

Her answer had to be clear, which meant her question did as well.

Once she was certain that she had the right wording in her mind—because she knew better than anyone that wording mattered—she set free her question into the world.

There was only one way she was going to be free to find her sister, only one way she was going to be able to find her mate and bind him to her.

Only one way her sister survived.

Her voice was a mere whisper that couldn't possibly travel outside of her shadowy space and reach the ears of another. "How do we save Dabyr?"

CHAPTER SEVEN

Morgan waited for Link to get into his rental car, then parked his truck behind it so the man couldn't follow Serena.

She was going to run. There wasn't a single doubt in Morgan's mind. He'd seen it in her eyes the second Link had walked into the room—a desperate need to get away. Flee.

A couple of minutes later, she raced out of the hotel and left the parking lot in a screech of burning tires.

He'd find her again, but Link wouldn't.

The gaunt Brit got out of his car and came up to Morgan's window, fuming.

Morgan greeted him with a smile. "Can I help you?"

"I don't know who you think you are, but you have no right to interfere in my personal affairs."

"I'm not. I'm simply helping a woman in need."

"What need?" Link asked, indignant.

"The need to get away from a self-important asshole like you. Obviously."

"Do you want me to draw steel on you?"

Morgan shrugged, unconcerned. "Can if you like. I'd hate to hurt you, but I will if you insist."

"Who's to say I wouldn't hurt you?"

"Anything is possible, but I can guarantee that if either of us sheds blood in this part of the country, a lot of demons will come running for a snack. An area as populated as this is bound to suffer some human casualties. I'm not willing to have that on my conscience. Unless you make the first move."

"This is ridiculous. No one has to die. Serena is mine by law. Just accept that and get out of my way."

"Nope."

Link bristled and his cheeks flushed red with anger. "What do you mean, *nope*?"

"Serena doesn't like you. She doesn't want to be with you. If she did, she would have asked you to stay. Ergo, nope."

"So, you'll sit here all night, blocking me in like some kind of child throwing a tantrum?"

Morgan shook his head. "I'll move in a few minutes—once Serena has a decent head start. What you do after that is your own business."

"You know I'm going after her, right?" Link asked. "She belongs to me."

Morgan shook his head. "With an attitude like that, you've already lost her."

"She has no choice. The law is on my side."

"I have a feeling that if Serena were here, she'd tell you to go fuck the law."

Link clenched his jaw and stomped off. Morgan remained alert, waiting for an attack, but it never came.

The Brit might have been a self-important prick, but at least he wasn't risking human lives. Morgan had to give him credit for showing that much restraint.

Morgan had only one play left to make, and he wasn't sure how well it was going to go over.

He called their leader, Joseph, and made sure he knew not to give Serena's location to anyone. He explained the situation in as little detail as possible, and told the man that until they knew who Link was, he was to be considered a threat.

If nothing else, he'd forced Serena to flee again.

Once that call was over, the one Morgan had to make now was as uncomfortable as it was necessary.

Iain—the man Serena had been in love with years ago—answered on the third ring. "What's up, Morgan?"

"Staying busy. You?" Morgan asked.

"Life in the shelter sucks. Everyone is bored and scared. The place reeks with all these people crowded in together."

"How are people doing there? Are the kids adjusting?"

"Kids always adjust. Just wish they didn't have to, you know? Still, beats having to fight off demons every night because we have no safe place to go." He let out a long sigh. "It's going to get worse. Let's hope Joseph is able to get the walls back up soon."

"How's Jackie?" Morgan asked.

"Struggling. Pregnancy isn't for pussies." He sounded worried, almost scared.

Things must not be going well for a man as calm as Iain to be freaked out.

"Fortunately, the baby will be here any day now," he said. "But small talk is not why you called, is it?"

"No." He pulled in a deep breath. There was no easy way to say this, but at least the direct approach was fastest. "Serena and I are compatible."

Iain didn't even hesitate. "That's great news!" Genuine joy colored his tone.

"You're not jealous?"

"Not even a little. Why would I be?"

"You two were…close."

"We were more than that. We were in love. We were going to tie our lives together permanently. She was an amazing woman and I was lucky to have her for as long as I did. But that's all ancient history. I have Jackie now. And a kid on the way. How could I want any less happiness for Serena? After what she's been through, she deserves it. You two will be great together."

The feeling of relief Morgan had weakened his knees. He hadn't realized until now just how much he wanted Iain's blessing to pursue Serena. They'd been friends a long time, as close as brothers. The idea that Iain would be pissed at him had grated on his nerves and made him edgy.

Now, all he felt was free.

"What do you know about Link Tolland?" he asked.

Iain's voice lost its warmth. "Why?"

"He showed up out of the blue with a contract stating Serena was *given* to him. Can you believe that shit?"

Iain sighed. "Yeah. I can. Serena's mother was a heinous cunt. She didn't care about Serena or what she wanted. All she cared about was appearances and status. I was never good enough for her, but Link was."

"Is he a bad guy?"

"He's full of himself, but who am I to say who's a bad guy and who isn't? I'm the dude with no soul, remember?"

Morgan stared out his windshield at Serena's hotel room. He knew she wasn't in there anymore, but he couldn't help but remember how close he'd been to striking a bargain with her.

Maybe.

"I want her, Iain," Morgan blurted. "I didn't realize I would, but here we are. The pain—"

Iain cut him off, his voice soft, sympathetic. "I know. I understand."

And he did. Iain had lived with his own pain for a long time. It was not the kind of thing a man easily forgot.

"I'm on your side," Iain said. "You want to know how to convince her to love you, right?"

Something cold and hard clenched in his gut. "No. Not love. I'm not foolish enough to think that's where we're headed. But I do want a partner. I need one if I'm going to keep fighting. And honestly, binding her to me is the best way I can think of to protect her."

Iain's tone was one of complete understanding. "Whatever you do, don't tell her that. Serena hates to be coddled. She spent her whole life being bossed around and controlled by her mother. If you try to use force—even for her own protection—you'll lose her forever."

"So, what do I do? She keeps running away."

"Indulge her wishes. Respect her. She's about as tough as they come, and smart enough to know what she wants and doesn't."

But what if she didn't want him? He didn't know how much longer he had, and now that he'd touched her and had a moment free of pain, the burden he carried around seemed so much heavier. That one moment of reprieve she'd granted him had revealed just how far he'd degraded over the years without even noticing.

Too far.

"Thanks, Iain. I owe you."

"Then find a way to make her happy and we'll call it even. She's a good woman, Morgan. She deserves to be happy."

Could he do that? Morgan wasn't sure, but he did know he had to try. There was too much at stake for him to half-ass this.

His life was on the line. So was Serena's freedom. Not to mention that one more bonded pair of Theronai could mean the difference between life and death for thousands.

"One more thing," Iain said.

"What's that?"

"If you hurt her, I will kill you."

Morgan grunted. "Only if Serena doesn't beat you to it."

***

Link Tolland had the law on his side. He didn't care if the contract was old, or that the laws had changed. He didn't care about political correctness or public opinion. Right was right, and Serena legally belonged to him.

He was running out of time. With only two leaves left on his lifemark, and his agony expanding by the day, he knew that Serena was his last chance at survival.

And he had to survive. His people were suffering, their numbers dwindling by the week. Another bonded pair of Theronai in Europe would make all the difference in saving the lives of those he was sworn to protect.

Not to mention Serena herself.

He didn't want to use force to make her do the right thing,

but he was nearly out of options. It had taken him months to learn of her return from wherever she'd been held for the last two centuries. It had taken him weeks to convince his leader that he needed to take time away from the fight to seek her out.

He'd landed in Atlanta and driven two days to find her, only to be rejected. Again.

Link wanted to be patient with her, but how could he? His leader had given him only a short time to seal the deal with her and bring her back to England. Three days of that was already gone, with the remaining few falling through his fingers like water.

He'd asked Nicholas, the Theronai who managed Dabyr's tech systems, to tell him where she'd gone again, but word had come down from Joseph Rayd not to cooperate with Link further.

Morgan Valens also wanted her—Link had seen that much in the man's eyes as he looked at her. And no doubt, the leader of Dabyr was going to give preferential treatment to one of his own over a stranger from another continent.

Link probably would have done no differently. The stakes were too high not to use every advantage one had.

And right now, his biggest advantage was his allies back home. One in particular had a knack for worming her way through the Web to find whatever she sought. If she looked hard enough, Link was certain she'd be able to find the location of Serena's vehicle.

After that, it was simply a matter of forcing her to see reason.

With little time left, Link hoped the force he would be required to exert upon Serena wouldn't cause her permanent damage.

Once they were bound and she had access to his thoughts, she'd understand why he'd done what he'd done. Perhaps then, she would forgive him. At least he'd still be alive to be forgiven.

CHAPTER EIGHT

Joseph Rayd, leader of the Theronai, called Serena's phone the next afternoon.

She'd just checked into a motel north of Austin and had settled in to eat a hamburger and fries before going out to hunt.

Like so many other rooms she'd stayed in, this one was bland and uninviting. The furnishings were shabby and worn, but at least they seemed clean this time. A faded painting of a field of flowers sat over the bed. The edges of the image were warped with moisture and slightly yellow. But at least it still matched the equally faded floral blanket covering the bed.

She leaned back in her chair as she peered through the sheers over the window. She checked the parking lot for unwanted visitors as she'd been doing since she'd arrived.

All she saw was frosty cars and trash and leaves being tossed by a cold, winter wind.

She'd kept her phone with her for emergencies, but had asked that no one but him have the number. She'd been very clear that if he abused her trust, she'd throw her phone in the nearest body of water and never carry one again.

She refused to be leashed—especially by a small, black box she didn't fully understand.

Like casting some arcane spell, it took three tries to make the right gesture in the right spot to connect the call. When it finally did, she said, "Yes?"

Joseph's deep voice came clearly over the device as if he were standing in the same room. Along with it were the sounds of battle in the distance—the clash of swords, grunts of men and howls of demons.

Serena still marveled over technology and wondered if she'd ever grow used to it. At first, she was convinced that the things she'd seen were magic. Lights glowed everywhere. Colors and sounds seemed to wrap around population centers as if summoned by those who lived in them. That words and pictures could travel through thin air was an astounding mystery to her, and one she struggled daily to accept as part of her new life.

Even toddlers were more versed in modern technology than she was.

"I know you don't want to be bothered," Mr. Rayd said, "but this is important."

"How is the battle?" she asked before he could take control of the conversation.

He hesitated. "We're doing the best we can."

Serena's heart sank. Those were evasive words. Words of defeat.

Not for the first time she wondered if she should return to the place her people called home and lend her sword to the fight.

"But that's not why I called," He said. "Do you know Sibyl Brinn?"

Serena remembered the name, though she hadn't heard it in years. "She's the daughter of Gilda and Angus Brinn, distant relatives of mine. I met them when I was young, but I don't believe I ever spent time with Sibyl or her twin sister. They were small children when I was imprisoned."

An awkward silence filled the space for a moment before Mr. Rayd cleared his throat. "She remembers you. She asked that I speak to you."

"Why?"

"She has the ability to see the future—at least a vague version of it."

"I'd heard rumors around Dabyr about a child seer. Is that her?"

"She's not a child anymore, but yes. That's her."

Serena's food was growing cold, and it would be the last meal she had before going into the field tonight. This conversation needed to be over soon. "Why did she ask you to speak to me?"

"Since the walls of Dabyr fell there have been some developments in the war against Synestryn."

"What developments?"

"You've seen the human-looking demons that have been popping up lately, right?"

"Yes. I've killed many of them."

"And the ones with red eyes?" he asked.

Serena thought about it. The detail wasn't one that she'd focused on in the midst of staying alive during combat, but now that he mentioned it, she had seen red eyes, though most were black. "Only a few, but yes."

"Have you seen where they come from?" he asked. His tone was almost desperate.

She frowned at his question. "Darkness and caves, like all demons."

"No, I mean the source. These creatures are new and we have no idea where they're coming from or how they're reproducing so fast. All we know is that their numbers are growing faster than we can kill them. They are the reason our walls fell and the reason they will stay fallen if we can't figure out how to stop them."

Serena had known the situation was dire, but she hadn't realized just how much of a problem these creatures were. Dabyr had stood for centuries. Demons had tried to breach the walls countless times, and never before had they succeeded so completely.

All those souls—some five hundred of them—out in the world, in danger of being killed and eaten for the traces of magical blood they carried.

Her appetite was gone in the face of so much suffering.

She pushed away the hamburger, sliding it across the small, round table in her motel room.

"I don't know much," she said. "I know these new demons are not poisonous like other Synestryn." If they had been, she would have been dead long ago, though she didn't feel the need to mention that to the man. "Their blood is more red than black and they seem to be able to communicate with one another."

"You've heard words?"

"More like clicks and grunts. I suppose they could be words, but if so, it's unlike any language I've ever heard."

"Have you been marking their locations on the maps I gave you?"

"Yes."

"See any kind of pattern?"

"I've looked for one, but so far, none have appeared."

"Have you ever seen any of their young?" he asked.

Serena paused, thinking. "Now that you mention it, no. I've been through many caves that housed the beasts, but I've never seen any but fully-grown adults. Unless, their children are also seven feet tall."

The line went silent, but she could tell he hadn't disconnected. The connection was so strong she could hear him breathing, hear voices in the background as they shouted across the field of battle.

Miraculous.

"What's going on, Mr. Rayd?" Serena asked.

"Joseph. You need to start calling people by their first names if you're going to fit into our time. And, to answer your question, I'm not sure what's going on."

She made a mental note to do as he'd asked. He wasn't her sworn leader, but he also bore her no ill will. He wouldn't correct her manner of speaking if it wasn't a problem.

"Then why did you call me?" she asked.

"Because Sibyl said you were the key to learning the source of the demons. In so many words, she said that if you don't find the source and destroy it, we're all screwed. We'll never rebuild the walls of Dabyr."

Serena's breath lodged solidly in her lungs, wedged in by thick apprehension. She'd heard rumors about the girl's ability, and that it carried a great cost. There were whispers that she only used her gift under the direst circumstances. If that was true, then Serena had no choice but to listen.

She hugged herself with one arm. "Is Sibyl always right?"

"As far as I know, yes."

Serena swallowed down a sick sense of dread. Visions of the future were real. She knew that. She'd witnessed the power of a woman in her own time who'd saved countless lives with her sight. If Sibyl was even half the seer that woman had been, then Serena would be wise to listen. "What were her exact words?"

"You'll have to talk to her directly next time. I'm too busy to record conversations. The closest I can get is, 'Tell Serena to find and destroy the source of the demons, or everyone she loves will be lost.' Or something like that."

She almost opened her mouth to say she didn't love anyone, but bit back the lie before it could escape.

Soulless or not, bound to another woman or not, Serena still loved Iain. She didn't want to, but that changed nothing.

He had a child on the way. Could she really let that baby grow up without a father? Or would that innocent life be lost as well if Serena didn't heed Sibyl's warning?

Joseph spoke again, his voice a soft warning. "She said that you're running out of time, Serena. Only you can find the source of those demons, and it must be done before the next babies are born."

"Which babies? Ours or those of these demons?"

Joseph paused. "I'm not sure. You really should call her. I'll text you her number when we're done here."

Serena didn't want to talk to the woman, but she said nothing. "Why me? Why would Sibyl have a vision about me?"

"Hell if I know. Maybe it has something to do with your unique talents. You never have told me what you can do."

Every female Theronai had a gift. Not all developed at the same time—some girls found their talent when they were children. Others had to wait until adulthood. But every woman born with the ring-shaped birthmark that signified they were Theronai had something special they could do. Even if they wished they didn't.

She hadn't told anyone that she could alter the flow of time. She couldn't reverse it, but she could speed or slow it within a small area for a little while. It was exhausting, but possible.

Not even Iain knew what she could do. Her powers were just beginning to manifest when she'd fallen in love with him. She would have told him after they'd bonded, but she'd been whisked away and caged before she could.

"Not much," she lied. "I have no idea what it is Sibyl expects from me."

"I think you do," Joseph said, his voice both kind and filled with regret. "I know you're not ready to take a mate yet, but we're running out of time. Morgan is running out of time."

"He told you that we're compatible?" she asked, furious that Morgan would share such a secret without her consent.

"It's kind of a big deal to find a compatible female. There may have been a lot of women running around when you were trapped away from the world, but there aren't now. Most of them were slaughtered the night you left. And until now, we haven't had any new generations born. It's going to be decades before Madoc and Nika's baby is old enough to choose a mate. We'll lose too many good men before that time. We could lose everything." Joseph paused for a moment as if gathering his composure. "I know you're dealing with a lot. I can only imagine how hard it was for you to come back and find the world so different and the man you'd loved with someone else. But please, Serena, set aside your anger and pain for just a moment and ask yourself what you want your life to look like. Do you want to keep running, constantly alone, in danger, or do you want a partner?"

After two hundred years, she didn't know how to be

anything but alone. It didn't matter how lonely she was or how much she craved companionship. She'd been so long without people that they all grated on her nerves now.

Joseph continued, "You have two men who can offer you power. I heard Link was a bit abrasive, but he's in a lot of pain, so we have to excuse him. Plus, there's a lot at stake for him."

"He's not the only one," she muttered under her breath.

Why was it that none of these men could see her side of things? They all wanted to be free from their pain, but what about her freedom? Hadn't she lost enough? Was it really fair of them to ask more of her?

"Morgan is a great guy," Joseph said. "He's a bit of a flirt, but I'm sure he'd give all that up for you. In fact, both of those men are in enough pain that either of them would give you whatever you want in exchange for your bond."

Would they? Permanently? She wasn't convinced.

"You're smart, Serena. Figure out what you want out of life and find a way to make one of those two men give it to you. Fast. Because if Sibyl is right, then none of us have time to waste. The attacks on Dabyr aren't getting any easier to fend off. Our temporary shelters are holding out, still secret, but that won't last long. We're spread too thin, working to protect too many humans in too many places. We need every bonded pair of Theronai we can get if we're to have any hope of surviving what's headed our way."

"That's a bit ominous," she said.

"I was sugar-coating it for you. Things are way worse—bad enough I'm not going to fill your head with any of it."

"I'm not weak."

"If I thought you were weak, I wouldn't be asking you to tie yourself to one of my men. Better you die alone than drag a strong sword arm down with you. My wanting you to take a mate has more to do with your strengths than your weaknesses."

Serena didn't know what to do, but she wasn't foolish enough to refuse to even consider what he'd said. "I'll think about it, Joseph." Using his name felt strange, but she'd become accustomed to it eventually.

"Think fast, okay? We need you on the front lines, at full power. I know you're good with a sword, but think of how much more damage you could do with a bit of magic fueling you."

She hesitated in asking, but had to know. "How are the babies?"

Joy and weariness wove through his tone. "Healthy. Strong. Nika's daughter is thriving, and Jackie's child will be here in only a few days. Andra's is a few months off, but it's just a matter of time. All of them are safe and healthy for now."

A few days wasn't long. If Sybil's warning was real and Serena had to find the source of those demons before the birth of Iain's child, she didn't have a moment to spare.

"I'll hurry," she said. "For the babies."

Serena hung up, put on her fighting leathers, and went to work. She had a lot of thinking to do, and she always thought best with a sword in her hand.

CHAPTER NINE

When Morgan found Serena, deep inside the belly of a cavern in central Texas not yet discovered by spelunkers or tourists, it was already too late.

He'd tracked her car here, then followed her footprints in the light dusting of snow on the ground. It led directly into a cave he'd never seen before.

The opening was little more than a narrow hole in the ground barely big enough for his shoulders to pass through. The tunnel angled steeply downward, out of the cold, biting wind and into humid blackness.

The air down here was thick with demon stench—a mix of animal musk, rotting corpses, feces and something cloyingly sweet. At one time he'd believed that he'd get used to the smell in his line of work, but after centuries of that not happening, he'd given up on the idea.

There were some things a man simply couldn't get used to.

He heard Serena before he found her. The rough, jagged tunnel split off into two branches. Her high, feminine voice could barely be heard over the guttural grunts of demons fighting her.

To the left. That was where she was. Fighting alone.

Morgan shoved his way down the tunnel, heedless of the rough scrape of stone against his body. This passage was barely wide enough for his body, and in some places, so short he had to crouch. In one section, he had to crawl to get through.

When the tunnel finally emptied out into a small cavern, Serena was there, only a few yards away.

It was dark, but he had no trouble seeing, thanks to the power he called to him without even trying. Minute sparks of energy fueled his night vision and showed him just how bad things were.

She was surrounded by those pale, gray, eerily-human demons, bleeding from a dozen wounds and barely fending off more.

In the distance, he could hear the echo of more Synestryn closing in. Every monster down here would have smelled her blood and come for a taste.

Before that happened, he needed to get her out of here.

Serena was too fast to track. Her sword seemed to be in three places at once, blurring into one continuous arc of dark red blood. That blood splattered the cave walls as well as her pale face.

Her lips were pulled back in a feral snarl of rage and bellow of determination. Even though there were far too many of the demons for her to survive the battle, she wasn't going down without a fight.

Morgan lifted his weapon and charged. He sliced through three of the demons with his first blow. Bone and tissue dragged along his blade, but he powered through until he hit nothing but air. There were three more rows of demons between her and him, and a few at the back had finally realized that she wasn't the only meal in town.

Demons spun on him and slashed at him with their rusty weapons. He managed to evade two of the blows, but that put him firmly in the way of the third.

The dull, rusty edge split the skin just below his shoulder. He didn't notice the pain. He carried around too much of that every day to register a bit more. He did, however, notice the way his left hand numbed almost instantly.

Morgan ignored it and kept fighting.

More demons fell at his feet. He climbed over them, careful not to slip on the blood and gore coating their bodies.

Finally, after what felt like a year, there were no longer any enemies between him and Serena. He was at her side.

She was in bad shape.

The leather along her thigh, as well as the flesh under it, gaped open, revealing a deep wound that went all the way to the bone. She was bleeding badly. Her magically enhanced leather armor protected her from some of the lesser hits, but too many blows had powered through her defenses and injured her.

The sword she wielded was shorter than his, slimmer and lighter. The reduced weight made it faster, but also gave it little mass to block the heavy strikes of the demons' clunky blades.

As he watched, another powerhouse of a blow barreled down toward her. She lifted her sword to block it, but she wasn't strong enough to do more than change its trajectory.

Morgan shoved his body close to hers and rounded to face the thickest clump of demons.

They needed to move. Retreat. This cavern was a deathtrap, but if they could make it back to the narrow tunnel, there was no way for the enemy to slip around them if they fought side-by-side. As long as they both stayed standing, they could take on the enemy only one or two at a time.

The clang of metal on stone was loud, but the thunder of approaching troops eager for Theronai blood was even louder.

"We have to retreat," he called to be heard over the fray.

"Agreed," she screamed back.

They began backing into the tunnel, leaving a trail of blood behind her. Two of the gray demons bent to lap up the blood, taking the treasure they had now over the one they had yet to earn.

After a few yards, Serena's injured leg buckled and she went down.

If not for him blocking the sword headed toward her, she

would have lost the other leg.

He reached down with his numb hand and tried to pull her up. He couldn't feel her touch, but when he felt her weight tugging at his leather jacket, he lifted his arm to bring her to her feet.

"Lean on me," he yelled. "We're almost there."

He could feel the roof of the tunnel opening scraping his head and knew they were almost to the narrow spot where he'd had to crawl to pass.

"Go," he shouted. "I'll be right behind you."

"You won't make it. They'll kill you before you get through."

"Trust me." There was no time for more words. He needed every bit of concentration to stave off the mass of attacks aimed at him.

"I'm through!" she yelled, and by the echo of her voice he knew she was telling the truth.

Morgan was going to have to go through the narrow opening feet first. If he didn't keep his sword swinging, these fuckers would cut off his legs before he got to the other side.

The tiny opening was only three feet long, but those three feet were probably going to cost him his life.

He promised himself that if he made it out of this alive, he was going to start carrying grenades down into these caves with him. Or maybe some C-4.

Hell, even a gun might have done him some good against these things. They weren't as hard to kill as the demons he was used to fighting—which took decapitation or fire to kill—but there were so damn many of them, they were still just as deadly.

"Coming through," he bellowed, then lashed into a frenzy of attacks meant to drive his enemy back just a few inches. He was going to need every one of those inches if he was to have any chance of making out of this alive.

At least his carcass would plug the hole and give Serena a chance to make a run for it while the demons feasted on him.

Not that she was running anywhere very fast on that

injured leg of hers.

As soon as he'd gained a fraction of space, he dropped down and shoved his feet back into the opening.

The moment he did, the oddest thing happened. First, Serena grabbed his ankle. Her bare, chilly fingers brushed the skin above his sock. He thought she was going to try to pull him through the hole, but that's not what happened at all. Instead, he felt an intense wash of heat suffuse him, along with a giddy lack of pain as she touched him. All of that was expected. What wasn't, was a strange sense of vertigo, like his brain had been spun around inside his skull. The air around him shimmered and seemed to shrink in around him. There was a heavy, popping feeling, like he'd broken through the surface of a bubble.

The demons in front of him went still. Frozen.

No, not frozen, but they were moving so slowly, it was almost hard to detect movement.

"Can't hold it," Serena said through clenched teeth.

Morgan didn't know what she was talking about, but now was not the time for questions. Later, after they got out of this alive, that's when he'd interrogate her about what was happening, but right now, he was getting them the hell out of here.

He scrambled through the opening so fast he skinned his knees and shoulders, which were barely able to fit through the space.

As soon as he was on the other side, he saw Serena's face.

She was eerily pale and sweating. Her whole body shook with effort, as if sagging under its own weight.

Whatever she'd done to slow down those demons was costing her.

Without hesitation, Morgan swept her up in his arms and raced up the tunnel toward the exit. It was a tight fit and he had to turn sideways more than once to shove through, but he did it, and he did it fast.

Fresh night air hit his face and cleared his nostrils of demon filth. The winter air was cold and clean, but it carried with it the sound of an army racing toward them. He couldn't tell if it was coming from outside of the tunnel or an echo from inside, but either way, if he let that army reach them, they were both dead.

Morgan rushed for his truck. There were at least a hundred yards between this cave opening and the cattle pasture where he'd parked. He and Serena were both bleeding freely. If he didn't make the run fast enough, nearby demons would smell them and come hunting.

He spared one quick glance down at her, and knew she wasn't okay. Her head bounced against his chest as if she had trouble holding it up.

She was in no shape to stand, much less fight.

To his left, a piercing howl split the night.

He'd know that cry anywhere. It was sgath demons signaling they'd caught a scent and were on the hunt.

They were so screwed.

He rounded a patch of brush, and in the distance, his truck became visible. He'd left it unlocked with the keys inside, as was his habit. More than one Theronai had died trying to find his keys, and Morgan wasn't going to add to that statistic.

A rumbling growl of hunger came from the brush to his left. He couldn't tell how far away it was, but it was too damn close.

"Serena?" he whispered.

Her answer was a weak whisper. "Yes?"

She was fading fast, bleeding out.

Fuck.

Morgan finally reached the truck, ripped the door open and sent her spilling inside as he crawled in behind the wheel.

Losing contact with her skin made his world light up with agony, but he swallowed it down and forced himself to move. *Just fucking move.*

He pushed the ignition button as he undid his belt and jerked it free of his jeans.

The second the motor started, he hit the accelerator and spewed dirt behind him as he tore out of the field. The field gate to the road was closed, but he didn't bother to stop and open it. Instead, he powered through, wincing at the gouges in his new ride.

"Put this on," he said as he held his belt out to Serena.

Her tone was one of weak confusion. "Why?"

"Tourniquet your leg. Stop the bleeding."

She took his belt with shaking hands and looped it around her upper thigh.

He pushed the hands-free button on his steering wheel and said, "Call Tynan."

Tynan was one of the Sanguinar—a race of Sentinels that were more like vampires than not. Of course, they'd punch you in the eye if you called them that, but Morgan never had understood what all the fuss was about.

They were the healers—healers who fed on blood to fuel their magic. They also didn't go into the sun and were weak during the day.

As far as Morgan was concerned, a vampire by any other name was still just as creepy. But they were handy as hell, too, if you could get past the whole moody, dark brooding, living in eternal hunger bullshit.

Morgan liked Tynan better than the rest of the Sanguinar. He was more pragmatic than most and was almost always willing to come help if there was a payment of blood in the offering. Unlike a lot of Morgan's brothers, he didn't begrudge the Sanguinar for the blood they needed to survive. Some of his kind were suspicious of the bloodsuckers, certain that they had ulterior motives to their healing.

Maybe they did, maybe they didn't. Either way, Morgan would have been dead a dozen times over if not for the aid of a Sanguinar. And he wasn't alone. Everyone he knew had needed their help at least once.

Now Serena was the one in need.

A quick glance at her thigh told Morgan that she hadn't pulled the belt tight enough to stop the bleeding.

A quarter mile down the gravel road, he braked, grabbed the leather tongue and pulled it tight enough to make her lever up and punch the side of his head.

Funny, but that instant of contact with her bare skin against his eased his pain, even though that hadn't been her aim.

The effort exhausted her, and she lolled back against the seat, limp and still.

After several rings Tynan answered with a surly, "I'm neck deep in the injured. What do you need?"

"Serena is bleeding out."

"It's not that bad," she said, but her breathless words proved it a lie.

As soon as Tynan heard her, his tone shifted to all business. "Where are you?"

"A few miles north of Austin."

"That's too far. Joseph called me back to Dabyr to heal the fighters. We're being overrun every night. You're hours away."

Morgan saw the flash of creepy green eyes in his rearview and knew he was out of time. The demons were on their tail. While he loved his new truck, it wouldn't stand a chance against the teeth and claws of hungry sgath.

With the tongue of the belt in one hand, he drove off as fast as his truck would go.

"I'll have to take her to a hospital then. It's bad, Tynan."

"Not that bad," she argued.

Morgan ignored her.

"No. Don't do that. Human blood won't help her. I'll ask Briant to come to you. He's the only one of us who is near you, in our Texas shelter."

"Where is that?" Morgan asked.

"Just outside of Dallas. South, I believe."

"I'll drive that way, but if he doesn't hurry, I'm taking her to the human doctors."

"How bad is the bleeding?" Tynan asked.

"Bad enough. We've tied a tourniquet around her leg. Should buy us some time, but not much."

"If you must, give her your blood, but none from humans.

I'll contact Briant and call back with a meeting location."

"How do I give her my blood?"

"There should be a large syringe in your medical kit. You do know how to hit a vein, don't you?"

"I do." All of the Sentinels had medical training. Morgan couldn't perform brain surgery, but he knew how to treat most injuries to keep someone alive until help arrived. After hundreds of years in combat, a man picked up the skills necessary to save those he was sworn to protect.

But he had no magical healing. He couldn't seal up her severed blood vessels from the inside out the way a Sanguinar could.

"Then use it if things get desperate," Tynan said.

Morgan feared they already were.

Behind him, more eyes appeared in the darkness.

"Gotta go. Demons on my back."

"I'll text you in a few minutes."

Morgan hung up and concentrated on driving faster than he ever had before in his life.

***

Serena was used to pain, but she far preferred the sharp sting of split skin to the crushing band of Morgan's belt around her thigh.

She tried to take over the job of holding the leather tight, but she was too weak to bat his hand away, much less maintain pressure.

Her heart was racing in an effort to use what little blood she had left to fuel her body. She couldn't catch her breath, though she was completely still. The world was spinning. Everything around her was turning cold, except Morgan's big fist around the belt.

She cupped it like a mug of hot coffee in an effort to warm herself.

Behind them, she could hear the cry of hungry demons. She'd bled so much, there would be no safe place to stop until sunrise, which was hours away. And even then, there were demons that could withstand sunlight now. Those demons would smell her blood and come for her.

If Morgan hadn't come in that cave after her, she never would have made it out alive. She was going to have to repay him the favor, assuming she lived long enough to do so.

"Sorry for the mess," she said.

His truck was meticulously clean. Or it had been before she'd bled all over it. He was bleeding as well, but fortunately, not as much as she was.

He spared her a quick glance as he careened over the gravel roads. "Live long enough to clean it up and we'll call it even."

She honestly wasn't sure if that was going to happen.

She'd never been allowed in combat before her imprisonment. She'd always been good with a sword and had trained to defend herself from the time she was a child, but Mother never would have let her step foot in harm's way. Since Serena's release from the prison of her mother's making, she'd fought dozens of demons. Perhaps hundreds. But her injuries had never been this bad before. She healed fast, but there was no way to know if it would be fast enough.

Maybe if they survived the night…

"You're not giving up on me, are you?" he asked.

"Never. Not my nature."

"Good. Then keep those pretty eyes open and those lovely lips flapping. I need to know you're still with me."

"Too tired," she whispered. And she was. Even speaking was too much of an effort. All she wanted to do was close her eyes and sink down into the soft, leather seat where no pain or fear could reach her.

"Are you telling me you're weak?" Morgan asked.

Anger flared in her chest, strengthening her. "Fuck. You."

His cheek lifted in a smile. "That's my girl."

"Not yours."

"You could be."

Was he really going to talk about this now? While she was

bleeding all over the place?

She let her disbelief color her tone. "As if you could handle me."

"Believe me, honey. When I get my hands on you, you won't question my ability to handle any part of you. You'll know."

Hot, consuming pulses of energy thrummed out of him where her hands met his. She absorbed them eagerly, and with each one, felt a tiny bit stronger. Maybe it was the magic of the luceria flowing through her, giving her strength, or maybe Morgan was somehow lending her some of his. She didn't know, but she wasn't about to let go and give up the advantage.

After a few seconds of silence, he said, "Sorry about that. I know that now isn't the time to seduce you, but when you put your hands on me, all I can think about is getting you naked, and tasting every square inch of that perfect skin of yours.

She grunted out a bleak laugh. "Not perfect anymore."

"A few scars aren't going to scare me off, Serena, no matter if I can see them or not."

She tensed slightly at his insight, then regretted it as her body rebelled with a fresh burst of pain. More injuries were making themselves known as the seconds passed, as if they were all vying for her attention like jealous, little children seeking their mother's approval.

Morgan was right. She did have hidden scars. Too many to acknowledge. She hated that he knew it, but she imagined that after living as long as he had, he likely had a few of his own. There was no way to travel through life without taking a few hits along the way, and some were far worse than others.

She'd been betrayed by the people she loved and trusted most. Maybe those people had their reasons, but the pain they caused her was still real. It still cut her open and made her bleed, far worse than any demon could. There was no tourniquet for those injures. No justification for their actions could ever change how emotionally savaged she'd been by both her mother and Iain.

Her internal pain wasn't the kind of thing she wanted to share with anyone. All it could do was make others suffer the way she did. Her mother was dead, but Iain wasn't. Did she really want his new wife to know how much he'd hurt Serena? Did she want his children growing up knowing how much pain their father had caused another?

She couldn't do that to them. They were innocents.

It was better for her to keep her wounds hidden from the world than to let anyone know just how much she suffered. That was the only way to keep her pain from hurting more people. If she did that, then she'd be as much to blame as those who had betrayed her in the first place.

No, she was the caretaker of this pain. Its keeper. She would hold it within herself so that no one else could ever feel its sting.

Bottle it up. Hold it tight. Hide it deep.

She sat in silence, listening for answers, but heard nothing over the crunch of tires on gravel and the howl of the winter wind outside.

"Are you still with me?" Morgan asked.

Her suffering tainted her words, making them come out bleak and hopeless. "Where else would I be?"

He let out a heavy sigh. "Serena, I hope that one day, when you say those words to me, you won't sound quite so defeated."

CHAPTER TEN

When Ronan arrived at the largest shelter, he could tell he had his work cut out for him.

The smell of fear and desperation was nearly overwhelming. With it was the faint hint of sickness, as if some kind of low-grade infection had just begun to spread through the group, now that they were housed together so tightly.

Justice was at his side, a fact that still thrilled him daily. He'd spent so long searching for her—so long fighting to be near her—that he still couldn't believe she was here, beside him.

She was a constant source of surprise to him, and a constant delight. Even in the midst of war, with injury, fear and illness raging around them, all he had to do was look at her and his spirits instantly lifted.

She was his world.

Her curly, black hair was pinned up in a messy bun that bared the slender lines of her throat. She'd taken to wearing it like that because he was in almost constant need of her blood these days. And she, generous soul that she was, wanted to make sure he had what he needed without impediment.

The long, sleek lines of her body were encased in clinging black leather so that she had at least some small protection from attack if they were caught off guard. She was good with her gun—which she lovingly called Reba and treated as a beloved pet—but bullets didn't work as well on most demons as a sword did. Still, he'd seen her take down enough of the bad guys to know that Reba was as effective in Justice's hands as it could be in anyone's.

She had caramel-colored skin that was flushed with cold and the very recent climax he'd given her. Her silvery-green eyes glowed whenever she was excited, which was nearly all the time.

Even in the midst of war, with problems on all sides and people counting on their every move, Justice still managed to rock his world on a daily basis. She loved sex, thrived on it, as if it somehow fueled her.

He didn't begrudge her the time their loving took away from their work, because he knew just how much more effective they were when they were joined so tightly.

Ronan had suffered in hunger and weakness for so long he still couldn't quite believe that his new world of power and love wasn't a dream.

He reached out and took her hand in his as they entered the shelter. His need to touch her and know she was near raged inside of him. She'd told him over and over that she wasn't going anywhere, that she was his, but he'd been chasing her for so long that he had to constantly reassure himself that she was still by his side.

This shelter was larger than the others and housed the most people. Its metal skin had been imbued with just enough magic to keep the inhabitants secret. Thanks to Justice's efforts and her guidance by an otherworldly power, she had worked for years to prepare these places and stock them with supplies, not knowing how or when they would be used.

If not for her, hundreds would have died.

Ronan squeezed her hand in silent thanks as he made his way through the crowded space. There was an aisle running through the middle of the warehouse with cots on both sides. Some of the residents had strung up sheets to serve as dividers. Others had upended pallets or used empty boxes stacked up to form walls.

He wasn't surprised by their need for privacy. They knew they were going to be here for a while, and many of them—especially the children—had been through hell. They had been hunted for their blood. Some of them had been captured and held prisoner. Some of the children had been fed demon blood in an effort to alter their basic physiology so that they could help breed more human-looking Synestryn offspring.

The nightmares these people had suffered were beyond what most humans could endure without going mad. Ronan and his kind had done what they could to soften the edges of those memories and ease their minds, but there was only so much they could safely do. The residents here knew that if they left this place, they'd be hunted as food or worse. They knew they were trapped. And they'd been through hell. It was no wonder they needed some small space to call their own.

Most of the children were playing in an area set up for just that purpose. There were toys for all ages and several video game systems set up in an area covered in thick, soft rugs. The ratio of adults to children was skewed. Many of these children's parents were dead, having given their lives to protect them. The adults who survived often adopted orphaned youngsters as their own in an effort to offer them some kind of parental love and support.

They all knew that it could have just as easily been their children who'd been orphaned.

People milled around, talking in small groups. There was an air of worry about them as they speculated how long they'd have to stay and whether or not they'd be safe. Some adults were in the breakroom, which had been turned into a kitchen, cooking in shifts because there wasn't enough space to make food for everyone at the same time.

Ronan's van was loaded with supplies, including more coffee, which had disappeared faster than Justice—or the forces that had compelled her to stock this place—had anticipated. Along with that were boxes of paperbacks to read and a stack of notebooks and pens so that people could make lists of what they needed in the future.

These people were going to be here for a while. Now that the confusion of battle and relocation had subsided and the majority of their injuries had healed—mostly cuts and bruises sustained when they'd fled—people were realizing just how dire the situation was.

None of them could go back to Dabyr until the walls were rebuilt. The magic surrounding that place was the only thing keeping the demons out. Until the protective barrier was strong and solid once again, the humans were trapped here.

As he and Justice moved through the group, several people asked for an update. He told them what he'd told everyone at the other shelters he visited. Lexi was working as fast as she could to rebuild the walls, but it was going to take a while.

Too long, he thought. It was only a matter of time before people became tired of living in such close quarters and began bickering. Turf wars would inevitably break out. People would argue, possibly even fight. Blood would be shed, and the scent of it would risk the lives of everyone present— including Jackie's and Andra's unborn children.

Once he'd delivered the status report, he gathered the Sentinels housed here and took them into one of the supervisor offices overlooking the space.

There were three such rooms, all raised up about ten feet, with a wall of glass windows that gave them a clear view of the space. It had been decided early in the relocation process that no one would be given these rooms as their own to avoid conflict. Instead, one was used as an infirmary, and two were classrooms so the children's schooling wouldn't be interrupted. Like the kitchen, the space wasn't big enough to teach all the children at the same time, so they were cycled through in groups divided by age and given daily lessons. The regular teachers had been spread out among the shelters, so some of the parents had stepped up to help teach.

For the most part, these people were calm, rational, peaceful adults who were concerned only with the safety of their children and themselves. There were always a few that caused trouble, but Ronan and his kind had been instructed by Tynan to find them and use their power to keep them subdued.

The last thing they needed right now was more bloodshed. It was already a strain to keep the warriors at Dabyr in fighting shape. The less healing his kind had to do, the better. Even more important, the less blood shed here, the less chance there was of the demons smelling it and finding this place.

While the mated Theronai housed here—Paul, Andra, Nika, Madoc, Iain and Jackie—could hold their own in battle, the women were pregnant or, in Nika's case, recently delivered. It was best to keep them out of combat unless absolutely necessary. The lives of their children were too important to risk. Without them, there was no hope for the future.

The three couples and Sibyl, an unbound Theronai, sat around a small conference table. Like the rest of the residents here, their first questions were about the status of Dabyr.

"Joseph's updates aren't coming as frequently," Paul said.

"He's as exhausted as everyone else," Ronan said. "There's really nothing new to report, so why bother."

Madoc jiggled his daughter in his arm. As he looked up from her, his expression turned from a goofy smile to a scowl. "Freakin', jerk-faced demons need to go down in a flippin' ball of fire," he muttered.

Ronan was so used to the man's foul mouth it was strange to hear him editing his speech for his daughter's sake. He couldn't help but smile, though he hid it quickly.

"The warriors are doing everything they can, but without the walls...." He trailed off. There was no need to finish the sentence when everyone present knew the score.

Jackie, Iain's wife, was hugely pregnant. When they'd found her in Synestryn caves, being used as a source of blood for demons, she'd been gaunt and hollow-looking. Now she was lush and rounded, her gray eyes luminous with the life growing inside of her.

Her daughter would be born any day. Ronan could hear her tiny, rapid heartbeat, strong and steady within her mother's womb. The sound was more comforting to him than he could have imagined possible.

But something wasn't right with Jackie. Her big eyes were darting around the space as if watching some invisible movie screen. Her features were pinched, and Iain hovered nearby as if he feared she might fall over.

"Is something wrong, Jackie?" Justice asked before Ronan could.

Her lips clamped shut. Beside her, Iain took her hand in a blatant display of comfort.

"It's okay," he said. "I'm sure there's nothing wrong. Just tell them."

"What?" Ronan demanded, more forcefully than he'd intended.

Jackie's voice was tremulous. She looked at him, but her focus was off, as if she were staring through him.

"It's the visions," she said.

Sibyl tensed, but Ronan ignored her. The only thing that mattered now was the health of Jackie and her unborn child.

"I can't control them."

"The lights?" he asked.

She nodded.

Ronan had been working with her for a while now. Unlike any of the other female Theronai, Jackie seemed to be connected to every other female of her race. Not only had she been compatible with every male Theronai, she had some kind of link to the women, too. She could see them in her mind, glowing like lights.

Two hundred years ago, nearly all of the female Theronai had been wiped out in a worldwide, simultaneous attack by Synestryn. At that same time, the men became infertile. For two centuries, no new Theronai babies had been born—or so everyone thought.

In secret, men from another world had snuck through the gate to Earth and impregnated human women. These women—half human, half Athanasian—had been able to bond to the remaining Theronai men who suffered under the strain of their growing power.

But there weren't enough women to go around. Only a few had been found, and there had been no way of locating others.

Until Jackie.

She saw the life essences of these women as lights spread across the world. Somehow, she was tied to every one of them.

She couldn't control her gift. It came and went as it pleased. She'd been trying to guide unbound men to find these women, but they were often moving targets. Without more control over her gift—some way to tie the lights to geographical landmarks—there was no way to locate them.

Several men had tried. So far, none of them had succeeded. And now they were all called back to Dabyr, forced to fight rather than search for suitable mates.

"I can't turn the lights off," Jackie said as she squeezed her eyes shut. "They're bright and flashing like they're in distress, warning me to hurry. But I can't do a damn thing."

Madoc covered his baby's ears and scowled at Jackie's language.

She didn't see a thing.

Andra spoke up now. "I tried to put a forcefield around her to block them out, but it didn't do much good."

Ronan nodded and forced his features to remain impassive. "There's nothing to worry about," he told Jackie. "It's common for women to have trouble like this toward the end of their pregnancies. Your child is a magical being. As she grows, that power can come out in strange ways."

"You've seen this before?" Iain demanded, almost desperately.

"I have."

"How do I make it stop?" Jackie asked.

"You can't," Ronan said. "Consider it in the same category as swollen ankles and back aches. It's all part of pregnancy. Once you deliver, you'll be fine."

At least he hoped so. While it was true that women sometimes experienced a surge in their powers, he wasn't at all sure that this was what was happening with Jackie. The only thing to do was to wait and see. If it didn't go away, they'd deal with the problem then.

"If you like, I can tie myself to you and see if I can offer you any relief," he said.

Jackie nodded. "Please. I'm so tired, but I can't sleep with this laser light show going on in my head."

"Okay," he said. "When we're done here, I'll see what I can do."

She slumped in relief. Iain pulled her against his body and held her close.

Ronan shifted his gaze to Andra. This next part of his mission was going to be tricky. Joseph had asked him to do a job, but Ronan wasn't convinced it was a wise decision. Still, he'd said he'd speak to her, so that's what he was going to do.

"Joseph wants you to go back to Dabyr," he said. No sense in wasting time mincing words when there was too much for him to do before dawn.

"What?" Paul bellowed as he rose from his seat.

Ronan held up his hands. "Hear me out. No one is going to make her do anything. But you need to know the situation."

"What situation?" Andra asked.

"Lexi isn't making any progress." The blunt words were harder to say than he'd hoped.

Beside him, Justice shifted in her seat the way she did when she wished she had a gun in her hands. Across from him, Paul shook his head in disgust. Nika, who'd been silent this whole time spoke up.

"You can't take my sister," she said. Her voice was calm, but there was a hint of a threat running through her words.

Justice shifted restlessly. Ronan put his hand on her thigh to silently tell her to mind her manners. Reba was not necessary in this situation.

Ronan gave Nika his attention.

Her white hair had been recently cut. It swayed just above her shoulders without touching, like a child's swing over the ground. She was no longer as frail and thin as she'd been when they'd found her. Madoc had taken good care of her through her pregnancy, and she'd come out the other side healthier than before conceiving. Her skin glowed with health. Her eyes were clear and lucid. Her pulse was strong, her breathing even.

She had the same pale blue eyes as her sister, but Nika's were filled with the kind of pain that came from years of witnessing the suffering of a loved one.

"I've already lost Tori," she said. "I won't let you take Andra too."

Madoc moved the baby from his right arm to his left as if preparing to draw his weapon.

Ronan wouldn't let it come to that.

"I'm not taking anyone," he said. "This is just a discussion."

Paul bristled. "Andra isn't going into combat. End of discussion."

Andra turned to her husband and raised her eyebrows. The look she gave him was so pointed it could have drawn blood.

Some private conversation passed between them in the way of their kind, both swift and silent. After a few seconds, Paul sagged in defeat.

"Fine," he said. "Discuss."

Ronan nodded. "The fighting at Dabyr is almost constant. Lexi can't make any progress. Every time she almost gets finished fortifying a section of wall, the demons tear it down. Until she can connect the whole thing and keep them out, she's just spinning her wheels."

"She needs me to put up a forcefield so her work doesn't get undone."

"Exactly," Ronan said. "I don't like it. Neither does Joseph. But if we don't make some progress soon, the warriors are going to wear out. They can't keep fighting around the clock like this forever."

Sibyl, who'd been so quiet Ronan had forgotten she was here, stepped out of the shadowy corner where she'd been standing. The movement was smooth and purposeful, seemingly choreographed as if she knew it was coming.

Maybe she did. She could, after all, see the future.

She'd grown taller since he'd last seen her. It was odd seeing her in a woman's body when she'd been a small child for so long. But this new shell suited her. Like her mother, she was beautiful. Like both her parents, she was powerful.

Her voice was sweet, almost childlike, but filled with absolute certainty. "Dabyr cannot fall."

Every head in the room turned toward her.

"Why not?" Madoc asked

"We won't survive it," Sibyl said simply, as if that were all that needed to be said.

Ronan winced inwardly. They didn't need dire predictions right now. What they needed was hope and nice, steady nerves. Sibyl's statement wasn't going to help matters.

"You've seen something?" Iain asked.

Sibyl inclined her head slightly. "Many people must act if we are to live. Andra is one of them."

Andra covered her rounded stomach with her hands as if she could protect her child from the future. Beside her, Paul's face blanched with fear. Madoc pulled the baby closer to his big body and Iain tightened his hold on Jackie.

Everyone here had so much at stake.

Ronan glanced at Justice. She was as tough and fierce as any woman ever born, but even she was also vulnerable. The idea of something happening to her made him want to bare his fangs at the world to keep it away from the woman he loved.

He found it strange how love changed things so fast, how his entire world had been altered by the presence of another person. There was magic in love, but it was a fragile kind of magic—one too easily destroyed by the choices of others.

"What do I need to do?" Andra finally asked.

Sibyl's gaze was hard and unwavering. "Your job. Protect the gate. We're going to need it soon."

The gate was a portal accessed through a series of magically enhanced stones put here eons ago. These Sentinel stones were the only way in or out of Athanasia, which was the world that was the source of all magic. Centuries ago the gate had been shut by the ruler of Athanasia—or so everyone had thought. It was only cracked open now, but that crack was enough to let in the dark things that thrived on the blood of those who lived there.

The Sentinels had been created to guard the gate and keep out those nasty creatures. It was why they existed—their sole purpose. At some point, the gate had been shut, leaving the Sentinels here to fend for themselves without the guidance of those who'd created them.

"Why will we need the gate?" Ronan asked.

Sibyl shook her head. "I don't know. All I know is that we will. Soon. If Dabyr falls, the Sentinel stones will be stolen. If we lose them, we lose everything. They must be protected at all costs."

"We're still finding those stones spread across the country," Ronan said. "Logan found one in downtown Kansas City not long ago."

"The other stones must be located, along with the women—the Theronai." Sibyl looked at Jackie now, but it was unclear if she could see. Her eyes were still wide and darting, haunted. "You must find the women before it's too late. Without them, we all die."

Iain spoke for his wife. "She's doing all she can, Sibyl. Don't push her."

"Now is exactly when she must be pushed," Sibyl said. "While the power of her child fuels her, while her gift is the strongest."

"How?" Jackie asked.

Sibyl frowned and shook her head. Uncertainty crossed her dainty features, making her look much like the child she'd once been. "What I've seen can't help you."

"What is it?" Iain demanded as he rose to his feet. "What have you seen?"

The seer held her ground, refusing to be cowed by the man's massive size. She lifted her chin and warned him, "It won't help."

"What. Have. You. Seen?"

"Pain," she said finally, her voice quiet.

Iain deflated. He let out a long breath and removed his hand from his sword. "You're right. That doesn't help."

There was no satisfaction in Sibyl's expression. "We all have our role to play. Yours is no easier than mine. I'm sorry for that."

Andra shifted her chair away from the table. "So, you've seen what I need to do?" she asked. "I need to go to Dabyr?"

"Yes."

"What about the baby?" Paul asked.

"His life is tied to Dabyr as strongly as all of ours is. Without it, none of us will survive."

Paul and Andra shared another meaningful look. After a moment, they both seemed to be in agreement.

"When should we go?" Paul asked.

"Sunrise," Sibyl said. "Your passage will be safer."

"And me?" Jackie asked. "When should I start trying to find those women?"

"Now," Sibyl said. "You must hurry. For some of them it is already too late."

CHAPTER ELEVEN

Three hours later, Morgan pulled in front of a little brick house just south of the Oklahoma-Texas border.

It was a modest structure with low ceilings and few windows—the kind of house a young family might buy when they started a family, or an older couple downsizing after the kids were grown. The warm, red brick was solid and impervious to the Texas heat and spring storms. The yard had minimal landscaping—just a narrow band of shrubs and mulch around the foundation.

Like many gerai houses, there wasn't much around. These places were often used for emergencies which included plenty of blood. Nosy neighbors wouldn't understand how people could go in bleeding and come out whole without any kind of standard medical intervention. Not only that, but wherever there were Sentinels, there were demons. It was best to stay as far away from populated areas as possible.

And this place was definitely that. There were no houses in sight, just a vast swath of rural pasture with a few cows grazing in the distance.

Briant's van sat in the driveway. Inside the little house, the lights were on behind gingham curtains. The single attached garage door was open. The Sanguinar stood next to it, waving them inside.

"Where are we?" Serena asked, her voice weaker now than

it had been a little while ago.

The bleeding had stopped, but only because of the tourniquet. Once he let go of the belt, all bets were off.

"It's a gerai house," he said. "Lexi warded it recently, so with any luck, the smell of our blood will stay contained."

Lexi was one of the new female Theronai that had been discovered recently. She was bound to Zach, a kick-ass warrior who Morgan had always respected. The couple had been overseas helping rebuild another fallen Sentinel stronghold. They'd only returned from Africa when Dabyr fell to bring with them the lessons they'd learned there.

Lexi was gifted with the ability to magically fortify structures against attack and protect those inside from being detected. Too bad there had been no power great enough to stop a flood of demons from overrunning Dabyr's walls, even after Lexi had repaired them once.

As soon as Morgan pulled his truck inside the garage, Briant hit the button to lower the door.

Morgan waited until they were closed inside the dim confines before he dared to open his window. When he did, it was only a scant quarter inch. "Is the garage warded?" he asked Briant.

The man was tall, with a lean, ropey build. His hair was dark brown and his eyes a pale, glowing green. As soon as he smelled their blood, light flared in his eyes and fell on them like a laser beam.

Like all Sanguinar, he was beautiful, with features so symmetrical, he looked like an artistic rendering, too perfect to be real. Also, like all Sanguinar, his hunger was evident in every word he said and every look he gave them.

Theronai blood was food to the Sanguinar, as well as fuel for their magic. And while Morgan wasn't the kind of asshole who begrudged them the blood they couldn't help but need, he also didn't trust them. At least not when Serena's life was at stake.

When a Sanguinar took a man's blood, it bound them to him. He could see their thoughts, even alter them if he chose.

And from that moment on, he'd always be able to find them.

Morgan had long ago accepted the price for healing and tried not to dwell on the downside. There were too many other things to worry about than what an ally might or might not do when healing him. They were all fighting the same war, on the same side. He chose to trust the Sanguinar would act accordingly.

Briant's voice was soft and musical, with a hint of desperation. "I believe Lexi was thorough. If not, we won't have to wait long to find out. The smell of blood is nearly overpowering."

"Sorry about that," Serena said. "It's mostly mine."

"I am aware," Briant said as he came around to her side of the truck and opened the door. Light from his eyes splashed against her wound, highlighting it in gruesome display.

He touched her temple for a moment, to assess the damage, then met Morgan's gaze. "Whatever you do, do not let go of that belt."

Morgan nodded.

Serena's head fell back on the seat in exhaustion. "Is it truly that bad?"

"Possibly worse," Briant confirmed. "I don't understand why you're still alive, much less able to speak." Again, he looked to Morgan. "I'll need blood to heal her."

"I figured as much. I'll give you what you need."

Serena bristled. "I don't want anyone paying my debts. I will pay my own blood price."

"Sorry," Morgan said, "but you're broke, honey. And there's no time to argue."

"We don't dare move her until the worst of the damage is mended," Briant said.

He walked around the truck to Morgan's side, and opened the door.

He lifted his wrist to the Sanguinar, willingly offering his blood. "Don't leave me too weak to fight. That's all I ask."

Briant nodded his agreement. "Do you have a firm grip on the belt?"

"I do."

"I'll try not to hurt you more than necessary." His green eyes were glowing brighter now, eerily similar to those of the demons hunting them.

"Don't worry about masking the pain," Morgan said. "I can take it. No sense in wasting your energy."

"Very well."

Briant lifted Morgan's wrist to his pretty mouth and bit deep. His bony grip tightened until those fingers were an unbreakable shackle.

Morgan ignored the pain and the sucking sensation. He ignored the slight feeling of invasion and focused completely on holding the belt tight.

Strength fled his body at an alarming rate, but he didn't fight it. There was no choice but to trust Briant to take only what he needed to keep Serena alive.

Her gaze met Morgan's, and what he saw there startled him.

She was all spines and acid, shoving him away every chance she got. But now, with his life's energy draining from his body in an effort to save her, all he saw in her expression was relief and gratitude.

"Thank you," she whispered. "I'll find some way to repay you."

Take my luceria, is what he wanted to say, but didn't.

He might have saved her life, but that didn't mean it belonged to him. If she was to tie herself to him, he wanted it to be of her own free will. It was the only way they could ever be true partners. He knew better than to believe that theirs would be some kind of fairytale romance, but at least they could respect each other.

And that started with giving her the freedom to choose her own path, even if that meant bonding to Link, some other Theronai she was compatible with, or no one at all.

He prayed she'd pick someone, because not only was it the only way to keep her safe, but it was also the only way she could take her rightful place among their people as a warrior.

With the way the war was going, they needed every warrior they could get.

***

Briant was in no mood to be gentle.

He'd spent every day for the past two weeks healing the injured. Most of them were humans, with weak blood that did little to fuel his efforts.

Since Dabyr had been compromised, wave after wave of demons had pushed through the Sentinels' meager defenses, leaving both dead and injured in their wake. Joseph had managed to relocate the most vulnerable residents—humans, Theronai and Slayers too injured to fight, and Sanguinar in a deep, magically-induced sleep—to a series of warehouses stocked with food, water and supplies. These places had been magically warded against detection, but they were still high-risk targets.

Theronai and Slayers had been positioned at each location to protect those inside, and the few Sanguinar still strong enough to heal had been dispatched to deal with any injuries before the scent of blood could draw their enemy to them.

But it wasn't enough. There weren't enough warriors or healers to go around.

Even now, Briant was risking the lives of over seventy souls he was ordered to protect to come here and save Serena. If not for the fact that she was a female Theronai capable of turning the tide of war, he never would have taken the risk.

But she was too important to lose. Tynan—the Sanguinar who led their kind—had been clear about that. There were so few women like her, they couldn't afford to lose even one, no matter how hungry or weak he was.

Briant was so tired that he hadn't bothered to take more than a cursory peek inside the Morgan's head as he took his blood. It was the custom of the Sanguinar to do a mental inspection of those they healed to make sure that all was well. The strain of battle often wore down the warriors, and on rare occasions, the Sanguinar were able to uncover and solve problems before they grew too large to handle.

The souls of the Theronai were at risk. As they aged, as the strain of the energy they carried became too great, they lost small pieces of themselves. And once those pieces were all gone, their souls began to decay. They became dark, dangerous creatures.

All of them knew their fate. Some of them hid how close to it they were. It was Briant's job to make sure that the men he healed weren't hiding any ticking time bombs that could risk the lives of hundreds if they exploded.

In Morgan's case, he was stable. His lifemark was nearly bare, but he still had some time. The most interesting thing Briant saw was his attraction to Serena.

The only thoughts rattling around Morgan's skull at the moment were of Serena's safety.

The two were compatible. That much was displayed prominently at the forefront of Morgan's mind. He wanted her, both as a partner and a lover.

Which surprised Morgan.

And that surprised Briant.

Morgan was known to be a flirt, a womanizer. But now that Briant was in his head, he could see how wrong that assumption was.

Morgan played the part, but that was all. He hadn't slept with a woman in a long, long time.

The image of an Egyptian woman's face appeared in Morgan's mind, and with it was a deep sense of love and devotion.

Briant had no idea who this woman was, but if she was getting in the way of Morgan claiming Serena and bringing more strongly blooded children into the world, then it was Briant's duty to fix it.

There had been a time when he would have felt guilty for meddling in the affairs of his allies, but that time had long passed.

His Sanguinar brothers and sisters were dying. Starving

slowly. They withered away as their bodies consumed themselves in search of even a faint flicker of power. And those who slept were even worse, near corpses.

He didn't know how many of his kind still slept, choosing oblivion to starvation, but he knew that if nothing changed, none of them would survive. Those that hadn't died in the attack against Dabyr had been moved, but they were vulnerable to attack.

So, Briant did what any good soldier would do given the chance. He infiltrated Morgan's thoughts and planted a compulsion to make Serena his in every way possible. And as soon as Briant got his hands on Serena, he'd do the same with her.

If his work was solid—if he expended the precious energy it would take to sway them toward their duty—it would only be a matter of time before the two created a new life that would eventually be strong enough to feed his kind.

Briant grinned with satisfaction. One more win for Project Lullaby.

CHAPTER TWELVE

Serena suffered through the Sanguinar healing without complaint.

Briant didn't have enough spare power to mute the pain of healing, so every ache and twinge she would have normally felt healing naturally over the span of several days was shoved into a few, brutal, agonizing seconds.

She clenched her jaw to keep from screaming, but sweat still poured down her temples from the strain. By the time he was done, she was shaking and nauseated.

Briant sagged as he sat back on his heels. He crouched outside the truck, in the dimly lit garage, leaning heavily against the open door.

She was in no shape to walk, and now, neither was he.

Once her breathing evened out, she felt much better. She was tired and starving, but that unnatural flutter of her heart that had scared her so much had passed.

"Are you okay?" she asked the Sanguinar.

His melodic voice trembled with fatigue. "As well as can be expected. I have no idea how you're still alive. A cut that deep on anyone else would have been fatal."

"I slowed time around the wound," she said, before she could think better of airing her secret.

"You what?" Morgan asked. He was beside her, still gripping that belt tight around her thigh as if her life depended on it. "Is that how we got out of the cave? Why those demons seemed to be moving in slow motion?"

Serena nodded. Her secret was out. No sense in being childish about it and lying.

Briant stared at her in speculation, his green eyes now dull, rather than bright and glowing. "That makes sense. I remember hearing about another female Theronai who could manipulate time that way—speeding it or slowing it in a small space."

Serena kept her gaze on the garage wall, on the shelf of old paint cans and rusting tools, refusing to look at either man. "My mother. Gertrude Brinn. That's how she caged me— trapping me in a place time could not touch. If not for the Athanasian woman, Brenya, freeing me, I might have spent eternity there."

And when she'd eventually gone mad from loneliness and boredom, she would have stayed trapped there until time ended, with no way to end her own suffering.

Silence filled the garage. No one spoke.

Serena squirmed in her seat, regretting her mistake to reveal herself to these men. She didn't know them, not really. She shouldn't have said anything at all.

Then why had she?

Perhaps she was simply too exhausted to filter herself. Or perhaps the effects of Briant's healing had left her tongue looser than usual.

"I need to go," Briant said, finally breaking the silence.

"Stay. Let me rest and hydrate for a few hours," Morgan said. "Then you can feed from me again."

Briant shook his head. "I have to leave. There's no time to rest. Lives are in danger."

"You're in no shape to drive."

"The only hope those people in my care have is for me to return to my post. But you two should stay the night here. Talk. Work out your differences. Both of you still have secrets to share so that you can bond properly."

Serena recoiled. "How did you know we're compatible?"

"I was in your mind as I healed you."

"You fucked with her head?" Morgan roared.

He shoved out of the truck, letting go of the tourniquet.

Blood flowed back into her numb limb, warming her flesh in a rush as it went. She could barely feel her lower leg, but she knew that when she finally could, she would wish she couldn't.

Briant stood and raised his hands to ward off the bigger man's approach. "I only touched her mind enough to make sure there was no other damage. While that may seem intimate or intrusive to you, it was nothing more than a routine examination to me."

Stinging wasps began attacking her leg from the inside as blood flow returned. She eased out of the seat, cringing at the way her spilled blood glued her to the leather.

She stood between the two men, balancing on one leg. "We don't have enough blood between us to shed even one more drop. Cease your bickering and behave like gentlemen."

"I'm no gentleman," Morgan growled. "It's one thing to poke around in my head, but he should know better than to read your mind. It's none of his fucking business."

"He saved my life, Morgan. Shall we call it even?" she suggested.

Briant shook his head in disgust, sneering at Morgan. "The next time someone you care about is bleeding to death, call a different healer. I'm done."

He went into the house, stomped out through the front door and started his van.

After a long minute, after Briant's van pulled out of the driveway, Morgan let out a long, weary sigh. "I was a bit of an ass, wasn't I?"

"More than a bit," she agreed.

"If I wasn't covered in blood, I'd go after him. Apologize."

"Use your box. It can apologize for you, right?"

"My box?"

"Your cell."

"You want me to text him an apology?"

"No. What I want is to shower off this blood. But I think you owe him one. All he did was try to help, apparently at great cost to him. You saw how tired he was, how thin? He's starving."

Morgan shook his head. "You're right. I'll have my box apologize to his after I get you inside."

She couldn't feel anything but hot needles in her leg, which put her off balance.

Morgan wrapped his arm around her waist to help steady her, and the moment his hand made contact with the bare skin beneath a tear in her fighting leathers, all her pain vanished.

He froze as though he felt it too. Someone groaned in bliss, but she couldn't tell if it was him or her. Perhaps it had been both of them.

"You feel amazing," he said.

So did he. She didn't know what magic his touch possessed, but it was potent. Overwhelming.

She looked up at him. Though flecks of blood had dried on his face, she still enjoyed the sight of him. He was darkly handsome, but there was more to it than that. Lots of men were handsome and couldn't hold her interest.

Morgan was…intriguing. She wanted to stare at him for hours until she'd memorized every line in his face and every golden splinter in his brown eyes.

As she watched, his pupils flared wide. "Bond with me, Serena. Tap into my power and use it to keep yourself safe." His throat moved as he swallowed. "I can't stand the idea of you coming that close to death again. What if you'd passed out and hadn't been able to hold the magic slowing your bleeding?"

She still wasn't sure how she'd been able to stay conscious. If not for the sparks of his power flowing into her skin, she probably wouldn't have.

Whatever the case, she owed him her life. She had no desire for a partner, but maybe this was the best way to protect her freedom.

"Let me think about it," she said. "I need to get clean and eat something. Then we can discuss it."

Hope brightened his expression, making him even more attractive than he'd been a moment ago.

How was she ever going to stop staring at him?

"Whatever you want," he said. "It's yours."

That's when Serena finally realized the power she held. His life was in her hands. All she had to do was figure out what terms she could live with and demand that he meet them.

They moved through the small house, doing their best not to leave a mess behind them. The pathway from the garage, through the kitchen and down the hallway to the bedrooms had wooden floors. Their bloody footprints would wipe up easily enough.

As they passed through the main room of the house, she saw plush, leather furniture in a scale grand enough to fit even Morgan's large frame. The bedroom on the right was dark, but the bed was neatly made with the covers turned back in invitation.

She so wanted to climb into that bed and sleep until her pain faded and all the big decisions in front of her were made.

She was so used to her mother making all the big choices in her life that it was hard to remember that she was now in control. Gertrude Brinn no longer called the shots. She didn't even have a voice, which was both a blessing and a curse.

It would have been so easy to simply go along with whatever her mother thought best, as she was raised to do. Even though Serena knew she wouldn't be happy, at least she could blame someone else if things went wrong.

Now that she was making her own decisions, the only person she'd have to blame was herself.

By the time Morgan had helped her to the bathroom, the sharp sting in her leg had reduced to an annoying buzz.

This room was small but tidy. There was no tub, only a shower just big enough for her to raise her arms to wash her hair. The space was tiled completely from top to bottom—clearly for making it easy to wash away the blood that would inevitably spill here.

The white and gray tile shower gleamed, inviting her to rid herself of the mess she wore and scrub herself from top to bottom.

Maybe once she was clean her world would seem clearer, her decisions easier.

Morgan released her, flinching as their contact ended. He made no complaint about the agony she could see clearly on his strained features. He didn't use his pain to make her feel guilty or to push her to hurry. He simply accepted the pain as his duty, and backed away.

"I'm going to clean up in another bathroom, then find something for us to eat," he said. "Take your time."

That gift of time was exactly what she needed. She didn't know how he knew that, but she was grateful for it all the same.

She had a lot of thinking to do.

From the front of the house, she heard a door slam shut. Morgan was by her side. Someone or something else was here.

She froze. This house was supposed to be warded to hide the smell of their blood from demons, but there was no way to know if those wards still held. There was so much blood on their skin and clothes. Her shoes slurped with every step from the pools inside them.

Morgan drew his sword and rushed from the bathroom whispering a quick, "Stay here."

She bristled at his order. Typical male Theronai, all overprotective and demanding.

Serena was no child to be ordered around.

She drew her weapon and followed him down the hall. Before she reached the living room, she heard Link's voice, loud and frantic.

"I know she's here. I know she's hurt. Where is she?"

"Serena is fine. You have no business being here."

"Bullshit. I have more of a claim on her than you do. Now get out of my way!"

Serena saw the two men facing off, swords drawn, teeth

bared.

This kind of thing was never going to end well. She had to stop them from hurting each other.

She stepped in between them, still limping from the buzzing numbness in her leg.

Link eyed her up and down, taking in her tattered leathers and the blood covering her body. Horror widened his blue eyes and made the gaunt hollows under his cheeks sink deeper. "What the bloody hell happened to you?" His gaze flicked to Morgan, and narrowed with anger. "You let this happen to her?"

"He didn't let anything happen. I went into that cave on my own. If not for Morgan, I'd be dead," Serena said, giving Link a hard shove. Cold, sharp spikes of power bit into her at the contact. As much as she hated the sensation, she could feel the quick burst of his energy flow into her and buoy her lagging strength.

His power wanted to be a part of her, to find a home inside of her.

No matter how weak she became, she didn't know if she would ever get used to the harsh angles his energy bore.

Link's face flushed an angry red. "If you'd taken your rightful place by my side, this never would have happened."

She lifted a brow at him. Her tone was pure challenge. "Because I would have been able to use your power to defend myself, or because you never would have allowed me to go into a fight in the first place?"

He wrapped his fingers around her arm. "We'll discuss that properly later. Right now, you're coming with me."

"You can't take her out there covered in blood," Morgan said. "The smell will call every demon within miles."

"Not to mention the fact that I refuse to leave," Serena added.

Every second he touched her, more of that biting power flooded her. She tried not to let the discomfort show on her face, but she'd already been through so much tonight, she wasn't sure how well she was hiding it.

"You're hurting her," Morgan growled, his tone a clear threat of violence. "Let her go."

Link did as he asked, and the moment he did, he doubled over in pain.

A pang of sympathy for him shot through Serena, but she didn't dare touch him again.

She knew these men suffered. She knew the power they carried was a heavy burden to bear, and that the pain often made them desperate.

She also knew she couldn't save both of them.

Serena tried to forgive Link for his actions, but even if she did, he'd only let her down again. He was fighting his own nature, and not likely to win the battle.

She took a long step back on shaky legs. "I'm going to shower the blood off. You two are not going to kill each other while I do."

"I'm not leaving you alone with him," Link said, glaring at Morgan.

"He would never hurt me," she said, though she had no idea why she felt the need to defend him.

But what truly shocked her was that she believed what she said. Morgan had proved he was willing to protect her with his life, even without his vow to do so forcing him to act. He'd been ready to guard her escape while she ran from those demons. He had no idea she was able to manipulate time. As far as he knew, he was going to die down there in that cave so that she had a fighting chance of surviving.

Link must have seen something in her face, because his posture deflated and he let out a long sigh. "I know you don't like me, Serena, but we would make a good match."

He pulled out the yellowed paper and tore it in half.

"I release you from the contract your parents made with me," Link said. "I'm not the man your mother wanted you to think I was."

That surprised her. "Then who are you?"

"Let me show you. Spend some time with me. Get to know the real me, not the man your mother wanted to believe I was."

Serena understood what he meant then. Gertrude Brinn had a way of judging people even before she'd spoken to them. She placed a high value on appearance and status, as well as public opinion. She was always looking for a way to elevate her standing among her peers. If tying her daughter to a man could do that, then that's what she'd do.

But what if her mother had been wrong about Link? What if he was more than his social standing and the opinion of others? What if, beneath his arrogant, presumptive exterior he was a good man?

He must have seen her indecision, because he said in a soft, almost pleading tone, "All I ask is for a chance to show you that we belong together."

Of all the things he could have said or done to sway her, he'd landed on the only one that made her rethink her choices. Before this moment, Link had no chance with her. But now that he'd torn up that contract? Now that he'd pleaded with her for a chance?

She wasn't sure. There was too much at stake for her to make a hasty decision. Not only was she choosing a partner, she was also very likely sending one of these men to their death.

Serena looked both men in the eyes and said, "Give me some time to consider."

***

Morgan wanted to pick up the torn remains of that contract and shove it in Link's mouth. Every word he spoke was swaying Serena to his side. It was like the man knew exactly what words would soften her.

Morgan couldn't let that happen. He needed her too much to let her go without a fight.

So far, silence had been his ally in dealing with her. He acted, letting her see the man he was, rather than trying to bully her into agreeing to something.

She'd had more than enough of that from Link.

But now, here the man was, doing and saying the right things to sway her.

Power seethed behind Morgan's lifemark, making the branches of his tree whip wildly. A sharp, stabbing pain ripped through him, and it took all his willpower not to cry out.

Another leaf fell from his lifemark, putting his soul one step closer to death. There were only three left now, when he'd started with thousands. Three little leaves stood between him and death.

He pressed his hand to his chest, grieving for the time he'd just lost.

How much time did he have left? Months? Weeks?

He didn't know, but one thing was certain—Morgan wasn't going to be able to continue his duty to protect those weaker than himself without Serena by his side. His days were numbered. If Serena didn't choose him, he was going to have to find some way of giving his death meaning—maybe follow those furless, gray demons back to their nest and take it out with a huge pile of C-4.

Morgan held no grudge against Link, but there was only one Serena. Only one of them could be saved by her.

Didn't Morgan deserve that as much as any other man?

His lungs stopped working as he realized the truth. Maybe not. Maybe he didn't deserve her as much as Link did.

Morgan knew he would never love Serena the way she deserved. His heart belonged to Femi, and always would. Sure, he and Serena could be partners. They would be fantastic lovers, of that he was certain. They could even have children. But without love, her life would always be hollow. He knew because that's how his was now, without Femi.

He couldn't do that to Serena. She deserved so much more than what he had to offer.

"It's okay," he told Serena, meaning every word. "I won't make you choose. If you want Link as your partner, you should have him. I won't stand in your way."

With that, he turned and left the room. Once he was clean, he'd hit the road so at least he wouldn't have to witness her binding herself to another man.

Besides, he had work to do. His brothers needed him and he needed to find an honorable way to die. With the battle raging at Dabyr, he doubted his quest would be hard.

CHAPTER THIRTEEN

Serena said nothing after Morgan left. She simply walked away and locked herself in the bathroom. As she stood under the hot shower spray, she marveled over the invention.

So much in her life had changed, and it was about to shift again, just when she thought she'd gotten her feet under her.

She wanted to be angry with the men for upsetting her world, but all she could manage was confusion.

Anger had been Serena's only true friend during her two centuries of incarceration.

Before her mother's betrayal, she'd been carefree and easy-going. Those girlish traits had taken a long time to die, and when they finally passed, the only companion left to her was her anger.

It, at least, had never once left her side.

When she thought she'd go mad with boredom, fury would come play with her. When hopelessness left her drowning in despair, rage would come buoy her up and breathe into her lungs. And when her heartbreak threatened to consume her, anger swelled within her until she was too big for her pain to swallow.

Over the decades, she'd learned to love her anger—cultivating it so that it kept her going, day after day, year after year.

She was back in the real world now, surrounded by real

people and real distractions. She wanted a relationship with those things, but anger was a jealous lover and refused to let her go.

Why then, could she not find it now, when she needed it so much?

Was it because she'd gotten her way? Both men had backed off, leaving her to decide her own fate—something she hadn't been raised to know how to do. Her mother had made every important decision for her, and now she found herself missing that guidance when she'd hated it for so long.

There was too much at stake. She didn't feel capable of issuing a death sentence on either man, which was, in essence, what she would be doing by choosing between them.

As the last of the blood was washed down the drain, Serena decided that she needed some help, or at least someone she could speak to about her dilemma.

There was only one person she knew who might have the answers.

Serena dried off and dressed in drab clothing she found hanging in the closet. Nothing sparkled or made her heart pound, but it was clean, dry and not coated in blood.

She locked the door to one of the bedrooms and made the call.

It took her two tries to use the device. She'd only ever received calls before, but she'd been shown what to do in case she needed to call for help.

Deciding her fate definitely qualified.

Sibyl Brinn answered with a soft, "Hello?"

"It's Serena."

"Yes, I know."

"Of course, you do. Your ability to see the future was why I called."

Sibyl let out a small laugh. "That wasn't magic. I simply read your name on my phone's screen."

"Oh." Now Serena felt foolish.

"Joseph spoke to you." It wasn't a question.

"Yes," Serena said. "He made it clear that I must find the

source of the demons soon. But that's not why I called."

"Okay," Sibyl's tone was hesitant and distrustful, as if she expected the worst.

"I need to know who to choose to bind myself to. Morgan or Link?"

There was silence on the line for so long, Serena began to squirm.

Had she overstepped her bounds by calling the woman? Was there some protocol she should have followed? Did all request to know the future go through Joseph, so he could choose which he deemed important enough for the seer's time?

"I can't tell you that," Sibyl finally said.

"Why not?"

"Because it's not my turn to use our gift. And even if it was, there are other more pressing questions that must come first."

Serena didn't know what she meant by it not being her turn, but the rest she understood. "I'm sorry I bothered you."

She was about to hang up when Sibyl said, "No, wait."

"Yes?"

"Just because I can't see that part of your future doesn't mean I can't help. We're family, after all."

"Distant relatives. There's no need for you to feel obligated toward me."

"I knew your mother. She was much like my own. I understand how hard it can be to not be told what to do, even when independence is the one thing you crave most."

Was it true? Could a woman who could literally see the future also struggle in making her own decisions?

A tightness blocked Serena's throat for a moment before she could loosen it. Her words seemed to stick and grow thick and heavy. "I don't want either man to die. I don't want to be responsible for their fates."

"But you are. There's no way around that. The power we women wield is a glorious thing, but it comes with a heavy price."

"Have you had to choose between men?" Serena asked.

"I choose between people all the time, though not the way you are. There's not enough of my gift to go around. I must be careful what I ask of it, but no matter what I choose, someone is always going to suffer."

Serena hadn't thought that Sibyl's gift was limited, or that she couldn't use it whenever, however she wanted. To be forced to pick what part of the future she saw...?

"How do you choose?" Serena asked. "How do you decide who to help and who to abandon?"

The woman's voice was heavy and filled with regret. "My loyalty is to my people. All of them. I choose whatever I believe will save the most lives."

While simple on its surface, Serena could see how that decision would possibly be the most difficult one to make.

"Is that why you chose to see my future?" she asked.

"It wasn't your future I chose to see. It was all of ours. Your role was simply a large one in saving our race."

The pressure of that statement made what little blood Serena had left go cold. Her hands began to shake and her grip tightened on the little black box.

"I'm not a hero," she whispered.

"You must be. Without you, we all die. You must find and destroy the source of the red-eyed demons before the babies are born."

Again, that sense of inadequacy bore down on Serena. She wasn't fit to save her people. She couldn't even choose a partner. How was she ever going to be strong enough to finish the task Sibyl laid out before her?

"But how do I do that?" Serena asked.

"I don't know," Sibyl said. "I don't control what is shown to me any more than you control the weather. All I know is what must happen. What you do with that knowledge is your own choice."

Like so many other things.

Serena sighed. "Sometimes, I wish that we could be human, that we could live quiet lives not filled with monsters."

"All lives are filled with monsters," Sibyl said. "Only some of them are visible, but it doesn't mean they aren't monsters all the same. Besides, you wouldn't be well-suited to being powerless."

"You're right. I'm merely tired."

"Then rest, but do so quickly. The child will come soon. We're all running out of time."

Serena pulled in a deep breath and let it out in a slow, silent exhale.

She didn't envy Sibyl's role in the war. To know what the future held but not be able to do anything about it? Serena didn't think she'd survive that kind of torture.

All lives are filled with monsters.

Perhaps that helplessness was Sibyl's.

"If you ever feel the need to talk to someone," Serena said, "please call on me. None of us should have to face our role in this war alone."

"Thank you for your kindness," Sibyl said, and Serena thought she heard the slightest waver in her voice, as if she were struggling not to cry.

Then the phone's screen lit up, indicating the call had ended.

Serena sat on the neatly made bed for a moment as she wished she could go to the woman and hug her. She seemed so lonely, so isolated. Serena's heart wept for her and all she'd had to endure because of her gift.

That alone was one more reason to find the source of those red-eyed demons and kill them. Once the threat was gone and the walls of Dabyr were rebuilt, maybe she and Sibyl could become friends.

The girl could probably use one as much as Serena could. And they were, after all, family.

She sat for a long time, weighing her options. The men weren't going to leave her alone until she made up her mind. And she wasn't going to have the power to kill those demons if she didn't tap into the power of one of them.

She had to make her choice. Now. Tonight.

I'm not the man your mother wanted you to think I was....
All I ask is for a chance to show you that we belong together.

Link's words haunted her.

He'd been controlling from the first moment she met him. Mother had chosen him because of his wealth and status, but also because she saw something in him she recognized—the need to keep everyone in his life exactly where he wanted them.

Within an hour of meeting her, Link had given her a list of expectations. It covered everything from the way she dressed, to the way she wore her hair, to what she was allowed to eat and who she was allowed so speak to. He'd said that he believed that it was best to teach her how to behave from the start, so that they could deal with her mistakes early and move on with their lives in harmony.

But was that truly the kind of man he was? Or was that pompous assumption all for show?

I'm not the man your mother wanted you to think I was....
All I ask is for a chance to show you that we belong together.

Serena was all too aware of the way her mother manipulated people into doing what she wanted. She'd never liked the way Serena dressed or wore her hair, but had failed to force her to change it. What better way to gain the upper hand but to give her to a husband who would conveniently want Serena to behave the same way her mother did?

She hadn't given Link a fair chance to prove the kind of man he was. The only question was, did she owe him a chance?

Serena's parents had never loved each other. They'd been an arranged bond meant to aid in the war and produce powerful offspring. Her father had a string of lovers on the side, and Mother allowed it so long as they were *only human*—her words, not his.

Their relationship had been cold. Businesslike. Void of any warmth or compassion.

But they were deadly in battle.

As poorly matched as they were in love, they were perfect

on the field. Countless Synestryn died by their hands and countless lives were saved.

Serena had always wanted more for herself than that cold alliance, but maybe she was the fool. Maybe Mother had the right idea—find a man to tolerate, rather than love, and put all her focus into her work.

Serena was never going to love again—not after Iain. The joy of loving him was fleeting, but the pain of losing him lingered.

She wouldn't do that to herself again. The benefits weren't worth the risk.

So, if she was never going to love again, what did that leave? She knew if she didn't partner with one of the male Theronai, she'd spend the rest of her life looking over her shoulder, waiting for some man to snatch her away and force her to comply with his wishes. And if one of those men succeeded, she knew she'd lose little pieces of herself every day for the rest of her long life, until there was nothing left.

She'd rather die than suffer through that.

In a sudden moment of clarity, she knew that a union with Link Tolland was a mistake.

The way his power grated on her was proof that he was not the right man for her—not even as a battle partner. If she couldn't stand his touch, if she hated the feel of his power within her, they would never develop the connection they needed to take their place in the war.

That left Morgan, or waiting for someone else to come along with whom she was compatible.

After two hundred years of hoping every day to be freed from her prison, she was so very tired of waiting.

Besides, there was no way to know how long it would take for her to find another male she was compatible with, or if that person would be any better than Morgan.

She wasn't even sure if it was possible for a man to be more patient with her than he'd been.

When she'd been in the hotel room with him, she'd been seriously considering partnering with him, at least for a trial run. If they bonded, the luceria would give her a vision that would help her better understand him. It would also uncover his true self, so that if he was simply pretending to be kind, she'd know it.

Serena would use whatever knowledge the luceria gave her to her advantage, and ensure that she took any warnings to heart.

She was smart. She'd been raised by the queen of manipulation. If Morgan tried to trick her, she'd see it coming a mile off.

With her decision made, she went to find Link.

It was time to send him on his way for good.

***

Link knew the moment he saw Serena's beautiful face that he'd lost her.

She found him in the kitchen, heating up canned soup the gerai who stocked this house had left behind.

He paused as he pulled a steaming bowl from the microwave.

"Tell me how to change your mind," he said softly.

"You can't."

"I should have burned that damn contract decades ago. I thought it gave me a right to you over others, but that was never the case. Law or not."

"It wasn't just about the contract," she said.

"Then what?" he demanded.

Her red hair was the color of tarnished pennies when it was wet, and even wearing those sloppy sweats she had on, she was still the most beautiful woman to have ever walked the planet.

Serena poured herself a glass of water. "What do you feel when we touch?"

"Excitement. Anticipation. The potential for vast power." He paused, considering how weak his admission would make him appear. "But mostly, I feel no pain. After decades of growing agony, one touch from you washes it all away."

He wanted to feel that blissful pain-free state now, but held his ground. Pawing at her would get him nowhere.

She met his eyes over the rim of the glass. "When you touch me, I feel something completely different."

"What?"

"Cold sparks. Little jots of lightning. It's…uncomfortable."

The idea that he'd hurt her turned his stomach. "I had no idea."

"That's why I don't think it would ever work between us, even if we could find a way past our differences in personality." She pulled in a deep breath. "I can't stand to touch you, Link."

Her words were a hard blow to his gut that drove all the air from his lungs.

What more was there to say? If she couldn't stand to touch him, they had no future. They would always have trouble connecting, and the flow of power between them that was supposed to be easy and natural, would be strained and frustrating.

Still, he didn't know how to go back to facing his pain every day with no hope of it ever coming to an end.

"Perhaps the discomfort is because I carry so much power within me. If we were to join and you were to bleed some off, contact might be easier."

She shook her head. "I'm sorry, but I don't believe that. It was the same two hundred years ago, when we first met. I know what it's supposed to be like. With Iain…" She trailed off, unwilling to speak about him to someone who was practically a stranger.

"You loved him," Link whispered. "Of course, it was different. But who's to say you couldn't grow to love me? We have all the time in the world. I'd be so very patient with you."

Tears welled in her pretty eyes, and he knew the next words she spoke would slaughter all hope.

"I'll never be able to love anyone ever again, Link. I can't

be with a man who lives in hope that one day I will. I'm sorry."
She squared her shoulders, decision made. "I think you should
go now."

CHAPTER FOURTEEN

Morgan came out of the bedroom just as Serena declared she'd never be able to love again.

Relief fluttered through him, but it wasn't because he now knew she was sending Link packing. No, his relief was due to the fact that he'd never break her heart.

Like her, he'd had one true, great love. Like her, he'd lost that love. Only someone who'd gone through that kind of heartache could understand it.

He would never have to explain to her why his dreams were filled with the face of another woman. He would never have to justify why he kept himself at arm's length. And he would never let her down because she would know his heart belonged to another. Just as hers did.

They were the perfect union—two people who were scarred in the same way, who could bond over those wounds and develop a deep, abiding friendship and respect for each other.

It was more than he'd ever hoped to find.

The front door opened and closed as Link left.

Morgan stepped into the kitchen to see Serena slumped over the table, defeated.

The room was brightly lit, showing off appliances that would have been on trend in the mid-eighties. Everything was clean and in good repair, but the mauve countertops and blue tile backsplash covered in geese with ribbons tied around their necks weren't going to grace the cover of any magazines.

There was a table for four along one wall, scuffed and worn from decades of use. He could picture the family that might have once lived here, all gathered for dinner, laughing and sharing what had happened to them that day.

That was what he risked his life for—that simple, happy gathering of humans who knew nothing about the monsters that hunted at night. To him, family was the only thing that truly mattered, the only thing that really made a difference in the world.

Technology advanced. Trends came and went. Life got filled with conveniences and complications. But people remained the same. They needed safety, love, companionship, family.

That was why he fought and bled. That was why he suffered.

And now, with Serena in his life, he had one more reason to fight.

If she would have him, she would be his family.

Her head popped up as she heard him enter. Dark red waves of damp hair clung to her head as they dried, framing her perfect face. Her beautiful blue eyes were filled with tears, so heartbreaking he could barely stand to witness them.

Besides Femi, he'd never seen a woman more beautiful, more desirable than Serena. The part of him that was flesh and blood wanted her, craved her. Even now he was having to fight his need to cross the space and touch her.

He feared that need had more to do with lust than the luceria, though he couldn't be certain.

"I hurt him," she said. "I didn't want to, but I had no choice. I have no love left in me for any man."

"And me, Serena?"

"I won't love you, either, Morgan. You need to know that up front." Her chin was up, her tone nearly combative.

"I'm fine with that. I have no interest in love."

She blinked in surprise, then relaxed with relief.

He crossed to her, but didn't let himself touch her. "What I was asking is, are you going to send me away as well?"

"No," she said, the single word hopeless. "I'll give you my bond, but it's going to be on my terms."

Victory sang through Morgan's veins. She was going to free him from his pain and allow him to become what he'd been born to be.

She was going to be his.

"Name them," he said, unable to keep the eagerness out of his tone. It almost didn't matter what she asked of him. He knew he would give her anything that was in his power. So long as her request didn't betray Femi or the vows he'd already given, he would give Serena whatever she wanted.

"You have to promise to never try to control or manipulate me," she said.

"That's easy."

Her gaze was hard, stern. "That's not a vow, Theronai. I will need the words to bind you to your promise."

"And I'll give them, once I've heard the rest of your terms."

She dunked a spoon into a bowl of chicken noodle soup and idly stirred it. "I won't ever be caged again—at Dabyr or anywhere else. I will go where I want to go, when I want to go there."

"I can only promise you that so long as you promise me you won't be reckless."

"I'm not a fool, nor do I have a death wish. But I think about those women who were at Dabyr when it fell, trapped there while they waited for their babies to be born." She shivered in revulsion. "If we were to ever have children, I wouldn't allow you to use them to imprison me."

Morgan had been trying not to think about her in a sexual way. In fact, he'd been trying not to think of her like that since he'd stepped in the shower.

Tried, and failed.

His cock had been rock-hard and throbbing. He'd briefly considered taking matters into his own hands, so to speak, but didn't. There were too many dangers lurking in the night. If this gerai house was attacked while he was jacking off, he'd never forgive himself.

Duty came before pleasure. Always.

Now there was no choice but to let his mind go to the lovely place where the two of them were naked together. She'd laid the idea of having children with him out there, and he was obligated to pick it up. "So, sex isn't out of the question?"

Her deep blue eyes turned to midnight as she stared at him. There was longing there, though he couldn't tell if it was for him or a family.

She held his gaze as she said, "Eternity is a long time to go without children. And without release. Just because I will never love you doesn't mean that we can't enjoy each other physically. Does it?"

Even the idea thrilled him. He could hardly imagine what the real thing would be like.

His hands tingled with the need to feel her skin beneath them. His mouth watered at the thought of kissing her, tasting all those secret places that would make her gasp and moan. His cock swelled and his balls grew heavy at the thought of touching her, of taking her.

His voice trembled with lust as he spoke. "Hell, no. We even have a name for that now. It's called friends with benefits."

She tilted her head as if scrutinizing the term, then nodded once. "That is exactly what I would like."

He could hardly wait to oblige. Whatever desires she had, whatever naughty fantasies ran through that lovely head of hers, he was going to fulfill them all. And then some.

"Anything else?" he asked.

"If we bond, it will be temporary—at least at first."

"A trial run?" he asked. Some of his lust deflated as he began to wonder if he'd have enough time with her to do all the things he wanted to do.

"Exactly."

"We'll have to make up our minds before the colors of the luceria solidify," he reminded her. "After that, breaking up will kill me."

She nodded. "I'm aware. But we should have years before that happens. There's no rush."

Morgan shook his head. "Things are different now. I don't know if it's because we've all gone so long without binding ourselves to females, or because the sheer amount of power we carry has degraded the luceria somehow. Whatever the case, it's only taking weeks or even a few days for bonds to become permanent now."

She sucked in a sharp breath. "Perhaps we shouldn't do this at all then."

He wasn't about to let her get away now that he had what he wanted in sight. Even a few days with her could help relieve some of the pain his growing pool of power caused. If she could bleed off enough energy from him, then maybe he could go a few more years before his lifemark lost its last leaf.

And even if they weren't together that long, at least he could learn what she tasted like, what she sounded like when she came. That alone was enough to convince him to take a risk.

"I'm not afraid, Serena. I'd rather take this chance with you and fail, then take no chance at all and die anyway. All I ask is that you don't take too long to decide."

She considered for only a moment. "Okay, then. Let's do this now."

"You don't want to eat first? You said you were starving."

She pushed away the bowl of soup. "The last time I put off bonding with a male to eat, I spent two hundred years trapped and alone, thinking about how much I regretted the hesitation. I won't make that same mistake twice."

She stood and pointed to the floor. Her tone was imperious, demanding. "Take off your shirt and kneel, Theronai."

***

Serena was making what could possibly be the second biggest mistake of her life, but she wasn't afraid. During those two centuries of captivity she would have given anything to be able to take a risk—any risk—but her mother's magic had ensured her safety, leaving her frozen in time, stagnant. Now that Serena could take whatever risks she wanted she wouldn't be the kind of coward who backed down. She was resigned to the decision to claim Morgan, come what may.

His dark chest was bare and beautiful under the kitchen lights. The branches of his tree twisted across his torso, weaving up and over his left shoulder, down onto his biceps. She'd seen the marks before, but never had one captured her attention so completely. It was as if each curving twig, each swirl in the bark were real. Alive. More perfect than any photograph or artist's rendering, his lifemark spoke to her, whispering of the things he'd done and seen.

She wanted to know where he was when each leaf fell from his tree. She wanted to know what he felt when he'd been young, when the branches had been smaller, barely reaching his heart.

His jeans had slid down without his belt to hold them up— the same belt that had saved her life. Above the faded blue denim, she could see ridges of muscles across his abdomen, angling steeply down toward his manhood. The thick roots of the luceria shot down toward his thigh and groin.

The idea of following the path they took made her insides tremble with anticipation. Her skin heated. Her pulse and breathing sped. A deep ache clenched her core and sat there, hungry and restless. Something hot and liquid inside of her burst free and filled her veins with the kind of physical need she hadn't felt since Iain had last touched her skin and loved her with his body.

Before thoughts of him could ruin this moment, she shoved them away and focused on the man to whom she would bind herself.

Morgan's gaze was fixed on her, eager and excited. His

nostrils flared with each rapid breath, forcing the wide expanse of his bare chest to stretch and swell. Thick muscles covered him, gracing his frame with smooth contours her fingers itched to feel.

He would be hers soon, to do with as she pleased. And she would be his.

His luceria seethed with ripples of color, dancing in an almost desperate display.

She'd always found the necklaces so pretty and wondered why their creator had decided to give them to the male of the species. Now that the glittering band was to be hers, she understood. Seeing it around his dark throat, watching the colors dance as if alive, she wanted his luceria even more. In this moment, she would have done almost anything to make it hers.

That was why his luceria was so appealing. It wanted to tie them together. It displayed a beautiful plume like some exotic bird working to catch her eye, to coax her in and entrance her.

She wasn't sure how she'd ever give it up if they didn't suit one another.

As her gaze lingered on his magnificent body, she knew that he would suit her physically. Quite well. The lust prowling through her was a familiar beast. She had felt it with Iain and never once grown tired of his body. With Morgan, that beast was even hungrier, larger. She'd gone too long without physical release. It would take a long time for her to be sated.

Morgan stayed where he was, kneeling on the hard, tile floor, waiting for her to act. Physical power radiated out of him, along with an invisible shimmer of something illusive and magical.

All of that would be hers, soon. *He* would be hers, at least for a time. All she had to do was give him her vow.

She reached out and wrapped her fingers around the slippery band of the luceria. It fell away easily, draping over her hand like a living thing. Warm colors swirled in its depths, making her wonder which one it would choose for her.

Her mother had been the Iron Lady. Serena hoped her title would be less cold and hard.

Maybe she'd never find out how the luceria saw her. Maybe this bond she and Morgan forged now would only last a few days. Maybe they would annoy each other or find their personalities clashing. There was no way to know without taking a leap.

After two centuries of forced safety and isolation, she was more than ready to take a chance on him.

Morgan stared at the necklace he'd worn his whole life. There was reverence in his gaze, and a small part of her wished that she'd one day see him look on her with that same expression.

Before the girlish thought could take root, she wrapped the band around her neck until she heard the muted click of the ends locking together beneath her hair.

There was no turning back now.

Morgan sliced a small cut over his heart to symbolize his willingness to shed blood for her. The act was unnecessary on the heels of his bravery tonight, but the ritual demanded it of him.

She knew what would come next. He would offer her his vow to give his life for hers.

The idea was abhorrent to her. She'd always thought the ancient ritual was too bloodthirsty, too violent. Perhaps some women would find the notion romantic, but Serena had seen too many men die upholding that vow, literally giving their lives to save their mates.

She would never ask that of any man. Her life was no more important than his.

But instead of giving her the promise his kind usually did—offering to protect her with his life—Morgan gave her something entirely different.

"I know I'm supposed to say 'my life for yours,' but that's not what you want. That vow promises that I'll do whatever it takes to keep you safe, even if it means going against your

wishes. I won't do that to you. So instead, I offer you this."
He took a deep breath that expanded his chest to giant
proportions. The branches of his lifemark whipped and
twisted as if caught in a silent storm. "My power is yours,
Serena. I promise to never control, cage or manipulate you. I
promise to be a true partner to you, both in life and combat.
And I promise to never ask you to love me."

She stood there, speechless. He was giving her everything
she wanted. And now it was her turn to give him her vow.
Once she did, they would be bound in a way that could only
be broken if she left a loophole.

She had to be careful. Words mattered. Promises were
binding. Once she spoke aloud what she'd been holding
inside, there was no taking it back. The magic of the luceria
would bind her to her words.

Serena stilled her nerves and lifted her chin. The regal
pose made her feel more in control, though it was merely an
illusion. Inside she was shaking, half-terrified that she'd
misstep.

Her voice was deceptively calm, giving away none of her
inner turmoil. "Morgan, I promise to never be reckless with
my safety so that you don't have to regret the freedom you've
promised me. I will use your power wisely and for the good
of our people for as much time as we have. Before the colors
of the luceria solidify, I will claim you as my own forever, or
release you." She hesitated only a moment before she
mimicked his vow, adding, "And I promise to never ask you
to love me."

Morgan stared at her for a moment, then nodded once.

He touched the cut over his heart to gather a drop of blood,
then rose to his feet and pressed that to the luceria.

Their bond was forged, and now it was the luceria's turn
to show them what it willed.

Serena prayed that what she saw now wouldn't make her
regret her decision to tie herself to this man.

***

In the space of a few seconds, Morgan watched Serena suffer through two hundred years of captivity, alone and cut off from the world.

He didn't understand why the luceria would torment him like this—forcing him to watch her agony without being able to do anything about it. What good was there in witnessing her pain?

Frustrated and angry, he was left with no choice but to accept her endless boredom and bouts of rage and loneliness. Whatever he needed to endure to learn what made Serena tick, he would.

Their partnership depended on their ability to bond and communicate.

After a few years of screaming and begging for help, she finally realized no one could hear her. No one was coming. No one would save her.

Her mother had died in the attack she'd tried to protect Serena from, leaving no one to know her daughter was trapped here.

Slowly, Serena came to realize that if she was to break free, she was going to have to do it on her own.

She came up with countless strategies to shatter the protective magic, or at least crack it enough so that someone could hear her cries for help. But nothing worked. With no source of power to draw from, and no way to store more, the little bit of energy she could gather from her surroundings was tapped out quickly.

Frustration and rage consumed her, so powerful that Morgan didn't know how she'd survived it.

A few more decades passed, and she learned to meditate—to block out the world and let time flow around her without notice. She would go into these restful states for years at a time, only to come out and find that nothing had changed.

She lived for the moments when the stars would align—or whatever caused it—and her prison walls would thin enough that she could see or hear the world passing by. She would watch with rapt attention, striving to memorize the conversations and events she witnessed. Then, when she could no longer see or hear the world passing by her, she'd replay those memories in her mind, over and over, like a favorite song.

Then, finally, came a woman powerful enough to see through to where Serena was imprisoned. Brenya, Queen of Athanasia, wife of the Solarc himself, had freed her with a mere wave of her hand.

Serena's endless torment was over, or so she thought.

Now free of her prison and surrounded by her own people, she was still completely alone. Her heart was broken, the love of her life now bound to another. Everything she'd hoped for was gone. Every fantasy she'd used to survive her imprisonment would never come to pass. Iain was in love with someone else. They were expecting a child together. There was no place in his life for Serena, who had held herself together on the false promise of a happy future—one she now knew would never be.

Morgan was half-mad when the luceria finally let go of him and returned him to his own body and time.

He was shaking, cold. Stunned.

He didn't know how she'd survived that torment. Sure, he lived with physical pain, but that was far better than the mental torture she'd endured.

The whole time she'd been trapped, the one thought that kept her going was that Iain would be waiting for her. They were in love. Betrothed. They'd been moments from bonding when she'd been whisked away. She believed his devotion was so deep, that it never once occurred to her that he would have written her off as dead and moved on with his life. But that's what had happened.

Believing Serena dead in the attack that had killed so many of their women, Iain had met Jackie and bound himself to her, irrevocably. He was lost to Serena forever. The one hope that had kept her alive had been destroyed.

Morgan knew how hard it was to lose someone you loved,

but Femi had died of natural causes. Iain had chosen to walk away. Sure, he'd had good reason to believe Serena was dead, but the pain his willing decision to abandon her had caused was far deeper than any natural death could be.

Until feeling Serena's loss, Morgan didn't believe it was possible to hurt more than he had after losing Femi. Now that he'd felt what Serena had, he realized how ignorant he'd been.

Femi would have stayed with Morgan if she could have. Iain had chosen to walk away. One was unavoidable pain. The other was intentional betrayal.

Morgan didn't know if he should thank the man for keeping Serena alive during her captivity, or punch him in the balls for hurting her.

If not for what he was feeling now, Morgan might have done both. But now, thanks to Serena's bond, Morgan's pain was gone, and the decay of his soul had stopped.

He was almost giddy with relief, swaying on his feet as his body struggled to adjust to its new pain-free state.

He felt light. Free. Hopeful. His body felt a hundred years younger, stronger and more capable than he'd ever hoped to feel again. She hadn't just saved him. She had restored him.

Morgan's heart ached for her suffering and loss, but he would devote his life to helping her move past her pain. Somehow.

A delusional laugh bubbled from his throat, mocking him.

How could he help Serena get over what Iain had done when Morgan had never been able to get over his own heartache?

***

In the space of a few seconds, Serena lived an entire human lifetime with Morgan and an Egyptian woman named Femi.

They were married in the way of humans, and deeply in love. Their parents didn't approve, but rather than let the meddling break them apart, the couple chose to leave their home and find a new one—a place miles away where they could forge their own life together.

They were blissfully happy and spent every possible second together.

After a few years, it became clear that while Morgan wasn't aging, Femi was. She spent hours crying, wishing for children—wishing for time to slow its inevitable march. As her hair grayed and wrinkles creased her skin, she begged Morgan to leave her. She was no good to him as an old woman. She couldn't even give him children now.

But Morgan didn't care. He loved her, children or not. He was completely and utterly devoted to her in a way Serena had never seen before. She hadn't even known devotion this deep was possible.

Through sickness and aging, Morgan stayed by Femi's side. When she was too old to pass for his wife, they moved to a different country and she became his mother. They had to hide their passion for each other, but he still loved her with the same ferocity he had when she'd been a young girl.

When they moved again, Femi became his grandmother. There were no more adventures, no more talk of the future. All dreams of *someday* vanished.

Shortly after that, Femi died.

Morgan buried her and returned to his birthplace, where his family shunned him for his disobedience.

With his heart shattered and his soul weeping, he wandered aimlessly around the globe, grieving and lonely, aching for his Femi. He ended up in America, and made the war against the Synestryn his sole pursuit.

He hid his past behind a casual, flirtatious manner, making those around him believe things that were not true—that he was a womanizer with a string of satisfied ladies behind him.

In truth, there had been no one. He'd been in the world, but in some ways, had been just as alone as Serena had been.

His love for Femi was both beautiful and tragic. One human woman had stolen his heart, and to this day, it still belonged to her.

Morgan's decision to never love again wasn't just empty words. It was part of who he was—down to his bones. What he'd lost when Femi died could never be replaced. Not by anyone.

That was what the luceria wanted Serena to see—that the man she'd bound herself to was broken. Permanently, irrevocably broken.

Just like her.

***

When Serena opened her eyes and looked up at Morgan, tears glittered behind her lashes and sadness creased her brow.

"What did the luceria show you?" he asked, worried.

"Femi."

That one word had the power to rock him to his foundation. His human wife was the secret he'd kept for so long, he wasn't sure how he could talk about her now. She was a hidden part of his past—not because of shame, but because of sorrow.

Serena swallowed. Sniffed. "She was an amazing woman. I would never even try to take her place."

Morgan didn't know what to say to that. In some ways, it was a gift that Serena understood how he felt—that she wouldn't be struggling to replace what was irreplaceable. But in other ways, he wondered if having Femi between them would make their bond harder to forge.

He took Serena's hands in his, and let the play of heat and energy between them sooth his worries.

"You're not alone anymore," he told her. "We may never have what we could have before our hearts were broken, but that doesn't mean we can't have something special."

She nodded, her deep blue eyes huge and luminous with tears. "We have no choice. Too many people depend on us to have a strong partnership. We cannot fail."

"You deserve more," he said. "You deserve someone who could love you."

She gave him a sad smile. "So do you. At least this way, we both know what we're getting."

He took her beautiful face in his hands, marveling over the gift she was.

She'd saved his life and taken away his pain. He didn't know how long their bond would last, or if either of them would make it out alive, but for now, he was content.

He bent and kissed her forehead. Heat danced beneath his lips and curled through his veins.

His body reacted to the touch, lighting up from the inside. Desire swelled low in his abdomen and shimmered out of him.

Serena sucked in a small breath and looked up at him in shock.

"Too much?" he asked, instinctively seeking the connection that should have been formed between them when she took his luceria.

All he felt was a blank hum of nothingness. Static. Her thoughts and emotions were still hidden from him.

He reassured himself that their bond was too new for him to feel anything. They needed time and patience. He couldn't force their connection. It would happen in its own time.

She gave her head a little shake. "No. Our bond will never be strengthened by love, so we'll have to find another way. Physical intimacy, mutual respect, and deep friendship are all that are left to us." She squared her shoulders. "Respect and friendship take time. Your seer Sibyl told me that there is none to spare."

Morgan ignored her mention of physical intimacy, though only barely. Serena had been alluring before they'd bonded, but now she was becoming more enticing by the second.

Her skin seemed to glow now. Her eyes were bigger and more luminous. Her lips were damp and the most enticing shade of pink he'd ever seen.

He wanted to kiss her so badly he had to clench his jaw to keep his mouth off hers.

The luceria's doing, no doubt.

"What are you talking about?" he asked.

"Sibyl said that I must find the source of the new demons that are overrunning Dabyr before Iain's baby is born. That's what I was trying to do when you found me in that cave."

"But the baby will come any day now."

"Which is why there is no time to waste." She closed her eyes in concentration. "I can feel your power, but the conduit is tiny—barely more energy than I can gather from the air around me. I'm going to need more if I'm going to use your magic in combat."

"So...what? You want us to sleep together so our bond will strengthen?"

"Can you think of another way?"

He wanted her. There was no question about that. He hadn't been with a woman since Femi, but he wasn't sure if he was ready to admit that to Serena or not. He didn't want her to see him as pathetic.

He needed her respect. Not only for his own sense of self-worth, but also because it would strengthen their bond and allow her to access his power more easily.

"What if it backfires?" he asked. "What if we rush things and end up doing more harm than good."

He couldn't believe he was saying that. Here she was, offering him her body, and he was giving her reasons why she shouldn't.

If this kept up, he was going to have to turn in his man card.

She frowned. "I hadn't considered that. I'm ready to do my duty, but we don't have time for setbacks."

Her duty? That's what sex with him was to her?

He knew the idea shouldn't grate on him the way it did, but he couldn't get past the image of her lying under him, cold and robotic, taking one for the team.

That wasn't at all what he wanted, what he craved. He wanted heat, fire, passion. If he couldn't have love, he could at least have something more than a calculated merging of bodies, couldn't he?

Maybe that was all he deserved. Maybe that was all that

was left to him now that Femi was gone.

His words came out harder than he'd intended. "Eat and get some sleep. There will be plenty of time for you to do your *duty* later."

CHAPTER FIFTEEN

Serena had hurt Morgan's feelings. She wasn't sure how, but there was no mistaking the flutter of annoyance coming from him.

That she could feel anything coming through the luceria was a good sign. Too bad it didn't make her feel better.

She'd been raised to know what to expect of her when she bound herself to a male Theronai, and it usually took a long time for the connection to widen enough for emotions to trickle through. Her feeling him now—even his annoyance— was more than she could have hoped for.

Of course, Morgan had told her that bonding between Theronai was different now than it had been when she was a girl. After so long with few women to tap into their power, men had been pushed past all usual endurance, bearing more power for longer than was natural. That vast pressure they carried had changed the way couples bonded, so she had to discard her childhood lessons and learn new ones.

If he'd been Iain, she would have gone to his bed and used sex to strengthen their connection. Her mother had told her that she would be duty-bound to do so.

But he wasn't Iain, she wasn't Femi, and her mother wasn't here. They were going to have to find a way to get around their obstacles. Quickly.

Serena didn't mind the idea of bedding him. Morgan was

deeply attractive, with a wide streak of kindness running right through his core. She'd known when she'd taken his luceria that he would take her as a woman.

Truth be told, knowing that was part of what had swayed her to go ahead and bind herself to him. She hadn't been with a man since Iain, and two hundred years was far too long to go without physical release.

Unlike with Link, she loved the way it felt when Morgan touched her. She'd been hopeful that he'd touch her more, kiss her, hold her.

It had been so very long since she'd been held. She ached for the physical contact, the intimacy of lying naked with a man and feeling his warmth sink into her skin.

As much as she craved sex, what she needed even more than that was simple physical contact. A hand stroking her arm, the thick weight of a man's thigh cast over hers as she slept, an arm around her waist, pulling her close.

She was never again going to have any of those things with Iain, so she would have to settle with finding them elsewhere. Morgan, with his delicious body and kindness, was as good a choice as any. Even the luceria agreed.

Too bad Morgan had other ideas.

He'd closed himself away from her in one of the bedrooms, presumably to sleep. Even though the Sanguinar had done most of the healing, her body was still too weak to go out and fight tonight. She needed to rebuild her strength, to drink and eat and rest so her body could recover from the strain of healing.

Still, nagging pressure bulged at the back of her mind, urging her to hurry.

Sibyl knew what was coming. She'd warned Serena what had to be done. There was no time to waste.

While Serena didn't dare go hunting for the source of those demons tonight, there was one thing she could do that wouldn't be a waste of time.

She had been trained from the time she could speak what would be expected of her. Over and over, she'd watched her mother draw power from her father and force it to answer to her will.

The Iron Lady was capable of many things, but her specialty had been manipulation of time and its flow. She used that gift in amazing ways, to heal and to hurt, to protect and to destroy. Serena had once seen her kill an entire nest of demons by speeding time and making them die of starvation before the sun set and they could go out to hunt for food.

While specific gifts didn't always run in a family, Serena had most definitely inherited her mother's ability to bend time to her will.

She hoped that was the only part of her mother she'd inherited. The world did not need another controlling, manipulative bitch.

Rather than dwell on an unhappy past, Serena refocused her attention on the one thing that could help the most people.

She had to find the source of the demons that could withstand sunlight, and to do that, she needed power—power that was now right at her fingertips, thanks to Morgan. She could feel it glowing inside of her, seething with eagerness.

It wanted to be free, to be shaped by her hand.

Serena had seen the accidents caused by female Theronai new to their power—the fires, the buildings shaken to the ground. She wanted to believe that she'd have more control than that, but decided it was better to go outside and experiment rather than take chances.

The air was cold and clear, scented with frost and not even the barest hint of spring. Dawn would come soon, but not for another couple of hours.

The grass under her feet was dry and brittle. There were no houses within sight, but plenty of open pasture interrupted by clumps of trees and brush grown up along aging barbed wire fences and creeks.

The moon was a bright sliver in the sky, which seemed like the only thing that hadn't changed from her youth.

She didn't stray far from the house. The threat of attack hovered in the back of her mind like a vulture, reminding her to be alert.

Death was always near.

She'd found an oversized coat in a closet, which she now hugged around her body. She closed her eyes and focused inward, to the tiny glowing spot where Morgan's power entered her. She didn't know if it was a physical place or simply a construct of her mind, but when she concentrated on it, that light seemed to shimmer in response.

Tentatively, she touched it, and was surprised to find that it felt like Morgan—hot, kind, intense, consuming.

She shivered in reaction, but didn't pull away. Instead, she tried to coax that light into herself by opening up a cozy place meant just for it.

At first, nothing happened. His power stayed where it was, hovering just outside of herself, out of reach.

Her mother's lessons came flooding back. Her stern, demanding voice was always there, lecturing her on the value of her appearance, how beauty was power and she must learn to use that power to get what she wanted from life. But there were other lessons, too. Valuable ones, like how the flow of energy from a mate worked best when one was relaxed and confident. Power abhorred timidity, but bowed down to the bold.

Gertrude Brinn had definitely been bold.

Serena imagined the pool of energy inside Morgan as a feisty puppy, eager to obey. She straightened her spine, relaxed her shoulders and summoned every bit of confidence she had.

Once she felt completely in control, she summoned the power with a firm command.

Instantly, a burst of energy shot into her with so much force, she gasped in surprise. Light and heat flooded her body, seeping into bones and tissue, weaving through her blood and filling her lungs. As she exhaled, tiny sparks of magic swirled in her misty breath.

The clean, hot smell of Morgan's skin surrounded her like an embrace. She could feel his presence inside that light, as if he were hugging her from the inside.

The feeling was exquisite. She reveled in it, soaking in the mirage of human contact as if it were real.

One of the hardest parts of her captivity had been not being touched. As much as she craved company and conversation, her body had starved for the simple brush of a hand or the warmth of a hug. She hadn't even known how deep her craving for such things could go until she was sure that not feeling the touch of another would literally kill her.

Only it hadn't. She continued on in her endless life of boredom and loneliness without relief.

But now she had something new, something amazing. Even though he wasn't here, his power was. Morgan's magical touch filled her and comforted her in a way she never could have imagined before experiencing it.

She wanted to hold in his essence and keep that warmth forever, but that was not the way her body was designed to function. She couldn't store power the way he could. She could only carry a small amount for immediate use, and if she didn't let it out, it would damage her.

With the warnings of her mother clanging in the back of her mind, Serena grudgingly let go of the energy, forcing it to come out in the form of fire.

A strand of flame the width of her finger shot out from her outstretched hand and sizzled among the blades of dead grass a few yards away.

Heat left her body in a rush. There was an odd, sucking sensation that made her tense, as if she could stop it. When the flow of power finally stopped, what was left behind was a charred, black squiggle in the lawn.

Tiny flames flickered for a moment before the cold stole their life and snuffed them out.

Serena was left with a feeling of satisfaction, mixed with a strange sense of loss. Something vital had been hers for only a moment before she'd lost it. She was greedy for more, desperate for that rush of power flowing through her.

This was what she'd been born for. This was what she'd

been missing all her life.

She knew there was danger in what she sought, but didn't care. She was done living a life of safety, a life without risk. She deserved to feel alive and whole after what she'd suffered.

She wanted more of Morgan's power inside of her. All of it. Now. And no one was going to stop her from having it.

***

Jackie locked herself in a supply closet with Iain in an effort to find some quiet. She couldn't concentrate. Sibyl's ominous warnings played through her mind on a continuous loop, making it impossible to focus.

Lights danced in Jackie's vision, so bright she couldn't see past them. The headache the glare caused pounded at her temples, but even when she closed her eyes, there was no relief.

Her baby seemed to sense her distress. She stretched and punched at her confines, hitting Jackie's bladder with uncanny accuracy. The infant's tiny feet lodged against Jackie's ribcage and began to dance.

Her back ached and the skin of her abdomen seemed so tight it might tear. The hard mound of her belly protruded like the prow of a ship, with her belly button as the figurehead.

She was almost done carrying this child. She could sense her daughter's eagerness to join the rest of the world and take her place within it.

The thought made Jackie panic. What if she couldn't protect her? What if she couldn't keep this tiny, little life out of the hands of their enemy?

She had to figure out how to locate the lights before her daughter was born. There was no other choice. Her baby had to survive. Any other outcome was unthinkable.

Iain was right at her side while she worked to solve the puzzle of how to find these women. His worry funneled through their link, fluttering against her like frantic insect wings.

She wanted to reassure him, but she didn't have the attention to spare. All her effort was going inward, pointed toward the map in her mind.

A few times before, she'd seen a bird's eye view of the world in her visions. As if flying overhead, she could see trees, rivers, lakes and mountains. Even roads were visible when she got close enough to see them. Superimposed on that view were the lights that haunted her. They pulsed and flashed, colorful and glaring.

They needed to be found, to be saved before it was too late.

While there were many lights spread across the globe, the ones she focused on were in North America. But without map lines to guide her, she couldn't pinpoint exactly where they were. All she could gather was a general location, sometimes not even a specific state. Even more frustrating, the lights moved around, sometimes hopping across the country as one of the women drove or flew to a different destination. At least, that was Jackie's guess.

How was she ever going to find them, much less pin them down so they didn't move once she did?

For a few weeks before the attack on Dabyr, she'd been working with a handful of unbound male Theronai in an effort to guide them toward these women. But so far, the process had failed. Her vision wasn't like Google Maps where she had a blue dot to guide her. She couldn't even see the men in her mind, only the women. The men simply told her where they were, or she located them on an app Nicholas had created to track them.

Connecting a light with a man seemed impossible. Without a better system, she had no hope of ever guiding the two together. And now, with every able-bodied male swinging a sword in defense of Dabyr, there were no men to spare to go hunting.

Sibyl's warning echoed in Jackie's mind.

Dabyr cannot fall....We won't survive it.

She had to find a better way.

Maybe if she focused on just one light....

Jackie looked at the landscape in her mind and chose a particularly bright light. It was a blue so pale it was nearly white, with flickering bolts of yellow streaking through it like lightning.

She willed herself closer and felt a moment of vertigo as she zoomed in on the pulsing dot.

Everything was white here. The glow of the light seemed to bounce off a great, glittering expanse that stretched out endlessly.

Snow. It was snowing here, wherever she was.

Was this happening now? If so, maybe she could use some kind of weather map to help figure out the location.

Iain was inside her thoughts as he usually was. He heard her idea and was already acting on it. He shifted slightly beside her to pull his phone from his pocket.

Even that small movement made her lurch back into herself, away from the light.

"Sorry," he said. "I didn't mean to break your concentration."

"It's okay. I'll just try again."

He slid away from her so that their bodies no longer touched. She didn't like the distance between them, but realized he'd done it so that he didn't distract her again.

Jackie refocused herself and went back to that white, snowy place she'd seen before.

The blue-white light was still there, glowing like a tiny sun.

She hadn't lost it. The woman was still there. Not only could she see the light, but she could feel a quivering sense of power radiating out from it.

The frequency was strange—so very different from her own—but still identifiable as a deep source of magic.

This woman was definitely a Theronai. Jackie didn't need to see her ring-shaped birthmark to know that.

She looked around in an effort to figure out where she was. All she could see was snow. It fell through the air, covered the ground, clung to the trees and bushes and blanketed the rooftop.

A roof. There was a roof here, but she hadn't seen it because she'd been directly overhead. It had blended perfectly with the wintery surroundings.

With an effort of will, Jackie moved lower, descending toward the ground. The light grew brighter as she did, blocking most of her field of vision.

How was she ever going to see these women if she couldn't see past them?

"I need mental sunglasses," she muttered. "Maybe a welder's helmet."

"You can do this," Iain said, his voice calm and confident. "I know you can."

She wasn't sure, but what choice did she have? Lives were at stake.

Her baby's life was at stake.

That was the thought that refocused her attention and made her try again.

If she needed sunglasses, then that's what she'd find.

Jackie pulled on the link to her husband and siphoned off some of his power. It felt so good to have it writhing inside of her, eager to be used. It made her swell and grow in a way she couldn't describe.

It made her whole.

She concentrated on the light and what she needed to happen. As always with magic, there was an effort of will, an exertion that forced it to take the shape she needed it to take. Some things were easier than others, but new things were always harder.

Building a magical pair of sunglasses to dim the light emanating from a woman hundreds of miles away was definitely new.

She gathered up the power and directed it to her eyes like she did when she needed to be able to see in the dark. Energy shot through her body and streaked up her spine. It gathered into two tight balls as it went, then detonated like tiny bombs just behind her closed eyelids.

The snow disappeared. Everything vanished and went dark.

She'd gone too far, she realized. She'd dimmed her vision too much.

She dialed back on the mojo until she found a sweet spot where she could see the light but wasn't blinded by it. As soon as she was satisfied with her adjustment, she set the flow of power coming from Iain at a steady rate so she could concentrate on the woman.

She was inside a small house. No, not a house, a cabin. It was just one room, no more than fifteen feet across. There was a round, metal chimney coming out of the side, pointing skyward. Smoke billowed from it, melting snowflakes as it went.

Jackie floated downward toward the ground until she was at eye level with the small window in the front wall of the cabin.

Three wooden steps led to the front door. The little building was rough and shabby, as if it hadn't been maintained in years. Paint peeled from wooden siding. The bare bulb over the door was broken, the fixture crooked, as if someone had bashed it with a bat. An empty bird's nest was tucked under the roofline with bits of Easter grass and plastic straw wrappers stuck inside the intricate web of grass and twigs.

Pale blue light glowed through the dirty window. Inside, Jackie could see a woman crouched in front of a wood stove, rubbing her hands together for warmth.

She was shivering visibly from the cold. Her hands were bright red. Her jeans were soaked to her knees and her boots sat beside the stove, also wet.

Jackie couldn't see her face. The glow was too bright, obscuring her features.

She tried to dial down the glare, but all that did was black out the woman completely.

Maybe there was something nearby that would identify her or her location.

Jackie scanned the area, searching for newspapers or mail. All she saw was dirt on the floor and a distinct absence of furniture.

This cabin was empty. So why was this woman here?

Her car. Jackie could find her car and get the license plate. That would tell her either the state the woman was in or at least the one she was from, wouldn't it?

She backed out of the cabin and did a visual sweep of the snowy landscape outside.

All she saw were footprints in the deep snow. No car, no snowmobile, no nothing. Apparently, the woman had walked here.

Jackie found the tracks and followed them back through the woods. Surely the woman had left her stranded vehicle behind nearby and walked in the rest of the way.

But all Jackie saw as she moved away from the cabin was tracks that were swiftly filling in with snow. After about a mile, there was no longer any trace of the woman's passage left.

"What the hell?" she said aloud.

As soon as she spoke, she snapped back into herself as if attached to a rubber band.

Iain was still with her, in her thoughts. He'd been silent and still, but had monitored the whole thing.

She opened her eyes. Everything was dark. It took her a second to realize she was still wearing her magical sunglasses.

She dropped the magic, and for a moment, could see his handsome face clearly. Then the lights began to glow again, blocking her sight.

"I have no clue," Iain said. "But clearly, she's in trouble."

Jackie closed her eyes and tried not to let her frustration get the best of her. "What makes you say that?"

"She was alone in a snowstorm with no supplies. Her coat wasn't even that warm. She looked like she was dressed to go shopping, not to take a midnight hike in the woods. And she'd broken into that cabin, likely for warmth."

"How do you know she broke in?"

"The door knob was broken. There was a piece of firewood lying nearby with a fresh gouge."

Jackie hadn't seen any of that. She wondered what else she'd missed.

"Did you see anything that could tell us where she is?"

She felt his answer through the luceria before it came.

"Sorry," he said. "I didn't."

She sighed, gave herself ten seconds to feel all the frustration and worry her failure caused, then sat up straighter in her flimsy folding chair.

"Guess we need to try again," she said. "Maybe the next woman will make identifying her a little easier."

Her belly hardened, drawing so tight it nearly stole her breath.

Braxton Hicks contractions. That's what Ronan had told her these were. She'd been having them for a while, but now every time one hit, she worried that she'd run out of time.

Iain placed his big, warm hand on her belly until the contraction stopped. "You don't have to keep going if you're too tired."

"I have to," Jackie said. "We're running out of time."

CHAPTER SIXTEEN

Morgan tried to sleep and failed. He didn't sleep often, his body able to go days or even weeks without rest. But his body was tired from feeding Briant his blood, and the only thing that would help heal him was fluids, food and rest.

So, he lay in a bed too small for his body and tried to relax. When that didn't work, he rose and knelt beside the bed to meditate as he had thousands of times before. No matter what he did, his mind couldn't seem to settle enough to rest.

He and Serena were bonded, and yet it wasn't at all like he thought it would be. There was no celebration. The event had come and gone with as much fanfare as laundry day.

He was left unsatisfied, like something vital was missing from their union.

Other men had been in his position and they always walked around, grinning, like nothing in their world could go wrong.

Maybe his bond just needed more time to solidify.

Then again, maybe it would always be a hollow substitute without real love—something as cold as the negotiation that had formed it.

As his mind raged with worry, an odd sensation vibrated behind his ribs. He felt heat and a relief of pressure. It was so small it was barely a sensation at all, but he knew without a doubt what it was.

Serena was tapping into his power, practicing, which meant she was probably outside, alone.

He rushed from the bedroom, pulling his jeans on as he went. His sword was in his hand as he cleared the doorway.

A blast of cold air stole his breath. His leather jacket had been too hacked up, too bloody to save. There would be others stored inside the gerai house for just such an occasion, but he hadn't yet bothered to find one that would fit his shoulders and still allow him room to swing his sword.

The pre-dawn sky was bright with stars and a thumbnail moon. More light from the windows spilled out over the brown lawn. He didn't even need to draw power to his eyes to see clearly.

He scanned the area, searching for a glimpse of Serena's fiery hair and pale skin, but saw nothing. He could feel her, though, on the other end of their newborn link, guiding him to her.

Morgan walked around to the back of the house.

Winter wind sucked warmth from his bare chest, but he ignored the chill. Only Serena's safety mattered.

She was on her hands and knees in the middle of the back yard, inside what looked like a giant, black rune. As he approached, he could see that the squiggly line of black was charred grass. She was breathing hard, and even from a few yards away, he could see her shaking.

"Serena?" he said softly so he wouldn't startle her.

She jerked upright to her knees, then wobbled as if even that movement was too much effort. She stayed facing away from him, but he couldn't tell if it was because she was hiding her weakness from him, or because she simply didn't have the strength to stand and face him.

"It's not as easy as I thought it would be," she said.

"What isn't?" he asked.

"I didn't want to wake you. You needed to rest after feeding the Sanguinar for me."

He still didn't understand why she was risking her safety outside the protective walls of the gerai house. "What are you doing out here alone?"

"I need to practice wielding your power. I didn't realize it would disturb you." She was panting as she spoke.

He came around in front of her. The whites of her eyes were bloodshot, as was often the case with women who tried to wield too much power at once. Her usual pink complexion was pale with bright blotches of angry red. She kept blinking, like she was struggling to focus, and she still had yet to catch her breath.

"You didn't disturb me," he said as he knelt in front of her, concerned by what he saw.

Even marred by her efforts, she was still deeply beautiful—the kind of beauty that drove men past the edge of sanity, just for a chance to be near her.

She'd bound herself to him, but she still wasn't his any more than he was hers.

Something about that thought bothered him, but he didn't spare the attention to figure out what it was. She was his sole focus.

He smoothed her loose curls away from her face, because he had to touch her—make sure she was real and that he wasn't dreaming that she'd saved him and freed him from his pain.

The chill of her skin told him this was no dream.

"You're freezing. Come inside and warm up for a while, then we'll try again, properly this time."

"Properly? I know how the bond works, Morgan. I've been trained for this since I was a toddler."

"You've seen how the bond worked for your parents and others who've been connected for a while. We haven't been. The farther away from you I am, the harder it's going to be for you to draw on my power." He spanned his hand at the base of her throat until his ring came in contact with her necklace. As it did, sparks erupted from the point of contact and lit their faces. "See?"

Her eyes closed and her head fell back on a groan of pleasure. Her cold fingers covered his, gripping him tight so he couldn't move his hand.

"This is what I want," she whispered. "Your heat. Your power." She opened her eyes and stared into his. There was hunger there, hunger and desperation. "Give it to me, Morgan. I've been so cold and alone for so long. Give me what I need."

As she said the words, he got a flickering image of what she wanted.

The two of them together, naked, entwined. Fucking.

It wasn't a gentle, sweet image, but one of raw, carnal need. There were no girlish fantasies in her head, tricking her into thinking that sex would lead to love. She was a woman who understood reality. A woman who wanted him.

He should have been bothered by her desire. He'd been hit on plenty of times before and never once had he been tempted. His thoughts had always been of Femi and how physical intimacy with another woman was a betrayal of her memory.

But now, with Serena in front of him showing him what she wanted, what she needed, he found his thoughts scattering so thin that his male instincts were able to surface.

She was his mate now, at least for a while. Sex was common between bonded Theronai. Instincts guided them to strengthen their bond, to join themselves together as tightly as possible. He wouldn't go so far as to say it was his duty to sleep with her, but no one would fault them for it.

With her here, so beautiful and hungry, he could hardly fault himself, could he?

"Physical intimacy will strengthen our bond," she said. "We're going to need all the help we can get to connect. I realize that now. And in this case, it's going to be so enjoyable to further the cause, don't you think?"

There were so many parts of him he couldn't give her, it seemed unfair to withhold one more. Especially when it was something he so desperately wanted to give her.

Would Femi understand? How many times had she begged him to leave her and find a suitable wife? Someone younger and able to give him children? He'd told her over and over that she was the only woman he wanted.

It had been true for centuries. But now…now he wanted another. Badly. His desire was purely physical, and likely a result of the magic flowing between him and Serena, but that changed nothing.

He needed to feel her skin under his fingertips, to hear her breathless cries of pleasure. He needed to sink himself into her so deeply he'd drive away all his doubts and guilt. If only for a little while.

Before he could lose his head and take her here, under the stars, where there was no shelter from enemies or the cold, he picked her up and headed for the house.

She was limp with fatigue and pliant in his arms—something he'd never associated with her before. Serena was prickly at best, always on guard and ready to fight at the slightest provocation. But now, under the stars and the cover of darkness, she'd let him see her weakness. For some reason that felt like more of an intimacy than when she'd stood completely naked in front of him in her motel room.

This woman in his arms was more than she seemed, just as he was more than people saw in him. He didn't know how long he would have to learn her secrets and uncover her layers before she chose whether or not to stay bonded to him, but he hoped that what he found would lead him to understand her better.

Morgan didn't want to die. He didn't want to live in pain. The only way to avoid those things was to convince Serena they made a good team, even in bed. Perhaps especially in bed.

She curled into his bare chest and buried her nose against his neck. "You smell so good—like the spring air I remember from my childhood."

Her lips brushed his skin, kissing and nibbling as they moved.

Morgan tightened his gut against a punch of lust that made his cock surge behind his fly.

Maybe it was the luceria fueling their desire for each other, but he didn't care. It felt real and if he felt it, then so would she. And right now, he was willing to use every advantage he had to tie her to him so tightly she'd never consider walking away.

Serena was going to be his. Tonight.

He made it as far as the back door before he gave into the need to kiss her. She turned her face up to his like a flower starving for sunshine, and drank him in. Her lips were sweet and soft, smooth as rose petals and just as delicate.

She sighed into his mouth, the sound one of a starving man finally tasting food again. There was so much relief in the sound, so much need, he almost wondered if he'd heard it right.

She deepened the kiss, driving her tongue behind his teeth to gather his taste. With every slick glide his mouth watered. It had been so long since he'd kissed a woman like this.

Not since....

No. He wouldn't go there again. Not now. This moment was between him and Serena. No ghosts allowed.

He tried to remind himself to be gentle with her, but those sweet noises of hers were making it hard to think of anything but stripping her naked and getting inside of her.

Morgan let her feet slide to the floor so he could shut and lock the back door. The way her body grazed down his bare chest made him forget about everything else. The monsters outside, Sibyl's dire warnings, the broken walls of their home...none of that mattered here and now. Only Serena and the raging heat of her body mattered.

He could feel her nipples under her shirt, so hard and stiff, they felt like fingers grazing his chest. The soft press of her curves seemed to fit his body perfectly. Even his lifemark shivered in response.

She took his face in her hands and held him still while she devoured his mouth. Her kisses were hungry, desperate things that left him struggling to breathe. She wasn't timid or shy. Not his Serena. She knew what she wanted, and was going to get it from him. He could either come willingly, or be dragged along against his will.

He'd never been more willing in his life.

She took one long step back and ripped off her baggy coat and borrowed clothes in a frantic rush. It was no slow, sultry striptease, but the end result was far sexier than any staged show the world had ever seen.

He'd seen her naked before, for a moment, but this time, she stood still, letting him look his fill. Letting him take his time.

Her breasts were perfect, sweet, pink-tipped concoctions meant for a man's mouth. Her tiny waist flared to womanly hips highlighted by a fiery tuft of hair he was dying to see beneath. Her legs were curvy in all the right places, and cushioned just right to wrap around a man's hips and stay that way for hours while he drove her to scream his name in release.

He wanted to possess her. Devour her. Claim her and leave a mark no other man would dare challenge.

The possessive streak startled him, but he shrugged it off as a by-product of their recent bonding—maybe a trick the luceria was playing on him. As soon as he had her a few times, he was certain all that caveman clutter in his brain would be worked out.

And there was no question that he'd have her. It would take more than once to work a woman like Serena out of his system. If such a thing were even possible.

"Take off your pants, Theronai," she ordered, imperious. "I want to see all of the man who may one day sire my children."

The way she talked about sex so brazenly thrilled him. He hadn't tied himself to a squeamish, wilting orchid. No, Serena was powerful in her own right, and clearly not afraid to ask for what she wanted.

He loved that about her.

Morgan stripped out of his boots and jeans, but propped his sword nearby, just in case. When he was completely nude, his aching cock thrusting out in front of him, dark and throbbing with eagerness, she went still.

She stared openly at his erection, as if it were some

priceless sculpture to be housed in a museum for all to see. Or perhaps, that look was more about a woman who wanted him all to herself. He couldn't tell. There wasn't enough blood left in his brain to puzzle it out.

She took two steps toward him, close enough to touch. He kept his fists clenched at his sides, letting her do what she wanted. Whatever it was, he was ready and willing to be on the receiving end.

His body quivered in anticipation. Lust wrapped around him like a second skin, so tight his breath was shallow and uneven. Heat poured out of him. His heart pounded hard behind his ribs, making his erection pulse and twitch with every beat.

Her hands pressed against his pecs, caressing his lifemark as they slid lower. The branches swayed across his chest, straining to reach her. He could hear wood creaking and groaning as if in a strong wind.

Was that his imagination or was it real? He couldn't tell.

Those slender, delightful hands lingered on his chest for only a moment before they moved straight for his groin. Both of her hands wrapped around his erection, but she couldn't hold all of him.

Maybe if she used her mouth, too, he'd be completely surrounded by her heat, her touch.

He wanted that so much, he trembled. He almost told her what he needed, but before he could, she spoke.

"I've chosen well," she said, her voice a little hoarse, her gaze locked on his groin. "You won't have any trouble at all planting your seed deep."

He almost spilled into her hands right then and there, just from the images her words sparked in his mind.

He'd wanted children for a long time. It had broken Femi's heart that she couldn't give him any. He'd told her that it was his fault—that he was infertile, not her—but she'd always felt guilty.

Since then, his people's fertility had been restored. The Sanguinar had developed a serum that cured the men. Babies were once again being born.

He and Serena could have one, too.

"You're not afraid?" he asked her. "There are so many risks with pregnancy."

She frowned at him in confusion. "Why would I be afraid of doing something that countless generations before us have done? I'm no child, Morgan. I'm not afraid of anything you have to give me, including children."

"And if we don't stay bonded?"

"Then we don't. I won't find a better specimen of Theronai than you anywhere." Her gaze heated as she openly stared at his body. "Whether or not we stay bonded, our children will be beautiful, powerful."

She hesitated and tilted her head to the side. "Are you afraid of having children?"

Surprisingly, the answer was as simple as it was easy to find. "Not even a little."

"Good. We're not a prolific people. Chances are it will take us years to conceive."

Morgan thought about how easy it had been for the other couples, but didn't dare bring that up now. Not when he was standing at the gates of heaven, being welcomed inside.

Besides, he didn't think there was anything he could say to warn her off, as fiercely determined as she was. His heart might have been off limits, but his body was hers to enjoy as she saw fit.

She offered him a sultry smile. "We may have to practice a lot to get it right."

"I can be very diligent," he offered. "Put in long, hard hours."

She smiled, a secret, womanly smile that made his head spin. "Just what I wanted to hear."

Before he could speak again, she pulled his head down and covered his mouth with hers.

CHAPTER SEVENTEEN

Controlling a man as powerful as Morgan was going to be impossible, especially when he made Serena's insides go soft and liquid with a single, hungry glance. Besides, control wasn't really what she wanted. That was her mother's domain.

Any man who would allow another to control him—even his wife—was too weak to please her for long.

And after what the luceria had shown her, she didn't think she'd ever find a man more perfect for her than Morgan. He would never expect impossible things from her, or demand she give him something she could never bear to give.

Sex, partnership, power, children. That was all this arrangement would be.

For her, it was enough. It had to be.

Rather than dwell on whatever she might find lacking later in their relationship, she focused on what she found bountiful.

Morgan was very likely more man than she could handle. At least without a bit of practice. But, oh, was she going to enjoy practicing.

Her body was starving for his, empty and aching to be filled with his impressive manhood. The width of his shoulders and the visible power of his limbs sang to that deep, feminine part of her that reveled in their physical differences. He was hard where she was soft, dark where she was pale. He was thick and sturdy where she was delicate. He was all bold angles and sharp planes, and she was sweeping curves and yielding flesh.

And all she wanted right now was to push him down and mount him until he had no choice but to bask in the dichotomy of their flesh right along with her.

Before she could, he lifted her up in his big hands. She wrapped her legs around his waist, and felt the hot, hard weight of his manhood against her bottom.

Serena wanted to wriggle down and fit herself around him, but he didn't let her. Instead, he carried her into the living room and sat on the couch, her heated body straddling his.

His mouth covered hers, claiming every nook as his own. He tasted like spice and citrus, and the joy of Christmas morning. She breathed him in as she feasted on his kisses, until her head spun from lack of air.

She pulled away to ease the dizzy spin in her head, but the moment she did, he leaned her back over his thick forearm and drew the tip of her breast into the heat of his mouth.

Pleasure. Keen, pure pleasure raged through her with every flick of his tongue, every suckling draw of his lips.

Sparks danced between them, blinding her. Searing energy rushed through her limbs until they trembled. Her nipples drew tighter against his tongue and sent a wash of quivering desire straight to her loins.

The smell of her arousal filled the space between them, heady and wanton. He pulled back just enough to slip a hand to her sex and gauge her readiness.

She was slick and ready, and nearly mad with need. In truth, she'd been that way since she'd met him, her body knowing what it wanted before her mind decided to follow its lead.

Serena was certain that he would take her now, but instead, he gave her a slow, wicked smile that showed off his bright white teeth. A moment later, he flipped her back onto the couch and lowered his head between her thighs.

"Just relax, sweetheart. This may take a while."

The instant his mouth covered her sex and his tongue

began to dance, she knew that it wasn't going to take long at all.

***

Serena climaxed within seconds. Morgan had barely even begun tasting her, and she was already rewarding him with the sweetest cries of release any woman had ever made.

He wanted more. Needed it. A man couldn't feel the rush of making a woman like her come once without craving it again and again.

She gripped his head as he savored her. She was trying to pull him up to cover her body with his, but he wasn't ready for that yet. He needed to make sure she was satisfied before he got inside her, because he didn't think that after so many years of celibacy that he was going to last long. Especially not with a woman as sexy as she was.

Morgan slid two fingers inside her pussy, and was bathed in the same slick, silken heat that wet his lips and tongue. He wanted nothing more than to sink his cock into that welcome embrace, but some things were more important than his immediate gratification.

He couldn't remember what right now, but he knew it had to do with making Serena scream in pleasure.

His tongue loved her clit, sending tiny sparks of power into the tender bud. Each one made her gasp and arch her back.

The seething ocean of energy inside of him wanted to be inside her as much as he did. As close as he was to her now, it churned and crashed against his bones in an effort to reach her.

She wasn't ready for that much power yet. She wouldn't be able to hold it all. But much like his cock, if he took his time and was patient with her, eventually, she'd take everything he had to give.

"Take me," she whispered. "I can't wait."

He almost gave in. Heaven knew he wanted to. His balls were aching for release. His cock was throbbing with need. But she wasn't relaxed enough to take him yet. Her pussy was too tight, and the last thing he wanted to do was hurt her.

"I'm not breakable," she said, as if she'd heard his wayward thought.

Maybe she had. The luceria was designed to allow them to merge, both mentally as well as physically. In battle, words took too long when split seconds counted. Thoughts were far faster to convey.

But he'd thought it would take longer for them to connect that deeply. Weeks, at least.

Maybe sex was helping speed the bonding process along, just as Serena said it would.

If they bonded completely, and then she walked away, he wouldn't survive.

But what a way to go.

The scent of her arousal went to his head. It mixed with the lavender fragrance of her skin, melding perfectly into a new, more intoxicating smell. Blood pounded through his veins and pooled in his aching cock. He slid another finger inside of her and sucked on her clit with renewed focus.

Her hands tightened against his head, and her scream of completion echoed in the quiet house. A rush of hot liquid bathed his fingers, and he knew that there was no more restraint left in him.

Before the last shimmering whimper of her pleasure had died, he rose over her body, and slid all the way inside her in one long, smooth stroke.

Searing perfection gripped his cock, so tight he couldn't breathe. He wanted to stay still and give her time to adjust to his size, but there was no more self-control left in him. Instincts and hunger ruled him now, forcing him to move.

A flicker of something crossed her beautiful features, but he couldn't tell what. Pleasure? Pain? Need? He was too far gone to figure it out. All that mattered was fucking her. Claiming her as his own.

So that's what he did.

His hips moved in hard, powerful thrusts. Each one made her full breasts jiggle and sway. Each one shoved air from her lungs in a soft sigh. Her lips were parted, the same raspberry pink color as her nipples. He levered her up against his chest, and the instant he did—the second her breasts were pressed against his lifemark—a waterfall of sparks spilled out of him, into her.

She let out a sharp cry that could have been anything from surprise to pain to enjoyment. Tiny flecks of light sprayed up between them, then clung to her skin for a second before soaking into her.

She glowed like some kind of golden goddess, powerful and mysterious.

And she was all his. At least her body was. For now, that was more than enough. For now, he couldn't handle anything more.

Morgan bent his head to kiss her, and the taste of her mouth made his head spin. She was intoxicating, making him forget that anything stood between them. Right now, their world was filled with pleasure and warmth and light. Utter perfection.

Her fingernails bit into his back as she struggled to get closer to his body. There was no room between them, but it still wasn't close enough.

It would never be close enough if he didn't give in.

Give into what, he wasn't sure, but his instincts were raging, pounding at him to listen.

Morgan shut it out and put all his focus on making Serena explode for him one more time. He knew she had it in her, and he was going to find that pleasure and drag it from her.

He pushed her knees up toward her chest, and angled her hips so he could slide a tiny fraction deeper. As soon as he did, he knew he'd found a sweet spot inside of her and was determined to make it his.

Stake his claim.

Before he was done with her, every inch of her would be stamped with his touch, his presence.

Her gaze met his, and the wildness he saw there thrilled him. She was strong enough to take everything he had to give, and hungry enough to demand that he hold back nothing.

That was exactly what Morgan did.

He moved, setting a demanding pace that had them both screaming toward climax. Her skin flushed a deep pink and her breathing sped even further. She clutched and clawed at him, until they were plastered together and moving as one.

Pressure caved in on him in a hot tidal wave. His orgasm hit him hard, giving him no time to slow down or retreat. All he could do was bare his teeth and roar out Serena's name as the pleasure crashed into him and stole the breath from his lungs.

Between the first heated jet of his semen and the second, Serena followed him into the storm. Her pussy clenched around him, milking every last drop of release from his body. He filled her to overflowing, and still had more to give.

The riot of sensations went on and on, lasting longer than he could ever remember. Each second stretched out into an hour, extending their pleasure to the point he didn't think he could take any more.

He hung suspended inside the storm, able to feel every flutter of her body against his, every minute vibration of release. He'd never known something so intense could last for so long.

Finally, when it was over, a familiar sense of vertigo wavered through him before passing a moment later.

That's when he realized what had happened.

Serena had used her gift to manipulate time to lengthen their orgasm and make it last far longer than usual.

Hell of a gift.

He panted as he held himself up. His arms shook. His heart thundered. His pulse was so fast he could hardly tell one beat from the next.

Careful not to crush her body, but refusing to move off of her, he propped himself on his elbows as their breathing evened and their bodies quieted.

It took a long time to come down from the heights of pleasure they'd just shared. He enjoyed the ride and simply basked in the feeling of relief and satisfaction.

After all those decades of celibacy, he'd really needed to come. So had she.

Her eyes were closed, and a peaceful expression of contentment shaped her features. Her red hair was spilled out across the cushions in a chaotic tangle. Her cheeks were flushed and her mouth was a deep, ruby red, the same shade as one of the tendrils running through the luceria around her neck.

She was the most beautiful woman he'd ever seen. Perfect. Exquisite.

The thought gave him pause.

There was a time when even the idea of someone else possessing qualities above and beyond Femi's gave him a sick sense of guilt. He didn't know when he'd lost the rosy glasses that saw only perfection in her, but his lack of loyalty to his beloved made him feel like an ass.

Serena opened her eyes and frowned at him. "It doesn't mean you love her any less."

"You can already hear my thoughts?"

"Just the loud ones." She touched his cheek and offered him a fragile smile. "We're forging new ground here. It's going to take some adjustment. Try not to be too hard on yourself. Femi would never want that for you."

Serena was right. Femi was the sweetest, most selfless woman he'd ever known, and she would have been horrified to think that anything having to do with her memory was causing him pain.

He owed it to her to cut himself some slack and stop judging himself for whatever random thoughts popped into his head.

Morgan slid himself from Serena's body and cringed at the mess he'd left behind.

This poor couch was never going to be the same again.

Neither was he.

She laughed, breaking his tension. "Next time, we'll put down a towel first."

And just like that, he was already thinking about the next time he'd get inside that perfect body of hers.

He knew sex wasn't love, and that it was impossible to cheat on a dead woman, but now that his body was cooling, that didn't mean he didn't feel just a little like a cheater all the same.

"I'm going to go clean up, then try to sleep for an hour or two," she said. "Between the loss of blood, learning to channel your power, and what we just did, I'm exhausted."

Morgan helped her to her feet. He almost followed her, but stopped himself as he realized he had no right. They hadn't discussed sleeping arrangements. They'd chosen separate rooms earlier. For all he knew, sex didn't change that. It's not like she asked him to come snuggle her or anything.

When she left the bathroom, went into her room and shut the door, her choice was clear enough.

Sex was all she'd wanted. She'd gotten it and now she was done with him.

For some reason he couldn't pinpoint, that pissed him off.

***

Link drove through the countryside, winding his way east. His flight would leave from Atlanta soon, and it was his duty to be on it.

His people needed him.

Things in the States were desperate—the war between Sentinels and Synestryn wasn't going well. Dabyr had fallen, but its leader hadn't yet given up on protecting the corpse.

It had been the same in Africa, where the stronghold had been destroyed in a recent attack. In Europe, things were also not going well. Their fortress still stood, but it was only a matter of time before it fell too.

Wherever Link went, the war would be there. Demons would stalk the night, and his sword arm would always be needed.

Perhaps he should stay here and try to change Serena's

mind. He didn't mind America. He'd lived here for over a century, when the countryside was still wild and untamed. He'd only returned home in the 1980s when his brother had fallen in combat and died.

Since then he'd stayed at home, doing his part to fight back the infestation of Synestryn. He was skilled in combat. He wasn't afraid to die. That combination made him one of the more deadly warriors in England.

If he stayed here, maybe another one of the female Theronai being found recently would pop up and be compatible with his power.

He had no prospects in England. All the females there were attached, bonded. At least here there was a shred of hope to cling to.

Without hope, he wasn't going to last another year. He didn't have enough leaves left on his lifemark to sustain him. And even if the death of his soul didn't kill him, the pain crushing him from the inside out would.

He couldn't continue like this. He had to change his path. Surrender wasn't an option, and returning home unbound would be the same as.

With that decision made, he already felt a weight lift from his shoulders.

Now all he had to do was convince the leader on this continent to accept him as one of their own. And the best way to do that was to prove just how indispensable he could be.

If Link brought Joseph proof of his prowess in combat, he'd have no choice but to welcome him here with open arms.

CHAPTER EIGHTEEN

Serena dreamed of children. Morgan's children. Her children.

They were beautiful, with midnight blue eyes and skin perfectly balanced between her fairness and his dark complexion. There were four of them—two boys, two girls— all playing in a valley filled with green grass. She and Morgan stood hand-in-hand, watching them with love and pride.

A moment later, the sky turned stormy. Rain slashed down from the heavens, racing lightning bolts as it went.

They rushed toward the children to scoop them up out of harm's way, but the ground seemed to stretch out in an endless treadmill they couldn't outrun.

A muddy wall of water careened down the valley, toward her babies. As it neared, she could see that it was more than just water. It was alive—a wall of demons.

The gray, furless bodies of the red-eyed demons churned inside the flood, arms outstretched, mouths open and hungry.

If those demons reached her children, she knew this would be the last time she'd ever see them.

Serena dove forward in an effort to grab her babies and jerk them out of the way of the flood of monsters, but it was too late. The wave washed the children away, into the clutches of monsters.

She was ripped from sleep, sweating and shaking, bolting upright in bed. A horrible sound of despair welled out of her, and there was nothing she could do to stop her sobbing.

Morgan burst into her room, naked, but armed with his sword.

She looked up at him, speechless. Tears streamed down her face and her throat was too tight to do more than gasp between sobs.

His dark gaze scanned the room, and when he saw no threat, he lowered his blade and propped it against the nightstand. He sat on the bed and took her into his arms.

She didn't even try to contain herself. There was no restraint after witnessing that tragedy. The nightmare had been too vivid. Too real.

A warning, something in her mind whispered.

A warning of what?

There was no answer, but Serena didn't need one. She already knew.

You must find and destroy the source of the red-eyed demons before the babies are born.

Had the seer been talking about Serena's babies, or those being born soon? Did it even matter?

Morgan rocked her as her terror faded. When she was finally able to stop sobbing, he wiped tears from her eyes and tilted her face up to his.

His voice was quiet and achingly gentle. "Do you want to talk about it?"

She shook her head with too much force. "No. Not now. It's just...we need to get moving. I can't go back to sleep."

The mere idea of subjecting herself to that terror again made her stomach churn. She needed to be out there, searching for those demons.

"Okay," he said easily. "Whatever you want. I cleaned the blood out of the truck while you were sleeping, so all you need to do is throw a few clothes in a bag."

She nodded, told herself that if they were going to leave, she had to let go of him. But her arms wouldn't obey. She had a death grip around his body and wondered if she'd ever be able to let him go.

He stroked her hair with gentle sweeps of his palm. "You're okay, honey. Everything's okay."

She could almost believe him, but that nightmare had rattled her.

What if it really was a warning? What if she was nearly out of time?

She couldn't stay here all day, clinging to a man, when her future children were at risk. She had to act. Now.

With an effort of will, Serena pulled away and wiped her eyes on the sheet. She looked up at him with resolve, and said, "That cave where we almost died last night, where I left my car? I need to go back."

He shook his head. "There are clothes here. I know you like your sparkly dresses, but we'll get you more. We can't go back for anything. Besides, your car has probably already been ripped to shreds, along with everything in it."

"It's not my belongings I'm after," she said.

"Then why go back?" he asked.

Serena squared her shoulders. "To finish what I started."

***

As soon as the sun broke the horizon, Paul and Andra raced back to Dabyr.

It was so much worse than she'd imagined, so much worse than when they'd fled to go stay at the shelter.

The sun shone down through the cold, winter air, hiding nothing of the destruction.

She remembered the first time she'd seen this place, with its gleaming stone walls and solid construction. The place was massive, with two huge wings jutting out from the back of the main structure like arms spread wide. The main building was at least three stories tall with glass ceilings in the center of the space to let in plenty of light. A parking garage large enough to hold at least a couple hundred vehicles sat to one side, joined by a breezeway so the inhabitants didn't have to face the brutal winter cold or scorching summer heat on the way to their rides.

Pristine lawns had circled the outside of the wall, as well as inside. Trees and bushes had been cleared all around to allow them to see any enemies who grew near. Inside the walls, the grounds were parklike, with plenty of trees for shade and walking paths built throughout the acreage. A small stream ran through one area, feeding a small lake with fresh water.

It had been the most beautiful place Andra had ever lived, and now it was destroyed.

Demon bodies littered the once-perfect lawn surrounding Dabyr. Fetid, black smoke billowed up from their remains as they burned up under the sun. Black and red blood left stains across the ground where battles had taken place. She knew from experience that nothing would ever grow on those black spots again. The ground was dead there—permanently scarred.

The main building was still mostly unharmed, with only a few broken windows and scorched stones serving as battle scars. But the stone wall—the tall, solid mass of stone that encircled their home with protective magic and kept out Synestryn—was ruined.

Large sections were broken, with piles of rubble beneath. Jagged openings perforated the thick barrier on all sides, leaving the warriors defending Dabyr scrambling to keep up with the influx of demons.

Even now, with the sun high in the sky, the battle raged on.

Those hairless, red-eyed demons were still here—the ones that stood seven-feet tall and fought with clumsy swords instead of teeth and claws. Their grayish skin looked sickly under the morning light, highlighting them as the abomination they were.

Their blood also stained the battlefield, an eerie mix of Synestryn black and human red.

Paul's distress mirrored her own. She could feel it vibrating through their link to clog it with a mix of disgust, anger and fear.

Only a few of their kind were left fighting—just enough to hold back the straggling forces dawn had left behind. Among them were also a handful of Slayers, some of them naked. Others wore armor, but fought with teeth and claws, ripping apart their enemies one-by-one. Still others had shifted into animal forms, their bodies covered in fur and rippling with otherworldly power.

She glimpsed more of their kind slinking along the perimeter as they sniffed out stray demons who wanted to slip in unseen.

There were no Sanguinar on the field. They couldn't tolerate the sun, and even if they could, the giant, crystalline Wardens that would have been summoned would have only made things worse.

The iron gate strung across the road leading to Dabyr was usually closed up tight, guarded by cameras, and men inside the walls controlling the heavy, rolling bars. But now, the black iron was a twisted mass of scrap metal, doing nothing to prevent intruders.

With so many other holes in the wall, one more hardly seemed to matter. And when would they have had time to fix the gate? It was a constant struggle just to hold their ground and keep the demons at bay. Repairs weren't even possible yet.

Paul navigated his SUV down the long drive toward the garage. They'd been given instructions to pull up to the front doors, rather than parking inside, because there was too much carnage inside the garage for safe passage.

Apparently, Synestryn had rampaged through the space, ripping apart tires, smashing glass and tearing metal until there was nothing left that was able to move.

To Andra, that seemed suspiciously like a calculated strategy, as if the mindless demons fighting them had someone smarter and more powerful calling the shots.

If none of the Sentinels could flee, they'd be trapped here. Easy pickings.

There were several trucks, vans and cars lined up right outside the stone steps leading to the giant front doors of Dabyr. Armed Theronai stood guard around the vehicles to protect them from attack. These men drooped with exhaustion. Many wore bandages over wounds. It was as if this guard duty was the closest these men were going to get to rest.

The fact that they hadn't been fully healed told Andra just how bad things must be. An open wound—the scent of Theronai blood—would draw Synestryn from miles around.

Assuming there were any who didn't already know to come here for a feast.

She wondered if there were enough vehicles here to evacuate everyone if things went from bad to worse, or if there were some who would stay behind and give their lives so that others could get away safely.

She felt her husband's desire to go help his fellow warriors flood their link. His need was like an itch in the middle of his spine—one that could only be scratched by wading into battle to lend his brothers a hand.

Only he couldn't. Joseph had given them explicit instructions to come directly to him when they arrived. With her pregnancy on the line, neither of them was to take any chances. They were here for a specific purpose and nothing else.

The men guarding the vehicles let them pass. Paul parked with the nose of his SUV facing out, just in case they needed to get out fast. Their ride was stocked with medical supplies as well as enough gas, food and water to get them across the country if they had to flee that far.

Andra knew they wouldn't. There was no way they were leaving their fellow Theronai to fight this battle alone.

They got out of the SUV and rushed inside. Paul's hand was at the small of her back. His other hand was filled with his sword, ready to cut down anything that came toward her and the baby.

Dabyr was usually warm and inviting, but now, the air was

as cold in here as it was outside. She could see her breath misting in a silver plume as they hurried away from the doors.

Joseph, their leader, appeared from the corridor leading to his office. He looked ten years older. There were ridges under his eyes so deep they looked like purple gouges. His skin seemed to hang on his frame. There was more gray in his hair than there had been only a few days ago. His entire body seemed to tremble slightly, though whether from worry or exhaustion, Andra couldn't tell.

What was clear was that he couldn't keep going like this for long. The man was burning out fast. If he didn't get some rest, he was going to crumble like the walls outside. And if that happened—if these people lost his leadership—they'd all be screwed.

"Sorry about the cold," he said. "Our HV/AC system was hit a few days ago. We're just glad we still have electricity and water."

Andra patted her belly. "I have my own internal heater. I'm good."

Joseph nodded. His expression was grim. "There's no time to chat. You have only one job besides staying alive and keeping that baby safe. That comes first."

Paul nodded. "Don't worry. We won't take any chances."

"Just tell us what you need," Andra said.

"Lexi is the only one capable of repairing the magic holding the wall together, but she's not making any progress. Every time she gets close to finishing an area, it's attacked again before her work is done. What we need is for you to stop that from happening."

Andra was good with forcefields. She'd been good from the beginning, but she'd gotten better with practice. She wasn't powerful enough to put up a field around the entire compound yet—at least not for more than a second or two— but she could cover a smaller area for a long time if she had access to Paul's power.

"You want me to put up a field around her while she works," Andra guessed.

"Exactly." He shifted his gaze to Paul. "All I want you to do is guard your wife's back and fuel her magic. No heroics. No running to help out the men."

Paul was still, but she could feel his frustration welling up between them. It buffeted the walls of the conduit that tied them together and made the luceria around her neck vibrate.

Joseph held up his hand. It shook so hard, Andra wondered if he'd eaten recently. "I know you can help in other ways, but I'm asking you not to. In fact, I'm going to ask that you give me your word not to leave Andra's side, no matter what. This is a marathon, not a sprint. It's going to take days for us to make any headway on the wall. You're going to need your strength." He looked at Andra. "And so are you. Don't do anything to push yourself too hard or do anything that will hurt the baby. Promise me."

Andra had no trouble giving the man her vow. "I promise I won't do anything to risk my baby."

As soon as she uttered the words, the weight of her promise settled over her, binding her to her word. No matter what, she wouldn't be able to break her vow.

Luckily, hers was far easier to give than her husband's would be.

"Paul?" Joseph prompted.

Andra felt his hesitation. He was a strong, proud man. He wanted to be capable of doing it all—protecting her and helping his brothers. That he couldn't do everything grated on his sense of honor and duty.

Finally, he said, "I promise. I won't leave Andra's side."

"Even if it means you stand and watch while other men die," Joseph added.

Paul nodded grimly. "Even so."

He stumbled under the weight of his vow, but recovered quickly. His voice was tight when he said, "Let's hope it doesn't come to that."

Joseph's shoulders seemed to bow under the strain of his position. He held Paul's gaze, his expression grim as he said, "Prepare yourself, Paul, because it will."

CHAPTER NINETEEN

Morgan drove Serena back to that cave against his better judgment. He'd underestimated how hard it was going to be for him to let her get close to danger. Talking about giving her freedom had been easy. Actually doing so? He wasn't sure his nervous system could stand it.

He'd been created to protect and defend those around him. He'd been raised to fight and keep others safe. He'd spent his entire long life taking risks so that those weaker than himself didn't have to. And now, thanks to his vow, he had to stand by and let the woman he should have sworn to protect above all others, walk into danger.

She hadn't had much time to learn how to channel his power. She probably didn't even know where her strengths and weaknesses lie when it came to magic. Some women were more gifted in certain areas where others struggled. Without experience there was no way to know when she might falter.

And here he was, powerless to stop her from walking straight into the mouth of danger.

It grated against every cell in his body, every spark of his essence, but there was no choice. He'd bound himself to his word and was stuck with his choices.

All he could do now was stay right by her side so that he was there to protect her when shit went down. Because it would. It always did.

They parked next to the ruined remains of her Nissan. Demons had clawed and chopped their way inside, leaving curling ribbons of metal behind. Every window was smashed, along with most of the mirrors. The tires were rubber streamers, and her belongings had been ripped out and spread around the area.

Frilly gowns and practical combat clothing were strewn in a fifty-foot radius around the car. Each piece had been shredded and stained with foul, greasy smears. Even the seats had been torn to shreds, stuffing exploding from the cuts like synthetic guts.

The only part of her vehicle that hadn't been penetrated was the trunk. Morgan guessed there wasn't as much of her scent there, making it far less appealing a target to the demons that had destroyed the rest of her car.

Serena eyed the mess. Her gaze lingered on some of the more sparkly clothing, filled with sadness and grief.

"So many pretty things, all gone," she said on a regretful sigh.

He vowed then and there that when they got out of this cave, he was going to take her to a mall and buy her all the frilly, sequined, ruffled clothing he could carry.

It was midday. The sky was a clear, blue field overhead. The caves would be stuffed full of Synestryn hiding from the sun, but that was part of her plan. She was convinced that the more monsters there were inside, the more likely she was to find whatever nest these new, red-eyed demons were coming from.

"Are you sure this is a good idea?" he asked. He didn't add that letting her walk into caves stuffed full of Synestryn was making him regret his vow.

"If the caves are empty, how are we to find the offspring we seek?"

"Maybe they stay behind while the adults go hunting. It could be that the nest will be easier to find without all the other monsters getting in our way."

She shook her head. Her fiery hair swayed around her face

to caress her soft cheeks.

He knew what her skin felt like now. He knew how she smelled when her body heated with arousal, how she sounded when she came.

His abdomen clenched against a hard punch of need. His cock began to swell, not caring that the timing was about as bad as it could get.

What he really wanted to do was find the closest gerai house, spread her out naked on a bed and devour her. He wanted to take her over and over until they were both too tired to even care what demons lurked in those caves, much less go hunt them.

But that wasn't going to happen. He'd given her his vow not to hold her back and that meant marching down into darkness with her.

Whatever it took, he'd keep her safe, because there was no way he was going to deprive himself the sound of her screaming in climax.

With a silent sigh for what he couldn't have, he led the way inside.

Even after centuries of fighting, Morgan could never get used to the smell of demon filth. It hung in the air, pungent and so thick he was certain he could see the fog hovering in the still air of the cave.

As before, he struggled to work his way through the tight confines of the tunnels. Rock scraped the shoulders of his new jacket as he went. A few times, he had to turn sideways to fit through a narrow opening.

And then there was that low spot where they had to crawl through—the place where they'd almost died the last time they were in here.

There was no trace of their blood on the rocky floor, only a sheen where grit and refuse had been swept away. Based on the smears left behind, he was certain that demons had lapped up their blood until there was none left.

Behind him, Serena whispered, "I hate this part."

Morgan did too, but he didn't respond. His voice was

deeper than hers and would carry much farther in the tunnels.

Once he was on the far side of the low tunnel, he rose to his feet and drew his sword. Not having it out had been a risk, but trying to maneuver with it out was also risky. He couldn't swing his weapon in that space and holding it only slowed him down.

But he hadn't been afraid. He knew that if Synestryn caught them in that tight spot, Serena would have been able to use his power to protect them.

It was strange having a partner after years of being on his own. Stranger still was the idea that he knew he could rely on her. There was no question about her motives or loyalty. He never had to wonder what she was thinking or what she wanted. She always made her wishes clear.

He knew without a doubt that she would do whatever it took to turn them into a killing machine. Together, they were powerful. Together, they were the dangerous thing that went bump in the night. They were the thing the demons feared.

He let that truth fill him with strength and resolve. People were relying on them to do a job. Dangerous or not, they were going to do it.

And maybe, if they came out victorious, Serena would decide that they belonged together permanently. She would save him from his pain, his isolation. She would stay by his side and perhaps together they could turn the tide of war.

Then again, if they failed, maybe she'd decide that she was better off with another man. Even if she didn't like Link, there were so many other unbound male Theronai that she would likely find another whose power was compatible with her.

As Serena gained her feet, Morgan saw the first flicker of movement up ahead.

Dark eyes landed on him, then lit with an eerie red fire as the demon realized prey was near.

Morgan charged.

The thing seemed to slow as it neared. Morgan had no trouble lopping off its head, as if it were waiting for him to do just that. Dodging the arching pulse of black blood coming from its neck was the more difficult job.

Before the demon's head had come to a complete stop a few feet away, more of those red-eyed demons came.

He felt a sucking sensation he wasn't yet used to as Serena pulled power from him to do her bidding.

A disc of almost invisible light streaked toward the incoming demons. It spun through the air, making a faint whirring sound that was instantly drowned out by the clicks and grunts of monsters.

That glowing disc sliced through the line of gray demons flowing out of a tunnel, neatly removing their heads.

Morgan had barely had a chance to warm up his sword arm, but he knew the day was still young. He'd get his fill.

They fought their way through the network of tunnels, slicing through demons right and left—his sword and her magic. It was messy, disgusting work, but someone had to do it.

Side-by-side, they scoured every inch of that cave system, only to find nothing more than bones, filth and gray corpses.

As they made their way back outside, Serena said, "I was sure this was the source." Her tone was desolate and defeated. If he hadn't been so dirty, he would have pulled her into his arms and offered her what comfort he could.

It was dark by the time they left the cave. They were both covered in sweat and plastered with grime. He'd earned a few shallow cuts along the way, but nothing serious, thanks to her ability to slow the blow of any enemy who came at him.

Unlike most Synestryn, these creatures weren't poisonous. Had they been, he wouldn't have made it through the first ten minutes.

His guess was that whoever had created these things had willingly traded that deadly Synestryn trait for a more human appearance. Not human enough to stop Morgan from cutting them down, but the new look was definitely creepy.

There were reports from the field that the Synestryn were altering human children from a young age so that they could breed more human-looking demons. Whether the intent was to allow those creatures to pass as humans out in the world, or if it was to tie the hands of those who'd sworn to protect humans, he wasn't sure. But what he did know was that the progress toward hybrids was moving far faster than any of them cared to think about.

And strangely, in all the places they'd looked, there hadn't been a single smaller, childish version of the gray demons. It was as if they had some way of hiding their young from sight.

"What made you so sure this was the source?" he asked.

"Joseph sent me some maps of all known attacks and sightings of those demons."

"We need a name for them," he said. "Let's call them baldies since they don't have fur."

She wrinkled her nose and laughed. "If we ever do have children, I'm naming them."

If she gave him a child, he'd give her the world—whatever she wanted would be hers.

"You don't like it?" he asked, grinning.

She shook her head. "How about daylight demons?"

"Whatever makes you happy, Serena." He meant that, from the depths of his soul. He wanted this woman to be filled with joy. Maybe he couldn't give her love, but he could give her nearly everything else. And he would, given the chance.

She beamed at his agreement.

"So, what did the maps show?" he asked.

"I didn't see a pattern until recently—until Joseph told me of Sibyl's prophecy. Her dire warning made me look closer at the notes I made on the maps. As it turns out, there is a high concentration of daylight demons near Austin, followed by a second, less-concentrated area in southern Missouri."

"Maybe they don't like the cold. They are bald, after all."

"You think they migrate?" she asked.

"Could be."

He followed her back to the gutted remains of her car. She tried to open the trunk with the interior release, but the battery cables had been ripped free along with most of the wiring under the hood.

"The maps are in the trunk," she said. "Can you open it?"

The metal was dented and bent, but hadn't been penetrated with claws, teeth or swords. He found a section where the edge of the trunk flared out from a dent, braced his fingers and pulled.

Metal squealed as it ripped loose of its moorings. With a sharp crack, the trunk latch broke free and released the lid.

Inside were some emergency supplies that all cars were stocked with as well as a few other items. She reached in and pulled out a long, plastic tube of maps. She opened the tube and spread out a stack on the hood of his truck.

"You might be right," she said. "Look."

She opened two maps side-by-side on the hood of his truck. They held down the curling edges so they could see the whole picture.

"This one is six months old," she said, pointing to the right. "This one is from a few days ago. Each dot is a sighting or attack."

There were red dots covering the maps like pimples, but there were definitely clusters in a few areas: Texas, Missouri, Arkansas, Kentucky, Tennessee, Alabama. Next to them were handwritten notes in Serena's tidy, curving script.

"See how the clusters shifted further south this winter?" she asked.

He did. There were still plenty of sightings surrounding Dabyr, but that place was a demon magnet without trying—especially now that it was easy to get in. "There aren't any sightings very far north, even though there are tons of known Synestryn caves up there."

"Maybe that's too far to migrate on foot. Or underground. I've seen underground passages that go for miles."

"Could be. Or it could be something else entirely. Maybe they're moving for some other reason."

She frowned. "Let's assume for now that they don't like the cold. We'll need another year of data to know for sure, but we don't have that kind of time. We have to find the source of the infestation and their spawning grounds."

"Spawning grounds? What makes you think they aren't reproducing wherever they are?"

She blinked at him like he'd missed something big. "They have no genitals."

"Oh. Well. That would make things difficult. Guess I don't pay much attention to demon junk."

"One of the Sanguinar dissected three of them and found no trace of reproductive organs, internally or externally. In fact, he couldn't detect gender at all—they're identical."

"And since they have to come from somewhere, it's our job to find how they're being spawned."

"I spoke to Sibyl. She warned me that I need to hurry."

Morgan hadn't told his boss that they'd bonded. He didn't want anyone to know yet—not because he was ashamed, but because he wanted to keep her all to himself. Once word got out, their little bubble of isolation would be burst as every unbound male Theronai would want to give her his vow to protect her.

He couldn't see Serena suffering through a pile of men who promised to protect her with their lives. She hadn't even wanted that vow from Morgan.

And if those same men got word that Serena had the power to end her bond to Morgan whenever she wished…there were too many desperate men in their ranks to risk the kind of chaos that news would cause. Men would start fighting each other for a chance at her, even if they weren't compatible.

Serena looked up at Morgan, her deep blue eyes troubled. "You're not thinking about going back to Dabyr or to one of those shelters, are you? Because I won't—"

He covered her lips with his finger. They were smooth and warm and made him think of how they'd felt against his skin as she'd kissed him.

He needed more of her mouth on his, more wherever she wanted to put it. Even the idea was enough to make him tremble with lust.

"I made you a promise. I have no choice but to keep it. Besides, there's not much Dabyr left to go back to, and I don't like the idea of sharing you yet."

She arched a fiery brow in challenge. "So, you think one day you will want to share?"

Never. He knew he was far too possessive to pretend otherwise. Still, he said nothing to give away the fact that he wanted to keep her all to himself. She might see that as too close to a cage for his peace of mind.

"I think today is the only one we have room to worry about," he said. "We don't even know what the source of the daylight demons is, much less where to find it."

"Or them," she amended. "There could be more than once source."

"So, how do you want to play this?" he asked.

"I remember hunting for game in the dead of winter," she said. "My father would bring me along to teach me. There was a lot of walking, endless hours of cold, numb feet, and sometimes days would go by without anything to show for your suffering."

"You're not saying you want to give up, are you?" he asked.

"Never. It's not in my nature to do so."

"Then what?"

She looked him up and down, then surveyed herself. "I think that if we want to go hunting, we're going to need warm boots."

CHAPTER TWENTY

Serena was glad the caves she and Morgan hunted in were dark, because otherwise, the daylight demons would have seen her coming a mile off in the new, sparkly boots she wore.

Women of this time were so lucky, with so many fine choices of clothing. It made her feel like a queen. A very warm, comfortable one.

For the last week, every day had been the same. They woke up before dawn, went into the next cave on their list, moving steadily northeast through Texas, Oklahoma, then into Missouri. They cleaned out each cave from one end to another, searching for signs of whatever it was that spawned the daylight demons.

After they could fight no more, they would go to the nearest gerai house where they would bathe, eat and sleep.

Morgan hadn't come to her bed, and she hadn't gone to his. They'd barely touched outside of combat. They were two distinct people who came together for their work, but that's where the bond ended.

The conduit between them that channeled his power to her hadn't changed much since the night they'd bonded, even with her intentionally trying to widen it every day. He had plenty of reserves to give her—she could feel a sea of power shimmering on the other end of the pipeline that connected them—but she could only take in a small amount of energy at a time.

She was beginning to think the fault was hers. What else could it be? Everything about him was healthy—it was she who must be lacking.

Serena briefly considered calling one of the bonded women at the shelters and asking for advice, but quickly tossed the idea aside. How could she get advice when she would never be able to explain to anyone the unusual vow she and Morgan had agreed upon.

Neither of them was interested in love.

No, that was not exactly true. She craved love, but the price was too high, especially with a man who was still in love with his dead wife. Even if she could bring herself to let go of Iain in her heart, Morgan's belonged to another.

But with Sibyl's warning still fresh in her mind and that eerie nightmare of her children coming back every night, Serena had to do something. She needed more of Morgan's power. She needed their link to grow.

A couple of times in combat, she'd almost been too weak to protect him. The conduit of magic between them hadn't been wide enough for her to send it in so many places, to block the path of so many swords headed Morgan's way.

What if they got in an even worse situation? What if she failed to protect him on all sides and it cost him his life?

She couldn't let that happen. He was a good man. His people needed him—needed both of them, together, strong and functioning as a team.

Friends with benefits, as he'd called it, only there hadn't been any benefits since that first night.

Like every night, she lay alone in her bed, struggling to find sleep. That nightmare continued to haunt her, lurking just behind her closed eyelids. Her children, swept away by a flood of demons.

She shivered at the memory.

It was a warning. She didn't know who was giving it—the seer Sibyl, the luceria, or something else entirely—but she would be a fool not to heed it.

The lives of her possible future children were at stake. No matter what else she had to sacrifice, or how much pride she had to swallow, she couldn't let them down.

She had to find a way to strengthen her bond to Morgan, and without allowing herself to love him, there was only one way she could think to make progress.

On bare feet, she padded through the gerai house to his room. She didn't knock, but turned the knob and slipped inside the dark space.

He knelt on the floor, meditating, gloriously naked, his sword on the floor in front of him.

As soon as she came in, he rose gracefully to his feet, sword in hand. "Is something wrong?"

He really was a magnificently built man, with powerful limbs covered in thick muscles under smooth, dark skin. He was unselfconscious about his nudity, utterly confident, which only made him that much more appealing.

The branches of his lifemark were still mostly bare, which gave her a moment of concern. Once they bonded, his tree was supposed to bud and replenish itself—proving she'd stopped the decay of his soul. But that hadn't happened.

"What's wrong with your lifemark?" she asked, forgetting her purpose.

He shrugged as if it didn't bother him, but the movement lacked his usual fluid power.

He was worried too.

"Give it time," he said. "It's only been a week."

"Is that normal?"

"Who's to say what normal is anymore. Don't let it bother you. Tell me why you're here." He lifted his jeans from a nearby chair to dress.

"Don't," she said, remembering why she'd come. "I like you naked."

He gave her a half smile. "Is this some kind of power play? I stay naked while you're fully dressed?"

"I would never manipulate you like that." And to prove it, she pulled her night gown over her head to bare herself. "See?

Now we're even."

Sultry heat took over his expression. "Hardly. But you won't hear me complain."

She stepped forward, forcing herself to be bold. Take what she wanted. "I want to make love."

Immediately, she winced at her choice of words. Love was forbidden.

"Sorry," she said. "I want to...fuck." That was the word one used when there was a physical act with no emotion, wasn't it? She'd heard it used often since returning from her prison, though it was possible she was missing some context. The word seemed to be everywhere.

He gave her a steady stare. "Why?"

"You don't want to?" She suddenly wished for something to cover herself. An embarrassed flush started at her brow and swept down her face and neck, then onto her chest.

She'd completely misjudged this situation. Morgan wasn't interested in her as a lover, and now she had to find a way out. Fast.

"I didn't say that. I just wanted to know why you want to do this."

"To widen our conduit."

He flinched as though she'd slapped him. "I see."

"Our bond isn't progressing the way it should. I thought if we..." she trailed off, unsure how to explain herself.

"You thought if we fucked, it would fix what's broken," he said, his tone flat.

"You don't think it will?"

"No, but I'll still fuck you. Any sane man would."

There was a strange look in his eyes, something dark and hollow.

She hadn't seen this side of him before, and she wasn't sure she liked it.

"Lay down and spread your legs, Serena." His cock swelled and lengthened as he spoke, and while it made her mouth go dry with need, this wasn't at all what she'd wanted. It was too cold, too empty.

"I think I've made a mistake," she said as she snatched up her nightgown and slid it over her head.

He caught her before she could slip her arms through the sleeves. His big hands slid around her body, caging her inside the soft cotton fabric.

"I didn't mean to scare you," he said.

Her chin went up out of habit, and she looked right into his eyes. "You didn't."

"Then why run?"

"I won't be used," she said, though that wasn't the only reason.

She needed his warmth, his passion. She wanted to get lost in the physical pleasures their bodies could provide so that her insides didn't feel quite so empty.

There was something missing between them. Something huge and vital. If she didn't figure out how to bridge the gap, she feared their bond would never strengthen.

If it didn't, how would they be strong enough to find the source of the demon invasion? How would they ever protect their children?

Her parents had never loved each other, but they'd found a way to be a formidable pair. Serena needed to figure out what she and Morgan were lacking—what her parents had that she and Morgan didn't—before it was too late.

He cursed under his breath. "Using you was never my intent."

He took a long step back and scrubbed a hand over his face in frustration.

"I don't know what to do," she said. Her voice wavered with insecurity as much as fear. "We're not strong enough yet. Your lifemark is still bare. I keep trying to figure out how to widen the connection between us, but nothing I try works."

He looked at her for a long moment as if making some important decision—a very difficult one.

She slid her nightgown in place and waited for him to wade through whatever was going on in his mind.

She thought she felt a flicker of guilt pulsing through their link, but she couldn't be sure. Her emotions were so chaotic right now, that feeling could have been all hers.

After a few seconds, he seemed to reach a decision. He nodded once, then took her hands in his. "You're right. What we're doing isn't working. It's time to try something else."

She opened her mouth to ask what, but his lips covered hers before she could.

The kiss was soft, sweet.

Loving.

Tears stung her eyes as memories of Iain's kisses filled her mind. He'd kissed her just like this when she'd been a young girl, when their love had overwhelmed them both and become their whole world.

She didn't want to think about him while with another man. She didn't want to think about him at all, but how could she not? He'd been the center of her universe for so long, she didn't know how to move past him.

Morgan lifted his face. "It takes time, honey. But I promise, the pain will fade. Just keep moving forward, and one day, he won't be your first waking thought when you get up, or the last one you have before you drift off to sleep."

Had he read her thoughts? Or was she merely that transparent?

"I've been where you are," he continued, his voice soft and low. "I know how much it hurts. But it does get easier to bear. Eventually."

She managed a weak nod.

He took her hand, pulled her to his bed and peeled back the covers in invitation.

Serena slipped inside the cool sheets. He got in behind her, but rather than pursuing sex, as she'd expected, he simply wrapped his arms around her and held her close.

His warm breath swept over her hair. His thumbs caressed her arms in a low, mesmerizing sweep that calmed her nerves and eased her worries. The heat of his skin sank into her, forcing her to relax, and the strength of his embrace made her feel safe, protected.

She lay there for a long time, simply listening to him breathe. It was nice not to feel so alone—to feel like she had a place where she belonged.

For the first night in a long, long time, Iain's face wasn't the last one she pictured before drifting off to sleep.

***

Link woke to pain.

He was used to the grinding pressure the magic he carried caused, but this was different—sharper and shallow, more about flesh than spirit.

He tried to open his eyes, but his lashes were glued together somehow. All he could manage was a thin slit through which he could see very little. His lashes formed a spiderweb network across his field of vision.

The last thing he remembered was marching into a cave near Dabyr, dead set on proving his worth to Joseph Rayd and all those who followed his leadership.

After that, nothing. There were no memories of how he got here, wherever here was.

Wherever he was it was dark. Humid. He pulled a few sparks of power from the surrounding air into himself and used them to fuel his night vision. Each pinpoint of energy stung his battered skin, biting at him like tiny insects. Even so, he continued drawing in the power he needed to see, because the giant pool of energy that lay inside of him was unreachable, off limits. Only a woman compatible with him could tap into that reservoir and ease the bulging agony of carrying so much.

When he'd finally collected enough sparks from the air to enhance his vision, he saw rock walls, tearstained from millennia of dripping water.

He was in a cave. The hollow echo of each drip and a strange, scratching noise told him that the space he was in must be large, though he couldn't seem to turn his head to see more of it.

At the base of the far wall opposite him was a pile of something gray. Rocks from a cave-in? Some natural formation? He couldn't tell. His vision was blocked by lashes matted together with blood.

That's when he smelled it. Blood. Lots of it.

Panic sparked along his skin. He tried to sit up, only to realize that he wasn't lying down. He was standing upright. Only that wasn't exactly right, either. There was no weight on his legs. All his weight was being supported by his shoulders, which were on fire. There were more sources of his pain—too many to sort them all.

He was tied by his wrists, dangling from some kind of rope or chain.

Link strained his neck to look down. His head wasn't bound, but something was wrong with his neck or back, impeding his movement. He hoped he was only stiff from being held here for too long, but instincts warned him that his injuries might be worse than that.

Below him were half a dozen gray, furless demons he'd heard reports about. They were humanoid, but taller, with wide heads and huge, shiny black eyes. There were more of them across the space. What he'd thought were rocks was a pile of them, either dead or sleeping—he couldn't tell which. They were all clumped up as if tossed there like bags of rubbish.

Link struggled to pull his lashes free. The strain made his eyes water, which helped to wash out some of the coagulated mess. He couldn't see perfectly, but his vision was less obstructed now.

As soon as he looked down again, he wished he hadn't been able to see a thing.

Blood dripped from his feet. He still wore his jeans and socks, but his shoes had been taken off or lost.

Past his bloody socks, he saw several of those gray creatures lurking beneath him, mouths open, scrambling and shoving each other to see who would catch the next drop of his blood in their mouths.

That's what the scratching sound was, he realized—demons jockeying for the best position.

He couldn't remember how he'd gotten here, but the throbbing in his head told him that he'd been hit there, hard. Possibly more than once.

Perhaps that was why he couldn't remember how he'd come to be here.

Link was dizzy and nauseated. His body was a mass of aches and pains. As he took a mental inventory, he guessed that he had at least one broken rib, and something was wrong with his left side. His neck didn't move right. He was bleeding from at least one place, possibly more. There was no way to tell without being able to better see his body.

What he could see was blood soaking his shirt along his left ribs. Something protruded from his side far enough he could catch a glimpse of rusty metal.

There were dozens of crude swords lying about. Chances were the thing sticking out of him was a piece of one of those.

Something about this whole situation was wrong.

These creatures didn't seem overly intelligent. How had they captured him, tied him up and hoisted him up here? And why had they bothered? Why hadn't they just eaten him when he'd been unconscious? Why was he still alive?

He didn't have any more time to ponder the question. One of the creatures saw that he was awake, and as soon as it did, it let out a howling screech. That shrill cry of alarm drew the attention of every demon present, including those that had been piled together, sleeping.

Dozens of huge, black and red eyes landed on his bleeding, broken body, and there wasn't a thing he could do to save himself from whatever they were going to do to him.

CHAPTER TWENTY-ONE

Serena woke to the most glorious sensation.

Sunlight streamed in through the curtains, gilding Morgan's dark hair with a golden glow.

Her nightgown was rucked up, baring her breasts to his mouth. He licked and suckled gently, while his clever fingers slid along the lips of her sex.

Without thought, she spread her legs to give him access, and arched toward his powerful body.

His fingers found the slick heat between her thighs. A low rumble of approval vibrated against her and sent an army of shivers marching across her skin.

He lifted his head and stared into her eyes while he moved over her and slid his thick, hard manhood inside her.

Her eyes fluttered against the pleasure of being filled so completely. She tried to find words, but he covered her mouth with his, effectively silencing her.

What good were words, anyway? She had everything she needed right here, right now. Her body was starving for his, and she wasn't going to let anything get in the way of having him.

His pace was slow and languid. Each stroke glided across nerves that set her body alight and pushed her right where he wanted her to go. As gentle as he was, he was also demanding, giving her no choice but to accept what he wanted to give her.

When he wanted her kisses, he took them. When he wanted her to look at him, he held her gaze captive. And when he wanted to drive her to the edge of pleasure, he did so with expert ease.

Everything he did heightened her senses and made her hover on the brink of climax. When she got close, he would slow down or change his rhythm so she couldn't quite reach the peak.

She was too groggy from sleep to understand what kind of game he was playing, and too swept away in the touch of his hands on her skin to care. She let him do as he pleased, and simply went along for the ride.

When she didn't think she could take any more of his teasing, he kissed her again and stared into her eyes. He said nothing, but she could feel his will singing through the luceria, urging her not to look away.

Serena didn't know why this was so important to him, but she could sense that if she didn't play along, he'd deny her release.

That, she couldn't allow.

His hips sped. He took her deeper, hitting a special place inside her she didn't even know she possessed. Each gliding stroke rubbed his erection across the tight bundle of nerves at the apex of her sex. In the back of her mind, she knew this amazing bit of flesh had a name, but her mother never taught her such things and she wasn't allowed time alone with friends who might whisper the word to her in a girlish giggle.

She made herself a promise to find out what it was called, because she needed to be able to tell Morgan what she wanted in the future.

What he was doing now definitely needed to happen again. Often.

He wrapped a thick arm around her hips and rolled his against her, pressing their bodies together in a slow, languid circle. That's all it took to send her careening into climax.

Morgan was only a split second behind her.

She grabbed onto his power and forced it to wrap around

them in a shimmering bubble. Inside, time slowed to a luxurious stretch, allowing them to linger in the sensations of the flesh for far longer than was normal for most people.

She held his gaze as she felt his seed fill her. She held his gaze as her body fluttered and shimmered in the midst of keen pleasure. She even held his gaze when the luceria throbbed around her throat, and the conduit between them stretched and widened.

When it was finally over, and she could once again pull in a full breath, she released his power and let time flow at its normal pace once again.

Sweat dotted his forehead. His breathing was fast, but steady. He brushed her hair away from her forehead and gave her the softest, sweetest kiss she'd ever had.

It was in that moment, Serena realized her mistake.

She didn't love Morgan yet, but she could. She didn't want to—didn't want to risk the pain of being hurt again. Even worse, he'd been very clear that he couldn't—wouldn't—love her back.

She believed him.

He'd had a lot of time to get over the death of his wife. That he hadn't, told Serena it wasn't likely to happen. He was committed to Femi on a level so deep, Serena knew she had no place there.

He and Femi had lived a lifetime together. Serena had only had a few years with Iain. How could she possibly understand the depths of Morgan's devotion? Of his grief?

He gave her another, briefer kiss, then rose from the bed and disappeared into the bathroom.

Serena felt his warmth dissipate from the bed and her body. She didn't understand how her world had changed so much in such a short time, but if she didn't do something to slow down her descent, she was going to end up in love with a man who could never love her back.

***

Morgan had made a terrible mistake.

All he'd wanted to do was draw him and Serena closer together in an effort to strengthen the flow of power between them, as well as revive his lifemark. Instead, he'd made love to her.

It hadn't been fucking. It wasn't just sex. It was more. Too much more.

He tried to lie to himself and say it meant nothing—that it was simply a merging of the flesh—but the truth was too glaringly obvious for that nonsense.

What they'd just done was far too sweet, and it had been all his fault.

A woman needed to be treated with gentleness and care. Serena deserved no less. Sure, she seemed to like it when he was rougher and more demanding, too, but she was a complex woman with a variety of needs. It was his job to satisfy all of them.

Except one. He wouldn't love her—he had promised himself that he would never again open himself up to that kind of risk—but love was the one thing a woman as amazing as Serena deserved more than anything else. It was the one thing that mattered most. Possibly the only thing that really mattered.

Morgan summoned Femi's beautiful face in his mind as he always did when he had a complex problem to solve. She'd been wise beyond her years, and had a knack for cutting to the heart of the matter. She'd always given him good advice, and after her death, he still turned to her memory to guide him.

What would Femi tell him to do?

He could picture her easily, her big, dark eyes framed in thick lashes, and her sweet, lush mouth that was an endless source of pleasure. He saw her at all ages, from the innocent girl she'd been when they'd met, to the wizened crone he'd held as she died. All of her incarnations had been beautiful and kind and filled with so much love he had no idea how to hold it all.

Still, she had no answers for him this time, no wisdom, no

encouragement. Just silence, as if he'd done something unforgivable.

Morgan had bound himself to a woman he would never love, and until now, he hadn't realized what a huge betrayal to Serena that really was.

Morgan had to let her go. If he didn't, her kind, loving nature would get the best of her and she'd fall for him. He could already see the signs in her face, the same soft smile that Femi had given him—the one filled with womanly secrets and unspoken dreams.

When he refused to return Serena's feelings, she'd start to resent him. That resentment would fester and grow until they were no longer able to function as a bonded pair of Theronai should.

Not only would he be putting her life at risk, but also the lives of everyone who depended on them to be strong and competent in battle with no barriers between them.

As Morgan stepped into the shower to wash away all signs of what they'd just shared, he felt a warm, comforting presence in the back of his mind, telling him everything was going to be okay.

At first, he thought it was Femi's memory strengthening him, but then he realized how wrong he'd been. That peaceful brush across his mind was Serena, filled with concern for him. With affection.

He cared for her too much to let her go down this path with him. She was an amazing woman, worthy of so much more than he could give her. And that meant he had only one course of action.

Pain or not, loneliness or not, death or not, Morgan had to let her go.

***

Serena felt Morgan shove her out of his mind with a single, unyielding push.

What they'd just done had left her shaken. Him, too.

She'd tried to reassure him that she wasn't upset that sex had veered toward something deeper than a mere physical outlet, but her connection to him wasn't strong enough to break past his resistance.

She was left feeling adrift, alone as she'd been in her prison. Cold.

Something was definitely wrong, and she had no idea how to fix it. She didn't even know what the problem was. Perhaps his sudden coldness had nothing to do with sex. Or maybe she'd done something wrong.

Before she could march into the bathroom and ask him what was going on, her phone rang.

Joseph's name appeared on the little screen. As soon as she answered it, she could hear worry tightening his tone.

"We have a situation," he said.

"What's wrong?"

"Link Tolland has gone missing. He's not answering his phone."

The news unsettled her, but there had to be some kind of mistake. "He was on his way back home when I last saw him. He's probably on an overseas flight and not answering his phone."

"He never got on his flight home. His people tracked his phone to a location in southern Missouri, but it stopped sending a signal several hours ago. We don't know if the battery went dead, or if he went somewhere with no cell service. Possibly underground. He was alone, Serena."

Now she understood Joseph's worry.

Her throat squeezed, making it hard to get out the words. "I...I rejected Link and bonded with Morgan. Do you think Link was staying in case I changed my mind?"

"First of all, congratulations. Morgan is a great choice. Second, if you think Link was going to give up on a chance to be free of his pain that easily, then you don't understand what it's like for our men. My guess is he was going to stay until all hope of a union with you was lost."

Guilt gripped her tight, until it was hard to breathe. "This is my fault."

"You can only pick one man, Serena. Someone was always going to get hurt. That's not on you. That's just the way things are."

"That's easy for you to say. You're not the one responsible for leaving a man in torment, facing certain death."

"You can't dwell on that. One of our own is missing, and you and Morgan are the closest people we have to his last known location. I don't want anyone leaving the shelters right now. We need all the swords we can get here at Dabyr. We're fighting off daily attacks on the stronghold and can't spare any firepower to go on a manhunt." He pulled in a long, weary breath. "Any luck finding the source of those demons?"

"We're calling them daylight demons, and no. We've had no luck, but we'll keep looking."

"I'm going to send you Link's last known coordinates. Go there first, try to find him."

"Of course."

"But if you can't, we'll have to assume the worst. We don't have time for an extended manhunt right now. You have to find that source, understand?"

"I do," she said, irritated that he felt as though he could order her around. "But I also understand that Link is here because of me. I'm not going to leave him behind unless I'm sure there's no chance of finding him."

"We're running out of time, Serena. You have to…" Joseph went silent for a moment. She could hear shouting in the background, along with the sounds of distant combat. Guttural screams mixed with rough shouts of warriors slicing through their enemy.

They really were running out of time.

"Use your best judgment," he said. "But remember what's at stake. Remember what Sibyl said. I have to get back to the fight."

"I'll remember," she promised. And she would. There were too many lives at stake for her not to take her job seriously.

"And Serena?"

"Yes?"

"You could not have chosen a stronger, more honorable man than Morgan to be your partner. Don't let guilt over what's happened to Link ruin what you could have with Morgan. It's too precious to waste."

Joseph hung up, leaving Serena feeling utterly alone again. When Morgan stepped out of the bathroom, barely sparing her a glance, that feeling didn't change.

The truth was clear on his face.

Whether they stayed bonded or not, Morgan would never truly be hers.

***

Link was well and truly fucked.

He wasn't just stuck in this cave, tied up, nearly blind, injured, weak and bleeding, surrounded by demons as clever as dogs. No, it was worse than that. He was here for a purpose. Some creature with a mind and a plan had brought him here.

How did he know?

Because he'd passed out not long after the gray demons had started screaming. Their voices pounded at his concussion until his mind finally checked out to avoid the noise.

When he'd next woken, he was still in the same place, tied up and dangling, but someone had cut off his shirt, removed the chunk of rusty metal from his side, bandaged him and healed the wound enough that he hadn't bled out.

Whoever had him here wanted him alive, and the list of things they'd need him for that didn't include using him as food, was very, very short.

His rattled brain could only think of one reason to keep him alive.

He was going to serve as bait for a bigger prize.

To die down here, alone and in pain was bad enough, but to bring others here to die as well...he couldn't tolerate the idea. He had to find a way to get free, before it was too late.

There were fewer of those gray demons surrounding him now. Most slept in a pile on the far side of the cavern. Three lounged beneath him, but with no more blood to seep from his wounds, they'd grown bored and fallen asleep as well.

Perhaps it was daytime, when all Synestryn grew weaker and sluggish.

If so, this was his only chance to escape. Only the red-eyed demons could follow him out in the daylight, but there had been only a few of them present. If he could make it back to the cave entrance, wherever that was, he'd be safe—at least until nightfall. By then, he'd be back in his rented car, driving toward the safety of the closest gerai house.

Slowly, so he didn't wake the creatures around him, he craned his aching neck to see how he was trussed.

Thick, rough rope bound his wrists in several loops. That rope led upward and over the edge of a rock outcropping. He couldn't see any farther so he didn't know if someone had levered him up here, off the ground, or lowered him from the rocks above.

Either way, he was in the same position—dangling well over ten feet from the hard ground and the hungry demons sleeping beneath him.

He thought if he could sway back and forth enough times, he might abrade the rope until it broke. Yes, that would mean landing on top of creatures who wanted to eat him, without the use of his weapon or—very likely—his arms. He couldn't feel much past his aching shoulders, and guessed that it would be a while after he was released before feeling, and use of his limbs, returned.

And where did that leave him?

Back to square one—well and truly fucked.

A low humming sound came from one of the openings into the cavern.

Link closed his blood-caked eyelashes until only a slit remained. He couldn't see much, but at least he wasn't totally blind.

The hum grew louder. As it did, the sleeping demons

began to stir.

They rose to their feet and backed away as someone else entered the cavern.

The creature walked on two legs, had a head and two arms, but that was where its resemblance to humans or Sentinels ended. It was grotesque, wearing only a loincloth so that Link could see every disgusting detail of its body. It had bulging patches of extra flesh on its joints that didn't belong. Its skin was a reptilian texture, the same gray as the demons that backed away in reverence. Its head was mostly bald, with too much skin hanging from it. Past its thin lips, Link could see pointed teeth. At the end of each of its gangly arms were three fingers, two with extra joints that made them eerily long.

As Link stared, he realized that there was an uncanny resemblance to the ugly creature and the demons that surrounded it, bowing low in reverence.

They let out a strange hum that grew louder as the seconds passed.

That's what Link had heard earlier—the sound of demons greeting this monster with reverence.

Maybe he'd been hit on the head harder than he'd thought. He'd never heard about behavior like this, much less witnessed it—not even on this continent.

The hideous, fleshy beast lifted a disfigured hand, and instantly, the gray demons fell silent.

"I know you're awake," the thing said, slurring his words through pointed teeth. "I smell your fear."

Link opened his eyes as much as his gummy lashes would allow. "That's not fear," he said. "It's disgust."

The creature stepped closer, seemingly immune to insults. "I am Vazel. In time, you will learn to respect me."

Vazel pointed at one of the demons, then at the rope holding Link aloft. The gray Synestryn scampered out of sight, and a few seconds later, Link was lowered to the ground. It wasn't a gentle landing, but he hadn't been dropped altogether, at least.

He landed in a clumsy heap, unable to control his fall. He

tried to protect his head, but the cost was something popping out of place in his left shoulder.

Pain radiated out from that spot, so intense he thought he'd vomit. He breathed through his nose until the urge passed, but knew he wasn't out of the woods yet.

Vazel planted a fleshy, stinking foot on Link's chest and pressed down hard enough to make a cracked rib break clean through.

More pain exploded through his body, leaving a sickening echo behind.

He'd screamed, he realized. That horrible, wrenching sound was his own voice bouncing off the cave walls over and over again.

"Stay," Vazel ordered.

As if Link had a choice. He couldn't even breathe yet, much less stand.

Over his shoulder, Vazel called, "Come, Mordecai. It's time for your lessons."

Link didn't think this situation could get any worse until he saw Mordecai.

He was a child—a toddler, wearing nothing but a diaper made from dingy rags. He sucked on his index finger as he crossed the uneven cave floor as easily as if it were smooth carpet.

Link's heart jammed up in his throat, cutting off his air completely.

This wasn't a demon child. He was far too beautiful for that. He had dark eyes, dark hair, and while a bit dirty, seemed to be completely healthy.

"Whose child is that?" Link demanded.

"Mine," Vazel said easily. "I delivered him myself, though sadly, his mother didn't survive."

Link had to get this baby away from the demon. Nothing else mattered now but that.

He caught the boy's gaze. "Come here, Mordecai. I won't hurt you. I'm a friend."

"You are food!" Vazel boomed.

All around them, furless, gray demons began to bow and hum.

The child didn't even flinch. He was clearly use to such outbursts.

"Enough!" shouted Vazel. And then, in a calmer tone, "Ignore your food, son. Remember what I taught you."

Mordecai looked at Vazel, then at Link. His chubby face was somber, accepting.

He toddled over to Vazel and held out his tiny hand.

The grotesque monster gave the perfect child a small, sharp knife.

Mordecai crossed to Link, so close he could smell his innocence—that subtle, hopeful scent that only babies possessed.

His pudgy fingers gripped the knife. They were barely long enough to reach all the way around the handle.

"What are you doing?" Link asked Vazel, both confused and disgusted.

"Teaching my son how to eat, as any good father would."

Mordecai's eyes were empty of emotion. They held no fear, no curiosity, no excitement. Whatever Vazel had done to this child, he'd stripped him of every normal human emotion he should have had.

Perhaps he wasn't human at all.

Mordecai climbed up onto Link's legs so he could reach his bare chest. He placed the short blade over the empty branches of his lifemark and pierced the skin over his heart.

Link flinched, more from surprise than pain. He couldn't get his head around what was happening.

"You don't have to do this," Link told the child. "Cut my ropes and I'll get you out of here. We'll leave together. I'll take you home to your parents. Your real parents."

Mordecai stopped cutting, but didn't remove the blade. His empty, dark eyes met Link's and stared.

Blood trickled down Link's chest. The demons in the room began to bristle and salivate at the smell.

"I'm sure your mommy and daddy miss you. Let me take

you to them."

Link was certain the child understood him. He didn't know how he knew, but there was no question that the boy had absorbed his words.

Vazel took one step closer. "Your food is trying to trick you, son. What do we do with tricky food?"

Mordecai plunged the little blade in as deep as it would go, then pulled it out. As Link watched in horror, the boy covered the wound with his mouth and began to drink Link's blood.

"That's my clever boy," Vazel said with pride ringing in his tone. "His blood will make you grow up big and strong."

CHAPTER TWENTY-TWO

Jackie worked for days trying to figure out how to pin down the location of the lights—of the women who emitted them.

For days, she went back to the woman in the cabin, hoping for a clue as to where she was, hoping she would leave and Jackie could follow her home.

Instead, the snow grew deeper. The woman stayed where she was, drinking melted snow to stay alive and burning her dwindling supplies of wood whenever she was too cold to stand the shivering that shook her starving body.

Once, Jackie had watched her cry. Fat, helpless tears had streamed down her cheeks, reminding Jackie of the first few months she'd spent in captivity. She'd been a prisoner of the Synestryn, used as food and as a caretaker for the children they tortured. She'd spent two years away from the world, in the dark, in complete despair. She'd watched so many children die, their small bodies too weak to stand what had been done to them.

She'd spent countless nights sobbing until she was too exhausted to lift her head. Her tears had been silent so the children couldn't hear, but they'd racked her body with physical pain and left her weak and dehydrated.

Those were the kind of tears the woman in the cabin shed.

Jackie wondered what she'd seen, experienced or done to leave her so desolate.

Her heart ached for the woman. All she wanted to do was go to her and pull her into a tight hug, to tell her that everything was going to be okay.

But she couldn't do that. She didn't even know what country the woman was in. The USA? Canada? Definitely somewhere cold, somewhere far north.

After days of trying to reach the woman, Jackie gave up. She couldn't keep witnessing her pain, cold and starvation without being able to do something to ease it. So, she moved on to another light and tried again.

Jackie was now constantly distracted by thoughts of the snowbound woman. She couldn't focus her mind the way she needed to in order to reach the lights. They glared in her vision, all but blinding her. They flashed and sparkled and taunted her, but she couldn't zoom in on them and make them dim enough to see what was going on in the other locations.

Every day ended with her too exhausted to do more than eat a meal and flop onto her cot. Sleep eluded her, both because of the noise and commotion of the shelter, as well as the lights dancing in her eyes, even when they were closed. The thumping kicks and stretches of her baby and the general discomfort of pregnancy didn't help her relax, either.

Iain walked the line between encouraging her to try again and making her rest. He was in her mind, so deeply a part of her that he seemed to know when she'd reached her limit before she did.

Once, she'd been so distraught that he'd used compulsion to will her to sleep. It wasn't the kind of thing she let him get by with normally, but in this case, she was glad he'd been so high-handed. It wasn't until she'd woken twelve hours later that she realized just how much she'd needed the rest, how much her baby needed her to sleep.

With her mind clearer than it had been in days. She decided to go back to the woman in the cabin and try something new.

Instead of trying to locate her, Jackie was going to try to contact her.

It took a long time for her to find a comfortable, relaxed state that allowed her to focus. But once she did, her consciousness flew through the air toward the cabin. Trees blurred by. She went up and down hills, following the contours of the land. Brown grass and trees gave way to silvery frost, then to gleaming white snow. She flew over a white expanse so flat that could only have been a frozen lake. A big one. Beyond that, she saw evergreens burdened with snow, their branches drooping heavily toward the ground.

The cabin sat in the middle of a little clearing, still as shabby and small as she remembered.

But now it was empty.

The stack of firewood was gone. The woman had burned it all, leaving her no escape from the frigid nights.

There were no tracks leading away from the cabin, though there were some slight indentations in the newly fallen snow that might have been footsteps. It was hard to tell what they were. All she knew was that the woman was gone.

Worry flickered through Jackie. Where had the woman gone? Had she survived the cold, or was her body lying frozen on the ground, covered in snow?

Jackie had no idea. All she could think to do was find the woman's light again.

She pulled back, flying up and outward to get a wide view of the countryside. That woman's light was so bright, it should have shone like a star, even against the sunlit snow.

But there was nothing. All Jackie could see was a glittering, frozen expanse.

She withdrew farther. Perhaps the woman had found a road and a ride out of the area. Perhaps she was simply far away from here.

A patch of red caught Jackie's eye. The color didn't belong here among so much white. It stood out like a bloody fingerprint on a clean, white countertop.

Jackie drew closer to the spot, and as she did, her heart began to constrict.

There were tracks in the snow—tons of them. They'd

churned up the white all around, leaving deep furrows and scuff marks. In the midst of that mess was a swath of red as if someone had dragged a paintbrush against a blank canvas.

It was blood. She could see that now clearly. There were splatters of blood all around and one body-sized path leading toward a cluster of trees.

Jackie saw the woman's light then. It was dim, barely a glow. It flickered like a flame blown too hard, in danger of snuffing out.

Panic ignited in Jackie's chest. Her baby gave a hard thump against her bladder, as if punishing her for the surge of adrenaline.

In her mind, Jackie followed the bloody trail to where it ended behind the trunk of a pine tree.

The woman sat there, slumped against the tree. She was covered in blood. Her skin was starkly pale beneath the red splashes and smears, almost the same color as the snow all around her.

One of her legs was missing below the knee. She'd tied off the stump with a torn length of plaid flannel, but blood was still slowly seeping out from the open wound.

There were deep claw marks dug into her torso and arms. The fluffy padding of her coat was soaked with blood. In her gloved hand was a pocket knife covered in black blood.

She'd been attacked by a Synestryn. Their blood was on her knife, proof that she'd fought back. But it hadn't been enough. The demon must have taken off her leg and dragged it away when it fled from the sunrise—a meal to feast on until nightfall, when it could come back and finish the job.

The horror of what was happening raged through Jackie's body like a storm. Her limbs shook with fury, with helpless, hopeless frustration.

She was supposed to help these women who didn't know what they were—didn't know the magic they possessed. She was supposed to find them and bring them home, where they could be treated like the rare treasures they were.

She'd failed so utterly her heart could barely stand the

strain.

Iain's warm, comforting presence filled her like a hug from the inside out. He was with her in her thoughts, and holding her body, though she felt so distant from that now, she could barely feel his touch.

The woman's eyes fluttered open. The light shining from her flickered faintly.

She was dying.

Let her go, came Iain's deep voice in her mind. *You've done all you can. Let her go.*

But Jackie hadn't done everything. There had to be some way to save her, some way to find her and send in the troops to rescue her. All she needed was a Sanguinar to heal her and stop her bleeding.

She's been poisoned, Iain said. *She's lost to us. Let her go.*

Jackie could see then that he was right. A sheen of sweat covered her pale skin, despite the blistering cold. There were dark streaks running through her veins. When her eyes opened once again, there was no clarity in them, only fevered confusion.

She was dying.

Come back to me, Iain said.

I can't. I need to stay here with her. She shouldn't have to die alone. It's the least I can do after failing her.

Iain's response was slow to come. *Then we'll both stay.*

He held her as the woman's light faded, then as it winked out.

She was dead.

She'd died alone in the cold because Jackie had failed.

"It's not your fault," Iain said, and this time his words were in her ear. He'd dragged her essence away from the woman and planted her firmly back in her body.

The feeling of being anchored by flesh, of being held down by gravity was odd. It took her a moment to remember how to move again.

Tears streamed down her cheeks. She felt deep despair, as if she'd lost a dear friend. Even though she hadn't known this woman, even though she didn't know her name or where she was from, they were still sisters. They were both Theronai, only Jackie had been lucky enough to have found Iain, rather than facing the demons alone, terrified and powerless.

She knew how that felt. She knew how horrifying it was to know you were going to die by the teeth and claws of monsters.

Only she'd been lucky. She'd been rescued.

"I have to find a way to save them," Jackie whispered through a throat tight with tears. "I'm running out of time."

"You need to rest. Then you can try again."

"No!" she nearly shouted. "No more rest. These women aren't resting. They're in danger. If I don't find them, then more will die the way that poor woman did. I can't let it happen again."

If she did, she knew she'd never recover from the guilt.

She had to save them.

Jackie put her hands to her belly to hug the child inside her.

Sibyl had warned her that she would have only until her daughter was born to find these women. After that, the power of the life growing inside of her would be gone and there'd be no hope.

She was so tired. So defeated.

Iain's black eyes softened between blinding blobs of light. His voice was calm, reassuring. "You'll find them, Jackie. I know you will."

His confidence in her was humbling. She only wished she could be as optimistic.

"Borrow mine," he told her. "I have enough confidence in you for both of us."

She loved him for that—for the way he always said the right thing to make her feel better. He kept her strong, gave her hope.

"There's still time," he said. "We'll just try again."

Jackie nodded, not trusting her voice. She didn't want him to hear it tremble and break. She needed him to keep believing in her so that she could keep going after so much failure.

A moment later, she felt a hot rush of liquid spill from her, soaking the soft maternity pants she wore.

Shock settled into realization.

Her water had broken. Her baby was coming.

Whatever time she had to find these women was now nearly gone.

Chapter Twenty-three

Morgan raced as fast as he dared toward Link's last known location. He'd never really liked the guy, but he was still Morgan's brother-in-arms. That meant something.

Almost as much as the bond he shared with Serena.

His lifemark was still bare. The colors in the luceria still swirled in an angry storm of reds and pinks. Their bond wasn't yet permanent, but there was no way to know how much time they had left before it was.

He'd intended to break things off this morning, but then he'd heard that Link was missing, and knew the timing was wrong. If they were going on a rescue mission to find a missing man, Serena needed to have access to Morgan's power. And Morgan needed to be free of pain so that he could fight.

It had taken three hours to reach the coordinates Joseph had given them, and in that time, Serena hadn't said a word. He'd felt her tentative poking at their connection, as if trying to read Morgan's mind, but he kept her blocked out completely.

He didn't want her to know that he'd failed her—that he'd convinced her to choose the wrong man. And now Link was missing. If he died, there might not be anyone else who could offer her his power.

Morgan prayed the man was still alive.

Cutting his ties to Serena would mean he'd go back to living a life of pain, but what choice did he have? He couldn't call himself an honorable man if he was only staying with her to save his own life.

What about hers? She deserved a man who could give her everything she needed. And a woman as sweet as her needed to be loved.

Femi had always said that Morgan's love for her was like the air she breathed. Without it she would perish.

Could Serena be any different?

He honestly didn't think so.

"Turn here," she said, pointing to a gravel road with no sign. She was following the map on her phone, navigating as he drove. "It's the only way to get to the coordinates."

Morgan took the turn, and as soon as he cleared the next hill, he saw sunshine gleaming off the hood of Link's rental car.

They pulled up alongside his vehicle, but he was nowhere in sight. Through the windows, they could see his cell phone sitting on his dash. He hadn't taken it with him, which meant either he didn't want to be followed, or he didn't think it would work wherever he was going.

"Are there any known caves around here?" he asked Serena.

She unrolled her stack of maps and found the one for southern Missouri. It took a moment to locate the right place.

"There's a cave entrance a few hundred yards away," she said.

Now Morgan knew what had happened to Link. "He went hunting in that cave."

"Do you think he saw something?" she asked.

"I don't know. How long ago since anyone last heard from him?"

"Yesterday," she said. "He must not have made it out yet."

"He's been in there too long. We have to go in after him."

"I agree."

"You need to be prepared," he warned her.

"For what?"

"Either a rescue, or a recovery. I'm not sure which it is yet."

She nodded once, brief and pragmatic. Then she stepped out of the truck and gathered her gear from the back. As she stripped out of her oversized coat and tightened her sword belt over clinging leather clothing, she said, "You're going to have to stop shutting me out. I don't know what's going on, but we can't afford to have anything standing between us right now. Seconds count."

She was right. He didn't know what she might see if he opened his mind to her, but there really was no choice. Link's life was on the line.

He lowered his defenses and hoped she wouldn't go poking around in his head. If she did, and saw that he would rather walk away than doom her to a loveless life, she was only going to get hurt.

Then again, no matter what she did, pain was likely her fate one way or another. He only hoped he wouldn't be the one to inflict it.

***

Andra wasn't sure how much longer she was going to be able to hold this forcefield. She'd been working for days, drawing power from Paul to keep a shield around Lexi and Zach so that she could repair the wall while he fed her power.

Watching the small woman work was amazing. Her dainty features were calm, almost placid, though Andra knew she had to be exhausted. After all, she'd been working for two weeks longer than Andra had—since the walls had fallen.

She stood inside the film of blue light no thicker than the skin of a bubble. Her hands moved in a slow, almost sinuous movement. Her eyes were closed, but she seemed to be able to see the stones clearly.

Zach knelt beside her. His fingers dug into the cold earth, connecting him to the source of his power so that he could gather it up and funnel it into his wife.

With each flick of her wrist, another chunk of broken rock moved from the pile of rubble to the exact spot in the wall from where it had fallen. Both giant sections as well as grains as fine as sand moved at her guidance, sliding into place like pieces of a jigsaw puzzle. Inch by inch, the physical barrier was reconstructed until the surface gleamed like it had been polished.

Then, when the section of wall was whole, Lexi would lay her hands on the smooth surface. Zach would slide his left hand around the base of her neck until the two parts of the luceria merged to ease the flow of magic between them.

Lexi would bow her head. Her pale brow would crease in concentration. Strands of soft, brown hair would lift from her shoulders as if electrified. Then the very air around her would change. Andra could smell the shift, filled with the scent of freshly-tilled soil and ozone. She could feel it buffeting her skin like tiny sparks. The temperature around them would warm, the air would grow humid and thick.

Then, after Lexi had gathered up enough energy, she would release it into the wall in a sudden burst.

The sound of rock grating, shifting, locking into place was deafening. Entire sections of hard stone would shrink slightly as if being compressed by some invisible machine. The surface of the wall would grow glossy and impossibly hard. Then, when it was all over and the shimmering cloud of energy around them dissipated, the wall would continue to sing in cracks and pops as it solidified even further.

Once this was done, Synestryn would avoid the completed section, as if they knew they couldn't break through. Or, perhaps, they feared to touch the newly empowered structure.

Lexi had just completed yet another ten-foot section of wall.

Zach caught her as her knees buckled and she sagged toward the ground. He gathered her into his lap, both of them panting and shaking with effort.

In those vulnerable moments, Andra's shield was the only

thing keeping the two of them alive.

Hungry demons pounded at her forcefield with rusty, blunt weapons. Andra felt each blow vibrate through her body as she struggled to keep the glowing, blue shield in place.

Now that the section of wall was done, Paul guided her toward the couple sitting on the ground so she could shrink down the size of the protective bubble to reduce the strain of holding it.

When it was just big enough to hold all four of them, she was finally able to breathe again.

"Sorry," Lexi said in a breathless, weary voice.

"Don't be," Andra managed. She tried to stay strong, to remain outwardly confident that she could do this job for as long as it took.

Inside, she wasn't so sure.

"They'll have to rest soon," Zach said to Paul.

The two men had become so close over the past few days that they rarely needed to say more than a few words. Their movements became choreographed and streamlined, both men of the same mind.

Neither was going to let anything happen to the women they loved.

Around them, beyond the shimmering blue wall of light, lay devastation and chaos. Daylight demons were everywhere. No matter how many of them they killed, there always seemed to be more marching on the horizon.

They crawled out of nearby caves by the dozen to lope over the ground on long, gray legs. Their bodies were hairless and disturbingly sexless. No one knew where they came from or how to stop them. They were a constant flood of danger over the landscape leaving devastation wherever they went.

Things weren't going well. Every day more Theronai were injured. As their bodies grew weary from weeks of constant fighting, they became slow and clumsy.

For the first few days, Andra had watched the battle play out, wincing every time one of their own took a hit. She ached to extend her magic to surround them and take the blows so they didn't have to, but her promise to Joseph stayed her hand.

She hadn't realized how hard it was going to be to watch her makeshift family struggle and not do something to help them.

But Joseph had realized it. That's why he'd bound them to their word.

Unfortunately, it was even harder for Paul to watch his brothers suffer.

After a few days, they'd had to learn to block it all out. Ignore the battle raging around them and focus on their task. If they could get the wall repaired, everyone would be safe again. Everyone could rest.

Even the idea made her eyelids flutter with exhaustion.

They'd been out here since dawn, but she was weaker today than she had been yesterday. With only a few hours of rest, she came to work more tired each day than the one before.

None of them were going to be able to keep up this pace for long.

"Just a few more hours," Lexi panted. "Then we'll rest."

The idea made Andra stifle a groan. A few more hours of exertion seemed like a lifetime.

Her son moved in her belly like he was swimming laps in there. She swore she could feel his eagerness to be born, his excitement to enter the world and join the fight.

She didn't want to let him out. She wanted to hold him inside her forever where she could keep him safe. Maybe it was a ridiculous thing to want, but she couldn't help it.

She needed her son to stay safe. She needed that like she needed oxygen. If anything ever happened to him....

"Don't go there," Paul said. His voice was weary, but firm. "You can't think about things like that right now. Stay focused."

He was right, of course. She needed to keep her concentration so her shield didn't falter. If even one of those sword-wielding demons got to Lexi, they were all dead.

Paul squeezed her hand. "Positive thoughts only, love."

She nodded.

They were going to fix the wall. Lexi was going to make it all the way around the perimeter. Andra was going to keep her safely shielded while she did.

Their son would be born inside these solid walls, safe and sound.

"Incoming!" Zach shouted as he had so many times before.

Andra pulled in a burst of power from Paul and channeled it into the shield just as a flurry of demons bombarded them.

They scrambled around the edges of the shield, hammering at it with their clublike swords. There were so many of them they had to crawl on top of one another in an effort to reach the juicy prey inside. Eventually, their numbers blocked out the sun.

It had happened before, but every time it did, fear bubbled inside of her.

She'd been afraid before, but always more for others than herself. First for her mother, then her little sisters, then Paul, and now for the life growing inside of her.

She wasn't afraid to die, but she was terrified of living on without those she loved.

After a few moments, the cloud of demons began to clear as warriors hacked them to pieces. Reddish-black blood streamed down the sides of the blue dome, leaving a sickly film behind. Severed, gray limbs piled up like firewood around the base of the shield.

They wouldn't burn up in the sun as normal Synestryn did. Their corpses had to be burned in giant pits dug for just that purpose.

Andra wondered if her home would ever be the same again.

Positive thoughts, Paul whispered to her mind as he held her close.

Andra wasn't sure how much positive she could find in this place with blood and bodies all around, but for her family, for her son, she would try.

CHAPTER TWENTY-FOUR

Serena struggled to concentrate on the task at hand. Something was upsetting Morgan, but right now, she didn't dare rummage around in his thoughts long enough to figure out what it was.

Link was down in that cave, and with any luck, they'd find him still alive.

The sun burned bright overhead, which meant that demons from all around had taken refuge down here. Even right inside the shadowy opening of the cave she could see piles of them sleeping.

One raised its ugly, gray head and stared at her with black eyes. She was too close to the sunlight for it to dare charge her.

"There are so many of them," she whispered.

"You know we can't charge in there, right? It would be a suicide mission."

She nodded and they backed out into the sun, out of sight of the demons inside. "We need a plan."

"Can you hide our presence?" he asked.

"You mean like the Sanguinar do?"

He nodded.

"I don't know. I've never tried. Give me a moment."

She closed her eyes to aid her concentration and latched onto the tendril of power emanating from Morgan. While still a meager flow, it came to her easily now, seething and eager to do her bidding. There was more at her disposal than there had been only yesterday, which gave her hope that their bond was finally progressing.

As soon as the thought entered her mind, she felt Morgan's resistance to the idea.

He didn't want them any closer than they already were.

Her concentration shattered before she could command her magic to take shape.

She looked at him, frowning. "You don't want me anymore?"

"It's not like that, Serena. Not even close."

"Then what?"

"Can we talk about this later?"

"Not if you want to live. I can't focus on our mission if I'm distracted by wondering what's going on. So, tell me."

He scrubbed his cropped, black hair with a broad hand, as if he could rub loose an answer she would accept.

Finally, he said, gently, "You deserve to be loved. I can't be the man to make that happen. As much as I wanted my pain to end, as much as I thought we could simply be partners, I see now that was a foolish idea."

Serena's stomach dropped at his words. A familiar pain radiated in her chest, a pale version of heartache.

"My parents did it," she said, her words sounding childish and petulant.

"Were they happy?" he asked.

She thought about it, but the answer was as bleak as it was clear. "Never."

His shoulders sagged in defeat. "I don't want a life like that for you. I don't want to be tied to a woman I can't provide for in the way she needs. And like it or not, Serena, you need to be loved."

Maybe he was right. Maybe her heartache over Iain was too new for her to really know what she wanted. The only thing she did know was that this morning, she'd seen a glimmer of how she could feel for Morgan if they stayed together.

She could fall in love with him.

And then what? Spend the rest of her long life tied to a man who didn't love her back? Tied to a man who was with her only because he had no choice if he wanted to survive?

She wouldn't do that to herself. As it was, ending things with Morgan now was already going to hurt. She wouldn't put off the inevitable for any longer than she had to.

"Once we're out of this cave," she said, though the words made her heart squeeze hard, "I'll set you free."

She didn't know why she felt like she was losing him. He'd never been hers to begin with. He'd always belonged to Femi. He'd never once tried to hide that from her.

He nodded slightly, but didn't meet her gaze, as if he was ashamed. "I think that's for the best."

She turned away and struggled to make her words come out steady and even. "Until then, we have a job to do."

It took her a moment to regain control over her emotions. They were rioting around inside of her, unsure whether she should be grieving over the impending loss of Morgan's company, or grateful that he'd spared her far worse pain in the future.

Either way, she was about to be free again, living life on her own terms.

Without looking at him, because she knew if she did, she'd burst into tears, Serena grabbed hold of Morgan's power and forced it to obey.

A shimmering blue film wrapped around them, clinging to their skin. Her vision was distorted slightly as she peered through it, but there was nothing she could do about that. Masking their presence was the only way they were getting in and out of this cave alive.

"I think I did it," she said.

"Only one way to find out." Morgan stepped into the shadowy mouth of the cave, sword drawn and ready to strike.

Serena was right behind him.

***

Morgan moved as fast as he dared through the winding tunnels and the caverns they connected.

Serena's magic had worked, shielding them from detection. They still had to be careful, but at least they had a fighting chance at going undetected.

Sleeping demons were everywhere. There were hundreds of them. Possibly thousands.

In some places, there was nowhere to step without touching one, which would have definitely woken them. Instead of risking it, Morgan used a piece of chalk he always carried into caves to mark those tunnels he couldn't scout and moved back until he found the next open route.

As they went deeper into the earth, the tunnels changed. They became wider, taller and perfectly round, as if something had drilled a hole straight through solid rock. The surface was burnished and far smoother than it would have been if this had been done by mechanical means. Something had bored this tunnel. It was definitely not natural.

The air changed as well. It became thicker, warmer, and more humid. It smelled horrible—a swamp filled with hot garbage and decaying corpses.

He felt Serena's disgust shudder through their link. The protective shield around them sputtered before she secured it back in place.

One of the daylight demons on his left stirred in its sleep. It lifted its head and sniffed the air.

Morgan froze. Serena did the same. Neither of them breathed.

After a few seconds, the demon lay its head back down and closed its giant, red eyes.

They'd been steadily descending for several minutes when they reached a spot where everything seemed to level out again. Unlike the other caverns they'd seen, this one was empty, with no sign of life.

There were three openings into the space—the one they

were standing in, the one to their left, and another to their right, which was glowing a pale fluorescent green. Light was such an odd sight to see down here that Morgan was shocked into stillness.

"What is that?" Serena asked in a faint whisper.

"No idea. I've heard some of the daylight demons have learned to use fire to help them see—that they were too close to human to be able to see in the dark—but that's not fire."

"Link?" she asked.

He shrugged. "Let's find out."

They crept forward. Morgan kept close tabs on her exact location through the luceria. He was amazed at how easy it was, how natural. He didn't even have to exert effort to feel her presence along his side, radiating out of her like heat.

She was easy to be around. If things had been different— if they hadn't suffered the pain of loss so acute it left them emotionally damaged—they would have made a great team.

But that was the thing about history. It hung around, coloring every decision and skewing every emotion. It was the house guest you couldn't get rid of, the chronic disease ruining your life despite your best efforts.

If there was a way to get past history and emotional damage, Morgan didn't know what it would be.

With a force of will, he brought his attention back to the matter at hand. Whatever they found down here in this glowing tunnel would be dangerous, if not outright deadly. It was their job to fight, and they were equipped to handle most things, but Synestryn always seemed to have more tricks up their demonic sleeves.

Especially lately. Things were changing fast. Demons looked more human than ever. They could even walk in the sun without bursting into flames. Something was shifting in the Synestryn world, altering the rules of the game in ways that left the Sentinels struggling to catch up.

Only those who maintained focus and kept their head in the game would survive long enough to be surprised another day.

As he stepped toward the glowing opening, he caught a glimpse of something far to the right. It was pale—like the underbelly of a deep-sea fish—and undulating. The closer he got, the more of it he could see. But it wasn't until his head passed the unnaturally round, perfectly smooth entrance to the chamber that he could see just how huge this thing really was.

At least twenty daylight demons surrounded it, each holding a sword. They looked sleepy, like they weren't able to stay alert and do their guard duty during the day. A few of them had given up and were slumped against a wall, snoozing.

The floor in here was wet and shiny. It reflected that green, pulsing glow onto the ceiling of the cavern, which was easily thirty feet up.

In the middle of the chamber, sitting on a huge nest of wet, dead grass and leaves was the object they guarded. It looked like some kind of larva, but was the size of a city bus. It moved just enough to prove it was a living thing, rather than some kind of construct. A faint green glow emanated from inside it, like a pulse, lighting up what it contained.

As soon as Morgan realized what he was seeing, his stomach gave a hard heave.

Inside this massive…thing were dozens of daylight demons, curled up inside translucent sacs filled with thick fluid. They varied in size from fully grown to as small as his fist, but Morgan recognized them easily.

As he watched, he could see them growing, visibly getting bigger as they progressed through the giant creature as if on some kind of conveyor belt.

Whatever this thing was, it was growing the daylight demons inside it. Fast.

This was the source.

As he watched, a wet, slime-covered demon was expelled out of the back end of the creature. It clawed at the sac around it until it burst and flooded the area with clear, mucus-like goo.

Within seconds, the newborn was up on its feet. A fellow demon nearby handed it a heavy, rusted sword, which it took without question. It then trundled off behind its mother into a tunnel Morgan couldn't fully see.

Just that fast, another enemy soldier was armed and ready for battle.

Another one was expelled only seconds behind the first.

Serena was right behind him. When she saw what had happened, what it meant, she sucked in a harsh gasp.

The sound wasn't loud, but it carried easily in the still, thick, humid air down here.

The guards came instantly alert, scanning the area and sniffing the air for the source of the sound.

She maintained the shield that hid them from sight, but Morgan didn't know how long that would keep them hidden. Even their heartbeats might give away their location if her magic faltered.

We must kill it. The thought was hers, but he heard it as clearly as if she'd spoken aloud.

Surprise rippled through him.

Their bond was strengthening faster than he'd thought possible. And as convenient as it was for them to be able to communicate in silence, he knew that it came at a cost.

He glanced at his ring. The colors within the surface of the luceria were still churning pinks and reds. They hadn't yet solidified—hadn't yet trapped her with a man who could never deserve her.

It took him a moment to steady himself and find the mental pathway she'd used to speak to him.

We will kill it, he told her. *After we find Link.*

He hoped she'd heard him. He was new at this telepathy stuff, and didn't dare ask her if she'd gotten the message.

Her body was shaking, but he couldn't tell if it was from the shock of seeing this thing, or need to kill it raging through her.

He put a hand on her arm, hoping to calm her either way.

The contact made the colors swirling inside his ring kick up like stormy seas. Deep ruby red and brighter, curling plumes of pink crashed inside the band.

Perhaps, if they'd been able to stay together, she would

have been known as the Ruby Lady. There was no way to know what color the luceria would pick for her with a different man.

The idea sent a jolt of jealousy through him, which he ignored completely.

They would find Link alive, rescue his ass, and she would tie herself to him so that she wouldn't be alone and defenseless.

End of story.

With that thought in mind, Morgan took Serena's hand and backed them slowly away from the chamber.

When they were out of sight of the daylight demons guarding the monstrous incubator, he led them to the next opening.

They hadn't made it twenty yards into the next perfectly round tunnel—a shape Morgan was now certain was created to allow the giant larva to pass—when they heard a low moan of pain.

"Link," she whispered aloud before taking off in the direction of the noise.

Morgan wanted to grab her and shove her behind him, but he didn't dare disrupt her concentration. If he did, the energy shielding them from sight could fail. Instead, he moved as fast as he dared, and let his long legs eat up the distance between them.

By the time he reached her side, she'd found the source of the sound.

Link was strung up by his arms, dangling from a rope, just out of reach of the demons sleeping below. He was shirtless. His body was a mass of cuts and bruises. His left shoulder was completely purple, and bulging at an odd angle. Dried blood from what appeared to be a head wound covered his face in a gruesome mask. More blood coated his lifemark.

Strangely, he wore bandages on some of the wounds.

She came to a dead stop, only feet away from one of the daylight demons.

Morgan grabbed her arm both to steady her and to keep

her from running in there to save Link. If she did that, she'd wake up every demon around.

Her sword quivered in her grip. Rage and regret thrummed through their link, so thick, he couldn't tell it the emotions were his or hers. Maybe both.

If they were going to get Link out of here alive, they needed a plan.

Serena sent him an image of what she intended to do. It burst into his head, fully formed and in living color. He'd never experienced anything so amazing in his life, which made him wonder what else she could do.

You're never going to find out, whispered her voice in his mind. *Your path is set. I am no longer yours.*

A flicker of grief hit him before he brushed it away. There was too much to do for him to be worrying about emotions at a time like this. Only actions mattered now.

Morgan gave her a single nod, indicating he understood, then went to perform his part of the rescue mission.

CHAPTER TWENTY-FIVE

Jackie's labor pains were making it almost impossible for her to concentrate.

Ronan was on his way to deliver the baby, though he was slowed down by daylight and lethargy it created in his kind. Justice—lead-foot that she was—was behind the wheel, which meant they'd be here soon, but there was no guarantee they'd make it in time.

Based on the way Jackie's body was trying to twist itself inside out, she was almost certain she didn't have much time to wait.

Their baby was almost here.

Iain had moved her to the infirmary, as if the three-minute walk up the stairs was going to take too long and that the baby might just pop out unexpectedly. She, on the other hand, was certain she wasn't going to get that lucky.

The pain was unlike anything she'd ever felt before. It was as if her body had betrayed her, using her own muscles as torture devices.

The contractions were still far enough apart that she had time to recover between them, as well as time to anticipate their arrival as one might anticipate a root canal or being burned at the stake.

Beyond the pain, fear and worry haunted her. Sibyl's warning rang in her mind like a gong. *You must find the women before it's too late. Without them, we all die.*

Jackie was almost out of time. She hadn't yet figured out how to locate the women and if she didn't do so before her baby was born, she might never be able to.

She thought about that poor woman bleeding out in the snow and her heart squeezed hard in grief and guilt.

Jackie had failed her—she'd failed to focus her gift soon enough to save the woman's life. That failure could never be undone.

She couldn't let it happen again. She couldn't lose another one of the lights. She needed to fight through her labor pain and figure out how to do what Sibyl had warned her she must.

The office-turned-infirmary was brightly lit, but she couldn't see anything past the lights in her vision. She knew there was a curtain spread across the wide windows overlooking the warehouse floor, but even that large sheet of fabric was impossible to see between the light the women put off.

She could smell disinfectant and hear the voices of people below, muttering excitedly about what was about to happen. Another Theronai baby was about to enter the world.

Jackie hoped like hell she didn't scream and scare the children. They wouldn't understand that what she was going through was normal, natural, joyful. Instead, they'd remember the horrors they'd faced in the caves and the screams of the kids who'd been deemed unworthy to breed. The screams of children being killed and eaten, hopefully in that order. They'd remember the screams of those unlucky enough to be chosen as breeders as they faced the horrors those demons had in store.

There had been so much pain and fear in those caves. Jackie didn't want to do anything to drag their minds back to that dark, hopeless place.

Screaming was definitely not an option.

"Don't go there," Iain said.

He was close, only inches away. She couldn't see his big body, but she could feel the heat coming from him, the gravitational pull of his solid bulk.

He wouldn't leave her. He'd *never* leave her. She was as certain of that as she was that she was nearly out of time to save those women.

Jackie redirected her thoughts and took a deep breath to try to clear her mind. Sweat dotted her skin. The cramps in her back and abdomen had receded but were never truly gone now.

The time between contractions was growing shorter. She was going to have to find a way to work through the pain, whatever it took.

As she had so many times before, she went to the lights and chose one at random. This one wasn't as bright as the dead woman's had been, but nearly so. It had a faint pink cast to it that seemed to glow with health and vitality.

That was what Jackie needed right now—a nice, healthy woman who wasn't on the verge of death.

She concentrated on that light and flew toward it.

Travelling to the lights was easier now than it had been. She'd learned how to guide her consciousness through space, darting and zipping like a hummingbird. There was no more sense of disorientation that had plagued her earlier. She could tell by the geography she saw that she was in Texas, right along the Gulf Coast.

That, at least, was more information than she'd been able to glean from all the other visits to the lights she'd made.

The woman was in a populated area. People and cars were everywhere. The buildings here were tall glass and steel constructions that gleamed under the sun.

The woman was in a shop in the shadow of one of those buildings, working. Jackie could see her as clearly as she could if she were standing right beside her.

She had dark brown hair that was tied in a knot at the back of her head. Her face was round and sweet, with the kind of uplifted features that made her look like she was smiling, even when she wasn't. She had beautiful peaches-and-cream skin that was flushed with health. A few strands of dark hair fell across her cheek, right next to a dusting of what looked like flour.

She wore a white T-shirt and jeans. Over that was a pink apron with tiny red and white hearts on it. Like the rest of her, it was simple and cute.

She smiled at someone who'd walked into the shop, revealing a deep dimple in both cheeks. As her expression warmed with welcome, her cuteness ramped up by a factor of ten.

There was a bright pink box in her hands that, like her apron, was covered in small hearts. On it was a store logo that Jackie couldn't quite make out. The box was moving too fast as it went into the hands of an elderly man.

Another contraction clamped around Jackie's middle, like a giant fist trying to squeeze her in half. A hoarse cry escaped her mouth before she could clamp her lips shut to trap it inside.

Her vision of the cute girl flickered, then disappeared, leaving Jackie looking at Iain's concerned face between blobs of light.

"You okay?" he asked.

She had to wait for the worst of the pain to die down before she could answer. "I thought I almost had something. I saw someone. A woman. In Texas."

"That's good," he said as he held her hand. "What else?"

Sweat coated her skin and made her hair cling to her forehead. She was wearing one of Iain's giant, button-up shirts since there were no hospital gowns to be had here. She was naked beneath it except for socks, which served to keep her feet protected from the cold warehouse floor.

A heart monitor was strapped to her belly. The baby's pulse was fast and steady, beating out a reassuring rhythm.

Iain had wanted her to lie down, but she'd chosen one of the folding chairs draped in a towel instead. She felt too vulnerable on her back, and right now, she needed to feel as strong and competent as possible.

"I saw a little shop. It smelled sweet, like a candy store."

"You can smell where these women are?"

Jackie hadn't thought that strange until he'd said something.

"Yeah. I guess I can."

"Can you hear anything?" he asked.

"I don't know. Let me check." With that, she closed her eyes and went back to the pale pink light the woman cast across Jackie's vision.

The little shop where the woman worked was bright and tidy. There was a glass display case at a serving counter with colorful objects behind it.

Cupcakes. The woman worked in a cupcake shop.

The air smelled of sugar and vanilla. It was cool, and there was a whir of a machine somewhere in the background.

The woman was behind the counter, adding beautiful, ornate cupcakes to an empty slot behind the glass. She hummed under her breath as she worked.

A small, plastic nametag flashed under the overhead lights. Jackie caught just a glimpse of it, but that was all she needed.

Genie was this woman's name, and, according to the shiny, silver star on the tag, she'd been working for Cuppy Cakes for three years.

Another contraction hit, this one worse than the last. It jerked her out of the little shop and back to the infirmary, where her body seized up against the grinding pain clenching her.

Iain's hand was on her back. It made wide, slow sweeps down her spine as she curled herself around her baby and prayed for the pain to ease.

With each pass of his hand, her pain lightened, as if he were wiping it away.

She touched his thoughts through the luceria and realized that he'd begun taking into himself some of her pain so that she didn't have to feel it all. While part of her wanted to tell him that she was strong enough to take the pain, most of her was grateful that he was sharing the burden. She didn't know how women did this without help from their men.

She hoped she never had to find out.

When the worst of the agony faded and she was able to pull in enough breath to speak, she told Iain what she'd learned.

"That's enough to find her," he said. "I'll let Joseph know right away so he can send someone to her."

"We can't bring her here now—not when Dabyr is under attack. We're a wreck. She'd never want to have anything to do with us."

He stroked her hair. "Don't worry about that now. We'll figure out the best way to proceed. You just worry about having the baby."

There were so many more women for her to locate. And all of them were in as much danger as the woman who'd bled out in the snow. They would all be hunted for the magic they possessed and the blood flowing through their veins. Without people to protect them and teach them how to survive, they were in grave danger.

Jackie had to find them. But how was she going to do that before their little girl was born and could no longer help fuel Jackie's magic?

You must find the women before it's too late. Without them, we all die.

"I have to find more," she said.

She couldn't see his face, but didn't need to. He was unhappy about the situation. She could feel his frustration and distress buffeting the walls of their connection.

"You're pushing yourself too hard," he said.

"There's no choice. We can't leave these women out there alone. And I can't be responsible for losing another one of them. I *have* to do this."

His thick fingers slid between hers. His voice was tense with worry. "Then do it, but I won't let you do it on your own."

Of course, he wouldn't. Iain was always with her, supporting and encouraging her. He'd taken care of her through her pregnancy and kept her safe when it seemed that every demon out there wanted her blood even more now that she was pregnant.

She didn't have much time until the next contraction hit, and she needed every second she could get.

There were at least a dozen more lights to find. Maybe more. It was hard to tell when they blinded her like this.

Jackie pulled in a deep breath and opened the conduit that connected her and Iain so deeply they shared a soul. As the connection widened, she could feel the shimmering heat of his power just waiting for her to call on it. Waves of energy pooled inside of him, seething and churning as if restless. That power wanted to be used, to be shaped by her hands into something different, something tangible and whole.

As she gathered up a thick strand of that energy, her baby responded. The pulse coming from heart monitor strapped to her sped. She thrashed inside the confines of Jackie's hard belly as if excited.

Jackie sent her mind soaring through the air toward one of the lights. Before she could make it all the way there, the next contraction grabbed her in its fist and squeezed.

She was jerked back into her body to endure every second of the pain. Iain was drawing some of it away, but there was still plenty to go around.

They panted together through the pain, holding hands. Their minds were merged, so no words were necessary.

They both knew that their baby was nearly here. The contractions were too close together now. She didn't have time to find another woman between them.

There was a knock on the door. Iain struggled to his feet to answer it.

Madoc's low voice came from the hallway. "Justice called. They're still over an hour away."

"She doesn't have that long," Iain said. "Her contractions are less than a minute apart now."

"Madoc delivered my baby," Nika said. She must have been with her husband. Her voice was low and soft. "He read all the books and knows what to do if something goes wrong."

Madoc had a photographic memory. If he'd read

something, he could always see it in his mind as perfectly as if the book were still in front of him.

Jackie felt Iain's protective side surge up, hard and fast. It clogged their link with aggression and testosterone.

None of the Theronai men liked others to touch their mates. Letting Madoc deliver their baby was definitely more than touching.

"Let him in," Jackie said, panting. "We need him."

Iain hesitated. Jackie couldn't hear his feet shuffle for several seconds. Then, slowly, she felt him relent, felt his need to keep her and the baby safe overcome his desire to keep Madoc away from her.

Finally, Iain uttered a grudging, "Come in."

Madoc donned a sterile gown and gloves then checked Jackie's cervix. The whole time, Iain was barely holding himself back from bashing in the other man's brains for daring to touch his wife in such an intimate way.

She stayed connected to him, soothing him, reassuring him.

Sometimes alpha males were so much work.

When Madoc was done with his exam, he said, "It's time."

"Time for what?" Iain asked.

"For Jackie to start pushing. She's fully dilated."

For some reason, those words sent a jolt of fear down her spine. She'd been looking forward to this day for so long, but now that it was here, she was terrified.

What if she couldn't keep her baby safe? What if she was a horrible mother? What if she did something wrong?

And then she realized what those words meant. If it was time to push, she wasn't going to find those women. They were all going to be left out there to fend for themselves.

She couldn't let it happen.

"Not yet," she said. "I need a few more minutes."

"For what?" Madoc asked, his tone sharp and confused. "No turning back now."

"I need to try one more time."

"She's trying to find the location of the other female

Theronai. Once the baby is born, it will be too late."

"This isn't like doing your taxes," Madoc said. "You can't put this off."

"Just for another few minutes." As she uttered the words, another contraction ripped through her, so brutal she let out a high, keening wail.

Iain was at her side again, holding her, easing her pain.

When it was over, she was dripping with sweat and shaking.

"There's no more time," Madoc said.

Jackie ignored him and went seeking the next light.

Chapter Twenty-six

Serena hid her weakness from Morgan. Simply holding the shield around them for so long had worn her down. The shock of seeing that huge, pulsing monster filled with baby demons had rattled her. The guilt of knowing she was at least partly to blame for Link's current condition had taken an even bigger toll.

She knew what she had to do, but she honestly wasn't sure if she was strong enough—if the bond she and Morgan shared was adequate for her to funnel enough power from him to get them all out of here alive.

Every second she hesitated only served to exhaust her more, so she closed her eyes, inhaled as much of the blazing energy Morgan stored as she could, and shaped it to do her bidding.

First, she sped the flow of time so that Morgan could move ten times faster than those around him.

As he began hacking the heads from sleeping demons at a pace so fast it was a blur, Serena did her part.

Her feet left the ground, giving her a giddy, buoyant sensation. She wobbled slightly before she got the hang of floating, but as soon as she was steady, she lifted herself up to where Link was suspended.

She wasn't strong enough to hold him up when she cut his ropes, but Morgan's power was. She wrapped it around Link in a tight embrace, then sliced through the tough rope binding him.

The second his body was free, he started to fall. She thought she'd been ready for his weight, but she hadn't realized just how heavy he'd be.

His eyes opened slightly, and past his blood-caked lashes, she saw shock and terror.

She strengthened her hold on him and exerted more energy to slow his fall. She wasn't quite able to stop him completely, but Morgan had started his killing spree with the demons directly below Link.

He landed on the relatively soft pile of stinking, gray flesh and rolled safely to the stone floor.

At least as safely as any ten-foot fall could have ended.

Serena dropped to his side and began to work on cutting the section of rope binding his wrists together. The second she moved his arms, he gave another one of those low moans of pain, as if he couldn't hold it in.

"I'm sorry," she whispered. "Just hold on."

Nearby, Morgan was a blur of shining steel and gleaming flesh. His work was almost done, with only a few creatures left on the far side of the room to finish off. They were groggy, slowly waking up from sleep, but Morgan would be done with them before they could reach her or Link.

Everywhere Morgan had gone, gray heads lay on the ground, rocking slightly as dark red blood leaked from the necks they used to inhabit.

The sight was hideous, but not nearly as disturbing as what they'd seen earlier.

Monsters birthing monsters, fully grown and ready for war.

The implications of that hadn't yet had time to settle in, but once they did, Serena knew she wouldn't sleep for a week.

"Baby," Link whispered through lips caked with dried blood.

He was delirious. The endearment proved he thought she belonged to him. Maybe that blow to his head had taken his memories of their last moments together. Maybe he didn't remember that he'd walked away from her willingly.

"It's okay," she told him. "We're going to get you out of here."

"No, baby," he insisted.

She wanted to tell him she wasn't his baby, but didn't waste her breath. She was still struggling to speed Morgan's movements, and the strain was starting to show.

His swings were slower than they had been. He was still fast, but not fast enough.

Before Serena finished slicing through Link's bonds, one of the daylight demons opened its mouth and let out a shrill cry of alarm.

In the distance, that cry was echoed, over and over again until the walls were shaking with the noise.

Every demon in this vast network of caverns and tunnels now knew the enemy was here.

Her plan had failed. There was no way she, Morgan or Link were going to make it out of here alive.

***

The moment Morgan felt Serena's magic falter, he knew how bad things truly were. Demons were everywhere. More were coming—too many to fight.

He was too busy to look beyond what lay directly in front of him, but she could see everything. She knew they weren't going to make it out of here alive. He could feel the dire nature of their situation shimmer between them, along the narrow walls of the link they shared.

He cut down another gray Synestryn, then another, moving faster than he ever had before in his life. Coupled with the burst of speed Serena fed him, he was still barely able to slay the monsters faster than they were flooding into the chamber.

His muscles burned with effort. His lungs felt like they were on fire as they struggled to funnel enough oxygen to his blood to fuel his body. Small cuts stung his skin, but there was no taint of poison running through his veins. That, at least, was a small blessing.

He wasn't sure how much longer his body could keep going like this. His limbs weren't designed to move at this pace. He could feel an unnatural heat building up inside his tissues.

She was struggling to rescue Link, all the way on the far side of the cavern. If anything broke through her defenses, there would be nothing he could do to stop it.

The idea of her falling in battle clogged his mind with worry. Even though he hadn't promised to protect her with his life the way his people always did, the need to do so burned through him as clear and bright as the sun.

If anything happened to her…

The connection between them flared suddenly as she sucked in a huge gulp of his power. As soon as it passed out of him, he could hear her thoughts, clear and unfiltered.

She'd been masking how exhausted she was from wielding so much magic for so long. She didn't want him to see her as weak. She didn't want him to pity her or stay with her because he thought she needed protection.

She wanted him to see her as brave and strong, an equal partner. Because of that, she'd covered up just how much of a strain she was enduring.

He swore that if they got out of this alive, he was going to make sure she never hid anything from him ever again.

To that end, he shoved his way into her thoughts, demanding their link to expand even further to fit the force of his resolve.

What he saw inside her was so beautiful, he almost forgot he was in the middle of combat. His sword swung out of habit, hitting where it aimed. But his mind was reeling from the warmth and selflessness that made up Serena's core.

She'd been forgotten, discarded and overlooked, but she hadn't been broken. She was still strong, if a little dented. She was kind, though she tried not to let others know for fear they'd walk all over her. She was smart, but had hidden the trait because her mother had pounded into her head that no man wanted to be with a woman smarter than he was. Beauty was all men cared about.

What a load of bullshit.

As Morgan's consciousness expanded inside of hers, he was instantly grateful that she had far more brainpower than he did. Because that was the only way they were getting out of here alive. He was too busy hacking down demons to come up with any brilliant ideas.

We'll never get out alive. It's impossible. Her words rang in his head, clear as if she'd spoken them.

Nothing is impossible for us, he told her. *Just pull what you need from me. Everything I have is yours.*

Her confidence faltered, but as fast as the speed of thought, she hardened her resolve to match his and started working on a plan to keep them all alive.

He didn't question what it was. His only thought now was of getting back to her side.

If they didn't stop more demons from flooding this room, there really was no hope.

As if responding to his thoughts, Serena aimed a quick burst of power at the opening of one of the tunnels. A deafening roar filled the space, followed by a deep, throaty rumble of rock on rock.

Tons of stone rained down just inside the opening of the tunnel. It crushed dozens of demons as it fell. They screamed and thrashed for only a moment before falling silent. Dark red blood leaked out from under the pile or rock which blocked the entrance completely.

Behind that wall, Morgan could hear Synestryn clawing and scrambling to find a way through the barricade. As many of them as there were, it wouldn't take long for them to clear an opening.

Morgan altered the trajectory of battle, taking out the remaining monsters as fast as he could. They didn't have much time before more found them, and they were going to need every second they could get.

Once the last gray giant fell, he rushed to Serena's side.

The room stunk of blood and death. He was so starved for oxygen that he couldn't help but gasp in the fetid stench with every breath his heaving lungs forced on him.

Every muscle and tendon in his body was on fire. Heat poured out of him, so hot that sweat rose from his skin in the form of steam. Everything around him seemed to be moving too fast, as if he could no longer handle time flowing in its usual manner.

Still, he regained his focus and assessed Link's injuries in a glance. The man was barely conscious, much less coherent. The only way out of this cave for him was if he was carried out.

Serena wasn't strong enough to do the job without magic, and every bit of magic she used had to count.

Right now, escape was their first priority.

Morgan flung the man over his left shoulder and nodded his head toward the exit.

"You go first," she said. "I'm right behind you."

That odd sense of vertigo hit him, and he knew that she was speeding their pace. Rock walls raced past them, faster than he could focus.

He was used to fighting in caves and tracking his path in so he could find his way out, but at this speed, the task was much harder.

He took one wrong turn, which landed them in a cavern filled with daylight demons.

As soon as they saw him, one of them let out that ear-splitting scream. The others joined in a second later, and after that, the whole cave began screaming like it had before.

They whirled around and headed back the right way, but now they had a shit load of demons right on their trail.

Serena was in front of him now. She stumbled on some loose rocks. The cave walls slowed as her magic faltered.

From their left, another tunnel connected, and a flood of daylight demons swarmed out as they passed.

Pain bit into Morgan's calf. He didn't slow down to see what had hit him or how bad it was. He knew that if they didn't move faster, they were going to be overrun.

As if she'd heard him, Serena sucked in more of his power and they began to speed up again.

Link was a heavy, awkward weight on his shoulder. To make matters worse, the man was pounding on Morgan's back as if he wanted to be set down. The blows weren't hard enough to injure him, but there was no time to stop and see what the man wanted.

Morgan thought he heard Link screaming about a baby, but the shrill cries of the demons echoing in the tunnels made it impossible to tell for sure.

Just when he thought they'd outrun the vast horde behind them, Serena skidded to a stop.

Morgan slammed into her, knocking her down.

A rusty metal blade swung in an arc where her head had been an instant before.

Had she not been unnaturally fast, that would have been the end of her life.

Once again Morgan was hit by how precious she was, how fragile. Sure, she was brave and strong and could kick his ass anytime she wanted, but her life was a thin tendril too easily severed. One wrong move and she'd be gone from this world.

Before he could drop Link and engage the enemy, the demon swung its sword again. This time, it bounced off of thin air, leaving behind pale blue sparks in its wake.

Serena had brought up a shield to fend off the blow, but it was too late.

There was an odd kind of pressure in the center of Morgan's back. He looked down, confused at what he saw.

Something red and wet with blood stuck out of his abdomen.

It took him a moment to realize that he'd been stabbed by one of those rusty demon swords. The weapon had gone clean through, but Morgan couldn't feel a thing.

CHAPTER TWENTY-SEVEN

Andra's shield faltered for a split second, but it was enough for one of the daylight demons to slip in and charge her.

Its gaze was fixed on her belly and the tiny life pulsing within.

The thing's eyes were huge, the same dark red as its blood. Its furless skin was knobby and bulbous over wide, thick joints. Heavy muscle covered its frame.

These things had been built for power, not grace. Every movement was a hard, jerky surge of strength meant to cut through flesh and bone. Even the swords they carried were clunky, dull and unrefined, but that didn't stop them from smashing through everything from bodies to metal to tree trunks. Even solid stone was at risk from the blunt, heavy blades.

Weariness like she'd never felt before wound around her until she could barely breathe. Her power had grown considerably in the time since she'd bonded to Paul, but she could see now that it wasn't going to be enough.

Already, she was slipping, letting in a random sword here or a long, gray arm there. Once, a demon's head had made it through a broken spot in her forcefield only to be lopped off by Paul's wickedly sharp sword.

But even he was growing tired. The strain of constantly feeding her his power was wearing on him, making him slower than usual. The casual grace she'd come to associate with his fighting style was gone now, leaving behind an almost frenetic rush to catch up to his enemy's attacks.

He lunged toward the demon, using its own momentum to send it stumbling. Once it was off balance, he brought his sword down hard in a two-handed blow that severed the thing's gray head. Dark red blood arced out to hit the blue dome of light before dripping to the cold ground.

Through the whole thing Zach stayed by Lexi's side, only lifting his head to make sure that Paul had the situation handled.

It was over, but there was no sense of relief in Andra. She was nearly at the end of her strength. If they didn't go inside and rest for a while, she was afraid she was going to get them all killed.

"Time to go!" Paul shouted to be heard over the snarling demons and sounds of battle all around them.

She couldn't see what was going on—there were too many of the gray demons beating against the forcefield for her to see a thing—but she knew it wasn't good. The volume of combat alone was enough to tell her that the place was being flooded with fresh Synestryn again.

Lexi didn't respond. She was too deep in concentration to even acknowledge she'd heard Paul. But Zach had.

"Ten more minutes," he called. "She needs ten more minutes."

Andra honestly didn't know if she could keep going that long, but if she didn't, all of their work for the past few hours would be ruined. If Lexi didn't finish, the demons would just tear the partially-repaired wall apart again and they'd have to start over.

Andra knew she didn't have the strength for that. As it was, there was still over half a mile of wall to repair.

Even the thought was enough to make her want to cry.

Her baby needed a safe place to be born, to grow up. Dabyr was the only hope of that. She had to stay strong for him.

Her legs were trembling but she didn't dare sit down. If

she did, she knew she'd never be able to get back up again. She was too weak to push herself up, and Paul needed his sword arm free to fight, so he couldn't carry her.

She was on her own.

She felt his warmth fill the luceria as he worked to reassure her, to encourage her.

She had to keep going no matter what. Her baby needed her to keep going.

Her eyes burned with the strain of channeling so much power. Like Lexi, her whites were shot through with angry red—a sign they'd been using too much magic.

Her body was shaky and uncharacteristically weak. She was used to being the strong one—the one her sisters leaned on for support. She'd always seen herself as capable of dealing with almost anything, but now...now she wasn't sure if she could even stay standing.

A new wave of daylight demons charged toward the gap left by those that had just been killed. It seemed as though they all knew that what was happening inside this blue bubble was important. Either that or they smelled her baby.

The idea made her shudder and strengthen the shield along the side where the demons charged. Unfortunately, that left the far side weaker.

Another gray demon shoved through a flickering gap only to be trapped as she tightened her hold on her power once more.

The creature was pinned in place, thrashing and biting at the shimmering blue light. As Paul moved toward it to put it out of its misery, it lashed out with its sword.

Exhausted from his efforts, Paul was a split second too slow. The rusty demon blade sliced through his leather jacket and left a deep gash along his forearm.

He tossed his sword to his other hand and lopped off the demon's head before it could get in another hit.

Without him saying a word, she could tell the injury was bad—bad enough that he couldn't fight with his dominant hand. Some vital tendon or muscle had been severed, leaving him unable to hold his sword.

Zach saw the situation, but didn't leave his post next to Lexi. "Nine more minutes."

Andra wasn't going to last that long. She just wasn't. There was nothing left in her to give and she still had to hold this shield until they were safely off the battlefield.

She shrank the forcefield smaller, almost to the point that it brushed their heads.

There was no room to fight inside now, but there was no one in shape to do much fighting, so she guessed that was okay.

Sweat poured from Lexi's brow. Her small body trembled like she was being shook. Zach's hand seemed to be the only thing holding her up, but he was shaking almost as badly.

More demons surged on their position and began slamming those heavy swords into the dome. Each time they did, Andra weakened slightly.

She couldn't do this. She couldn't hold out for three more minutes, much less nine.

Paul stripped out of his jacket and T-shirt, then staunched the flow of blood with his shirt. Andra managed to tighten the knot around his arm, but it took three tries to manage the small task.

She couldn't do this.

No choice, Paul whispered inside her mind. *You're strong. You can do this.*

Her baby boy thrashed inside her belly as if to remind her he was there.

As if she could ever forget him.

She could feel him inside of her. The connection wasn't as strong as the one she had with Paul, but it was there. She could feel his energy, his growing power.

She had to protect him at all costs, even if it meant sacrificing everyone else on the battlefield.

He punched at her ribs in denial.

If he were grown, she could imagine how he'd react to her willingness to let others die for him. He'd be as brave and honorable as his father, as strong and stubborn as his mother.

He'd fight to the death. She knew that as surely as she knew she loved him.

Andra focused her mind on him, on the miracle he was—the first male Theronai to be born in two centuries.

She'd do anything for him, including keeping up this damn shield as long as it took. Nine minutes, nine years. She didn't care. She wasn't going to let him down.

She could do this. She *would* do this.

Let the demons come. Let them hammer and claw and bite the blue dome all they liked. For her child, she'd keep up this shield until the sun burned itself out and all the stars went dark.

CHAPTER TWENTY-EIGHT

Serena knew the instant Morgan was hit.

She was still on her knees, trying to stand when the thick column of power fueling her magic sputtered.

The invisible shield she'd raised was gone. The magic that was helping cloak their presence and speed their exit—it was all gone.

For a split second, she was disconnected and alone, with no one to lean on and no one to give her strength.

In that instant, she realized just how empty her life before Morgan had been. Not because she didn't have a man, but because she had no power. She was only half of the glorious, powerful creature she'd been born to be.

And she didn't like it.

Without the magic he held, she was never going to be able to stop his bleeding and save his life.

And she had to save his life because she loved him.

How could she not? She'd seen inside of him, seen his honor and kindness. He'd shown her in a hundred different ways the kind of man he was—his honesty, loyalty and dedication. He'd opened himself up to her as much as he was able and given her everything he had to give, without reservation. He'd accepted her as she was without any thoughts as to how he might change her to better suit his wishes.

He didn't love her, but he cared for her. He'd give her whatever she wanted, and spend his entire life trying to bring her joy and safety. He'd give her all the children she wanted and love them unconditionally. It was only her he couldn't love.

Serena couldn't hold that against him. She understood his pain, his fear. She understood his need to protect himself from grief and loss. And because she loved him, she accepted that part of him, too, refusing to try to change who he was to better suit her wishes.

It hadn't been part of her plan to love him, but there was nothing she could do to stop herself. He might never love her back, but she didn't care about that right now.

All she could think about was saving the life of the man she didn't want to love, but loved anyway.

With a roar of defiance, she grabbed Morgan's hand. She issued a silent command that she sent directly into his mind. He was to give back what was rightfully hers—everything he had to offer. The power he carried was hers and she demanded that he give it back.

He obeyed. Even confused and stunned, he opened himself up, and poured himself into her without hesitation.

Power raged beneath her skin. It sizzled and sparked along her limbs. It surged around her, striking out at every demon it touched.

They fell back, fear and confusion haunting their huge, red eyes.

"Run!" she bellowed, infusing her voice with the ring of absolute authority. The sound was grating and guttural. Completely alien.

Rock walls cracked around them at the force of that single word. The ground shook. Dust rained down.

Daylight demons flew away from her as if an explosion had hit and flung them back. They couldn't scramble to their feet fast enough to flee, which made them claw and bite at each other to get away from the threat.

Serena didn't stop the flow of power. She sent it out

further, seeking enemies in the darkness. She sent it to that
glowing cavern where the abomination lay, birthing more of
her enemy every minute.

She was one with her power, part of it, seeing what it saw,
feeling what it felt. She could see through its many eyes as it
wove through the system of tunnels and caves, destroying all
it touched.

Gray flesh split as she passed, tearing away from bones.
Thick slabs of gore splattered against stone walls as demons
were turned into pulp.

When she reached the cavern that housed the giant larva-
like creature, she tore her way through it as well, sending
gouts of glowing fluid splashing against the ceiling. Like a
thousand swords, her power cut through the beast, until no part
larger than her hand remained.

Slowly, the faint, green light winked out. There was no
more movement, no more life.

The abomination was dead.

Her power continued through the caves, seeking more
enemies to slay. There was one area that she couldn't
penetrate—as if something were keeping her at bay—but the
rest of the cave was now her domain. After a few seconds,
there were no living daylight demons left in sight, either here
near her or anywhere else her power resided.

But it didn't matter. Serena didn't have the strength to drag
one man out of these caves, much less two. Even if she did,
Link's injuries were bad. Morgan's were worse. She could
slow the bleeding with her gift, but she didn't know if she
could buy him enough time to get him help—not in the middle
of the day when the Sanguinar were weak and sleeping off the
effects of the sun.

Morgan collapsed to his knees, and Serena wasn't fast
enough to stop him.

Link's unconscious body slid from his shoulder and hit the
sword sticking out of Morgan's back. The blade shifted,
allowing blood to flow freely and wet his clothing.

Panic unlike anything she'd ever felt before closed in

around her, as stifling and unbreakable as her prison had been.

He couldn't die. She couldn't let him die.

She was shaking with weakness from the magic she'd wielded, but refused to relent. Now was not a time to give up.

Morgan would never have given up on her. She knew that without a single hint of doubt.

From somewhere deep inside her—some hidden reserves—she found the strength to keep going.

Serena shoved down her panic with a force of will that would have made even her mother proud. She calmed herself enough to think, then used her gift to slow time inside his wound. The bleeding had all but stopped, but there was little else she could do.

Panic quivered, as if ready to spring again, but she tamped it down and forced herself to think.

"Save…yourself," Morgan whispered.

"I'm not leaving you. Either of you." Though how she was going to get them out, she had no idea.

Then an idea hit her—one that turned her stomach and made her want to cower and rage all at the same time.

Could she do that to him? To both of them?

Serena wasn't sure, but there was no more time for her to come up with a better idea. She had to act. Now, before they were both dead and lost forever.

She had only one play she could make—one chance to save them. She didn't know if it would work or if either man would forgive her if she failed, but she had no other choice.

She bent her head and gave Morgan a quick kiss on his lips. She thought about the hundred things he'd done for her in the short time they'd been together—how he'd risked his life for hers over and over, how he'd put himself in danger to keep her safe. She thought about his honorable spirit and his utter devotion to the woman he loved. She thought about how selfless he was, how he always thought about her and others before himself. But mostly, she thought about what her world would look like without him now that she'd found him.

He wasn't Iain. He was better. Braver, stronger, more

loyal. Her life had been fuller in the few days since she'd met Morgan than it had been in all the long years before combined. Including the years with Iain.

Morgan was everything she could have wanted in a mate, everything she could have hoped to find.

Her mother would have hated him, but that was just another added bonus as far as she was concerned.

"I love you, Morgan, and I will never abandon the man I love. I will come for you. Do you understand?"

He frowned at her, confused, but there wasn't time to explain.

Those shrill demon cries had started up again from somewhere her power hadn't reached. She knew there were only a few moments left before the horde descended on them again.

And this time, she didn't have the strength to destroy them.

Serena stood, picked up her sword and pulled in as much of Morgan's power as she could stand. When she was sure she had enough, she encased the men in a bubble the way her mother had done to her and tethered them to the nearest Sentinel Stone.

One second, they were there in the cave with her, the next, there was a pale blue streak of light that knocked her out of the way as it sped past.

The men were gone, imprisoned as she'd been.

As the magic fled her body, she was left so weak she couldn't stand. Her frame vibrated with exhaustion, only now, she could no longer pull strength from Morgan to replenish herself.

She was just a girl, powerless and alone, with only her flagging strength and her sword to rely on.

Somehow, she had to make it out of this cave alive, before the charging demons arrived. Because if she didn't, those two men would spend eternity trapped together, with no one alive who knew they needed to be saved.

CHAPTER TWENTY-NINE

Jackie was split into too many pieces.

Some of her was inside Iain, holding onto him and his power like a lifeline. Some of her was in her body, struggling not to scream from the pain of labor. Some of her was out in the world, searching for each light and the location of the woman emitting it. And then there was another part of her, a small, desperate part that was with her child, whispering to her to help her mama, to help these poor women who already needed her to be strong.

It wasn't fair to ask anything of her baby, but if there was one thing that Jackie had learned in the two years she spent in those caves, it was that life was horribly, terrifyingly unfair.

It wasn't fair that these women were in danger and didn't even know it. It wasn't fair that Dabyr had fallen and there was no safe place for any of them to go. It wasn't fair that demons needed their blood to survive. It wasn't fair that their men had suffered in pain for centuries with no hope of any relief or companionship.

It wasn't fair to beg an unborn child to step into her duties before she'd even taken her first breath. And yet Jackie had no choice.

She conveyed all of this to her daughter, praying she'd find a way to make her understand without scaring her. She sent waves of comfort and love along with her request for help.

What kind of help, Jackie wasn't entirely sure, but Sibyl had been clear that the baby was the key to finding those women.

With her body in torment and her mind spread thin, she struggled to connect herself to any specific light—she didn't even care which one. They were scattered and out of reach, almost like they were evading her grasp every time she tried to grab one.

As another grueling contraction wrapped around her, the lights seemed to dim and grow distant.

Desperation pounded at Jackie like giant fists, making demands on her to hurry, to figure out what to do.

But she didn't have any answers. She was too tired, too terrified, too distracted. Concentration was impossible. She couldn't even stop herself from screaming—not even to save the children in the warehouse from being afraid.

"You have to freakin' push," Madoc said. "You can't wait any longer. It's not safe."

He was right. She knew he was. The need to push was overwhelming. Instincts were screaming at her that there was no more time to wait.

Her baby had to come first.

As she realized she'd failed, Jackie mourned for those women and their glowing lights. She had to let them go. She couldn't risk her baby to save them. She wouldn't, even if it meant Dabyr fell and hundreds died. She'd easily trade all of them for the tiny child struggling to be free of her body.

She loved her daughter so much. Even though she'd never set eyes on her, even though she had no idea what her personality would be like, she loved that little girl with everything she had in her.

Let the world burn so long as her baby was safe.

"Okay," she said, her voice weak and breathless. "I'll push."

"On the next contraction," Madoc said, sounding relieved. "Help her, Iain."

Iain shifted closer and put his arm around her shoulders.

The lights in her vision began to dim as if they knew she was letting them go. A deep sense of loss gripped her, but there was no more she could do. She'd failed them.

A tear slid from her eye. She didn't have the energy to spare those around her from witnessing her grief.

Iain squeezed her tight and molded his body close to hers.

He was still bearing some of her pain, muting it so that she didn't have to suffer through it alone.

She could not have loved him more in that moment. It wasn't possible. She was completely full, overflowing with gratitude and love for this man.

She relaxed into the bed to regain her strength for the battle ahead. She would have only a few seconds to rest, but she was going to use every one of them to prepare for the birth of her daughter.

Before the next contraction hit, she felt something shift inside of her. It was a strange sensation, like a small box being opened to let out something primal and bright. That feeling ricocheted inside of her, bouncing off her flesh and bones until it had streaked through every part of her.

The whole sensation lasted only a second, but when it was gone, she felt different.

Something powerful and pure was inside of her, part of her now.

Her daughter.

Jackie wasn't sure how she knew what was happening—some kind of instinct, she guessed—but she did. Their baby girl had opened herself up to give Jackie access to her strength, her gifts and talents. The child couldn't possibly understand what they were or how to use them, but Jackie had told her how important her job was, how much she needed help. And their baby had responded.

Before she lost this last chance to find those women, Jackie flew out of herself once more in search of the lights.

They were so bright they nearly blinded her. It was as if she'd been blind before, but her eyes were fully functioning now and able to see everything at once.

She saw a woman in a salon putting highlights in a blonde's hair. She was in Omaha, Nebraska. Jackie could read the name and address of the place on the label of a magazine in the waiting area.

Excitement filled her, driving out all the pain and fear she'd been feeling before. She shouted what she saw and silently begged Iain to start writing it down.

Next, she saw a tall redhead crouched in a shipping container, hidden behind boxes to sleep. Her long body was folded up, dirty and shivering. As soon as Jackie saw her, her eyes opened as if sensing her presence.

"Who's there?" the woman demanded in a harsh whisper.

"A friend," Jackie said, though she wasn't sure if her voice carried to wherever she was.

The woman stood and pulled a long knife from her belt. "I don't have any friends."

"You do now. Where are you?"

The woman scoffed. "Show yourself and maybe I'll tell you."

Jackie didn't have time for this. She could already feel the next contraction getting closer as the seconds ticked away.

She backed out of the storage container and found a sign. She was in a railway company's intermodal terminal in Memphis. Then she found the number on the container the woman was in. Sure, she could relocate, but at least this was a starting point.

Jackie went from light to light, finding every detail she could. In some cases, she even had names and addresses. She blurted it all out, hoping Iain wrote it down or Madoc put it in that vault he called a mind.

The process took another three contractions, but by the time she was done, she'd touched every light there was to see. One by one they winked out, satisfied that she'd done her job.

Now that she was no longer blind, she could see the concern on the faces of the men. Iain's arm was covered in scribbles. Madoc was scowling.

"Can we have this freakin' baby now?" he asked.

Jackie nodded and then went to work.

She pushed twice and cleared her daughter's head. Twice more and the rest of her was born. She was screaming bloody murder, but the sound was the most beautiful, musical thing Jackie had ever heard.

CHAPTER THIRTY

Serena ran faster than she ever had before. Her legs trembled with every step, her lungs ached from expanding too wide, too fast. Her mouth was dust dry. She was so dizzy she kept bumping into rough cave walls.

Still, she ran.

Her only thought was that if she didn't get out of here alive, Morgan would be trapped forever, doomed to live on endlessly in the same prison that had nearly driven her mad.

With each step, she heard the excited grunts and howls of demons growing closer. She didn't know where they'd been hiding before—possibly behind that magical blind spot she'd encountered earlier.

While it hardly mattered how they'd hidden from her, what did matter was that there was something else down here with them—something powerful enough to protect them from her magic.

She didn't care what it was. There was no more strength left in her to fight whatever it was. If she lived through this, then she'd come back another day and finish her work.

But not today.

Up ahead, she saw the welcoming glow of daylight. The sight buoyed her spirits and gave her a little burst of strength to make it up the last steep incline to the cave entrance.

Cold, dry air sucked away her breath. Weak, winter

sunlight hit her face. The clean smell of nature filled her nose, so welcome she felt her eyes fill with tears.

She'd made it out into the sun, but she wasn't alone.

Demons were right on her heels.

She heard them howl in excitement as soon as they caught sight of her. She spared one quick glance over her shoulder only to see that they were almost within fighting distance.

There were too many of them for her to fight. If she'd been at full strength, with access to Morgan's power, maybe she would have taken on so many, but not now.

There were dozens, perhaps hundreds. They poured out of the mouth of the cave, swatting and biting at one another to get to her first.

Morgan's big, white truck sat only a few yards away. It was unlocked. The key was inside. All she had to do was push the start button and get out of here before the demons reached her.

She wasn't sure if she was going to get that lucky.

Morgan was no longer with her. She'd been cut off from him the moment he'd been swept away in that bubble. Still, he'd left an imprint within her—a little space hollowed out just for him. She knew that if he could reach her, he'd give her encouragement, strength and courage. She knew that he'd have total faith in her ability to do what must be done.

Because of that, she knew she would.

Serena raced over the frozen ground, using her natural gift to speed her along. As weak as she was, her power faltered over and over, but she kept trying, kept reaching for whatever scrap was left within her.

She reached the door of the truck and ripped it open.

Behind her, a wall of gray closed in.

If they reached the truck, they'd shred the tires and destroy her one chance to get away.

She punched the button. The truck started with a growl, as if eager to be of service.

She had to sit forward in the seat to reach the pedals, but there was no time to make adjustments now.

With a hard shove of the gear shift, she put the truck in drive and smashed down the accelerator.

The truck took off with a lurch that sent her sliding back in the seat. Her foot lifted from the gas pedal and the truck slowed over the uneven ground.

In the rearview mirror, she saw that wall of gray swarm and seethe, growing wider and wider with every passing second.

Two demons reached the truck before she could get it moving again. They leapt into the back and began hacking at the glass with heavy swords.

Serena shoved her foot down again, mashing the pedal as far as it would go. She braced herself with the steering wheel so she wouldn't lose her footing, but the demons weren't so lucky.

One of the demons fell out of the bed of the truck. The other dropped its sword, but held fast.

It still had claws sharp enough to wreak havoc if she didn't dislodge it.

The ground here was pasture, left to go to seed. The grass was long and hunched over in the cold. The blades hid dips and ruts in the ground which heaved the truck every time she shot over them.

Her teeth snapped together. Her arms felt like they were going to rip out of their sockets. It was all she could do to hold on and not slide back in the seat.

The demon punched through the shattered glass of the back window and reached inside.

It would only take one to kill her. And if it didn't do the job—if it merely slowed her down—there were many more to finish her.

Serena turned the wheel hard to the right in an effort to send the monster flying.

It grabbed hold of the hole in the broken glass. As its body jerked sideways, it ripped the hole in the sticky glass larger.

Large enough for it to crawl through.

Her mind raced for a way to stop it. She couldn't turn

around and fight, because doing so would mean taking her foot off the accelerator. She could throw her sword at it, but she doubted that would do more than nick the tough-skinned creature. She had no gun, no projectile weapons.

There was only one thing she could think to do.

At its heart, it was an animal, a demon, hungry and desperate for her blood.

She was going to let the thing have it.

She pushed the button to roll down the window, then used her teeth to rip a hole in her wrist.

Pain flew up her arm, but she ignored it.

She shoved her arm through the open window and let her blood fly out on the wind.

The demon smelled it. She saw the moment it did, the way it went still and began sniffing.

The scent of her blood was on the air slipping around the truck. The monster followed that scent as it poked its nose over the side of the bed, sniffing like a dog.

Serena didn't hesitate. Using one hand, she turned the wheel of the truck hard to the right—hard enough that she sloshed around in her seat.

The demon tilted off balance and fell over the side of the truck. It scrambled for purchase, but was unable to stop its body from careening out of the bed.

She watched as a blur of gray skin rolled behind her, as the horde on her tail overran it. Some of them stopped to lick her blood from the ground, but most of them kept chasing her.

She pulled her bleeding wrist inside the cab and closed the window.

The gate to the pasture was up ahead, open and ready for her exit.

She raced through it, out onto the gravel road.

A heavy sense of relief threatened to overwhelm her. She sagged in her seat until she felt the truck slow, then straightened back up again.

Serena had gotten out alive, but that was only half the battle. She still had to find a way to save Morgan.

CHAPTER THIRTY-ONE

I love you, Morgan, and I will never abandon the man I love. I will come for you. Do you understand?

He didn't. Nothing made sense to him. He couldn't see the cave walls, or hear the demons screaming. There was no pain from the sword that had impaled him, and no smell of blood and filth. No air moved around him. Everything was still and silent.

He was...nowhere.

And yet, he wasn't alone. Link was here—at least he thought so. He could smell the man's aftershave and sweat nearby.

There was someone else, too. Someone he knew. Someone sweet and feminine.

"Serena?" he said, only his voice made no sound.

He tried to reach her though their link, but it was gone. She wasn't part of him anymore.

He was alone, untethered. Empty.

Despair and grief grabbed hold of him and didn't let go. They fought over him like demons did scraps of meat, shredding him with their teeth until there was nothing left but useless ribbons.

He mourned the loss of his connection to Serena as strongly as he would have if she'd died. Maybe she had. Maybe they'd all died in that cave, and this nowhere was all that was left of them.

"You're not dead," came a woman's voice. "Just stupid."

He opened his eyes to see who'd spoken. All around him was shimmering light. He could see Link lying unconscious a few feet away, but no one else was here.

Was he dreaming?

"If it were a dream," the woman said. "I would be naked."

Femi. He realized now that was the voice of his late wife. But where was it coming from?

He couldn't see anything but Link. Wherever he was, it was light, but there were no lamps, no sun. He was surrounded by a globe that shimmered, but there was nothing beyond it. No trees, no sky, no cave, no nothing.

"The more important question is why am I here?" Femi asked.

He reveled in her voice, in the sweet sound of her youth. Gone was the cracked tones of age, and in their place were dulcet strains of music. And irritation.

Why would she be irritated with him?

"I don't even know where here is. Why can't I touch you or see you?" He kept looking around for her, but saw nothing.

He tried to stand but couldn't. His body was too weak. He could barely keep his eyes open.

Morgan looked down. A rusty blade stuck out of his body, covered in his blood.

Panic gripped him then.

"Be calm," Femi's voice said. "You can't see me because you're not dead. Yet. Your woman trapped you between life and death to give her time to save you."

Time to save him? That didn't make sense.

Until it did.

Serena had slowed time for him so he wouldn't bleed out. But if that was the case, then where was she? Why couldn't he see her, feel her?

"I don't understand," he said.

"No. You don't," said Femi, her tone curt. "Why are you hurting that poor girl?"

"Hurting her? I'm not." At least not intentionally.

His eyes drifted closed. He was so tired. He needed to rest and heal, but he couldn't slip away yet, not while Femi was near.

He wanted to be with her. But he wanted to be with Serena just as much.

How could one man want two things so badly when he knew he could never have either of them?

"Then why are you hurting yourself?" Femi asked.

"What are you talking about?" he asked, confused.

She appeared to him then, darkly beautiful, young and heartbreakingly perfect.

He tried to reach for her, but his body refused to move.

Her big, brown eyes settled on him, stern but kind. He remembered how she could do that—how she could straddle two separate things so effortlessly.

How many other small details about her had he forgotten? How many other bits of her had he lost with time?

Even one seemed like a huge betrayal of her. He should have kept all of her in his mind, every tiny aspect. They were all important, all part of who she'd been. How could he have let even one part of her go?

Morgan's heart squeezed at the thought.

She shook her head. Long, glossy hair swayed around her shoulders. "You are using my memory as a justification for killing yourself slowly, and I don't like it."

"I am not."

She lifted a black brow in question. "No? Then why won't you love Serena? I know you are capable. I lived a lifetime filled joy because of how deeply you can love. Why do you hold back now?"

He couldn't lie to her. Not to Femi. "Because the risk is too high. I gave you everything I had to give. When you died, you took it all with you. I have nothing left for Serena."

Femi's musical laugh echoed in this nowhere place. "Love is not a single cup of water, but a boundless ocean no one man could empty."

"And the pain of loss?" he asked, angry that she was using what little time they might have together now to talk about another woman. "Is that not a boundless ocean as well? I nearly drowned in grief when you died. How can you ask me to go through that again?"

Her voice was a gentle ripple of sound that stroked his skin. He wished she'd come closer, wished she'd touch him again.

"I am not the one asking you to take risks. You fight only yourself."

Morgan was losing his mind. That had to be what this hallucination was.

He missed Femi so much. The pain of carrying his dying luceria was nothing compared to the agony he'd endured when she'd died.

How could he ever ask himself to willingly go through that again with another woman?

The job of a bonded pair of Theronai was not just risky, it was dangerous. Their lifespans were long, but they weren't immortal. His kind died all the time. He'd lost enough friends and family to know that all too well. One well-placed blow, one sneaky demon, one random accident—any of that could take Serena from him.

Once they were completely bonded, he wouldn't survive her death for long, but even a few moments of the loss he'd endured with Femi was too much risk to take.

What if in the end, he loved Serena more? What if their elongated lives, shared experiences, or the magic of the luceria bound them together even tighter than he had been bound to Femi?

That would be the ultimate betrayal.

Her voice was a soft breeze of sound. "Loving Serena more does not mean you loved me less. You gave me everything you had to give. How could I ever feel betrayed?"

"How could you not?" he whispered, already feeling ashamed that he'd even considered betraying her with Serena.

"If I had lived on after your death, would you have wanted

me to remain alone?" She touched his face then. Just one small, soft stroke of her hand on his cheek. He ached for more. Needed more.

Instead, she drew away.

"Never," he said instantly. "You deserve to be happy, even if it's not with me."

"There is your answer, love. Honor me with your happiness, not your grief. I am gone now, but you are not. Live, my love. Live your life to the fullest. That is what I want for you."

Morgan felt Femi's presence leave. It drained away like water through spread fingers.

Once again, he was left with a gaping hole in his heart where Femi had once resided.

She'd been his everything. He didn't know if part of her was still alive out there, somewhere, or if he'd made up the entire conversation. Dreamed it, hallucinated it in the throes of death.

All he knew was that losing Femi again tore him apart. It shook his foundation and left him reeling in grief.

He stayed in that dark place of loss, so familiar to him, for a long time. Tears streamed down his face and wet his bloody shirt.

His body was made of dull lead, numb and heavy. He couldn't even lift his hand to wipe away the tears wetting his face.

He wished Serena was here to hold him until the pain passed. His grief didn't hurt so much when she was around. He was too busy soaking in her sweet warmth and innate goodness. He was too consumed marveling at her quick mind and seemingly endless strength. He was too swept away by her selfless spirit and her ability to love despite what she'd suffered.

His mind ground to a stunned halt.

He didn't just want Serena around because he liked her. It was more than that.

Way more.

He admired her. He respected her.

He loved her.

As soon as the truth of that entered his mind, he felt free. The grief and sadness he'd carried for so long, the pain of losing Femi, seemed to lift from his body, from his mind. He could remember her clearly now—every lost detail, every mannerism, every quirk. Femi was whole and safe in his heart.

But she wasn't alone.

Serena was there, too. And somehow, he found that there was more than enough room inside of him to love them both. Not only that, but his sense of betrayal—his worry that loving Serena would somehow diminish his love for Femi—that was gone.

He felt free. Light.

A sense of elation filled him up, but a split second later, his world exploded in pain.

CHAPTER THIRTY-TWO

Serena promised more people more favors than she ever had before in her life. But in doing so, she'd managed to lure a small army of Sentinels away from Dabyr to do what needed to be done.

It was dark and cold outside. The makeshift group gathered near a stream on private land in the hills of southern Missouri. Low clouds obscured the stars and reflected the faint light emanating from her palm.

She was exhausted and sore, but the worst of her injuries had been healed already—at least the ones others could see. There were more wounds she'd carried out of that cave— mostly the horror of knowing what lurked inside. Those would take time to mend, though likely not as long as it would take to get over watching the man she loved get skewered.

Serena still didn't know if he was alive. His luceria hadn't fallen from her neck, but she hadn't been able to sense his presence or feel his power, either. She didn't know if that was because he was inside the stasis bubble she'd created, or because he was dead.

Even with time for him frozen in place, if he were dead, the luceria would have fallen off, wouldn't it?

No one seemed to know the answer to that question, no matter who she asked. Her kind of magic wasn't common. As far as they knew, she and her mother were the only ones ever able to manipulate time.

Tynan, Logan and Hope stood huddled together against the chill. The Sanguinar were brilliant healers. She'd exchanged more favors to make sure they were well fed and ready to work.

Serena had told them everything she could remember about both Morgan's wounds as well as Link's.

The Theronai Nicholas, Samuel, Neal, and his wife Viviana had spread across the surrounding area to watch for possible attack.

"Are you sure we're in the right place?" Nicholas asked. His scarred face was cast into gruesome relief by the moonlight. "We don't have any record of Sentinel Stones in this area."

"We also didn't have record of the one in Kansas City, either," Logan said. "Serena may have inadvertently offered us a gift. Perhaps we can use her gift to find more."

"Later," she said, though she knew she'd follow through with Logan's wishes. After this, that would be the least she would owe him.

She lifted her hand higher, searching for a sign of where the men were. No one could see or hear them. She was the only one with even a chance to find them. Well, she and Brenya, who was by all accounts, ensconced on another world, completely out of reach.

Serena's hand hit something warm. The tips of her fingers hummed with an energy she recognized.

"Morgan is here!" she cried. "Over here!"

The group coalesced on her location just as she figured out how to break the spell.

Two big, bloody men tumbled to the ground, unconscious. A rusty sword protruded from Morgan's body. As it shifted, blood welled up from the wound.

A split second later, the Sanguinar went to work.

***

Morgan woke in a bed in a gerai house he'd been to once before. He was thirsty, and his fuzzy head told him he was suffering the effects of Sanguinar healing.

The fact that he woke up at all amazed him. Almost as much as the woman sitting next to his bed.

Serena had saved their lives. He wasn't sure how, but there'd be plenty of time to hear the stories later. He had more pressing things to worry about now.

Sunlight spilled into the room, painting the walls with a golden glow. It was almost as lovely as she was, but not quite.

"What happened?" he croaked. His voice was low and rough. His throat was parched.

She offered him a glass of water, which he drained in one long drink.

She watched him, his big, dark blue eyes troubled. "I knew I couldn't get you and Link out alive, so I put you in a stasis bubble."

He frowned as he tried to digest her words.

"It swept you away as it had me, tethering you to the closest Sentinel Stone."

That's where he'd been in that nowhere place?

All the pieces started to click together. "Like your mother did to you," he said.

She nodded. Her expression was troubled, serious. "I knew if I died in that cave, you and Link would spend eternity together. As fond of him as you aren't, I also knew that if that happened, you'd never forgive me."

Morgan could not even think about how hideous it would have been to be locked away with a man he really didn't like all that much. Maybe they would have found a way to make it work, but then again…

He shuddered.

"The idea of your endless torment was the push I needed to make it out the rest of the way," she said.

"How did you manage?"

"I ran fast and didn't even try to take down any of the enemy as I went." She sighed. "There's quite a mess left to clean up, but at least now we know what the source of the daylight demons is."

"We'll go back and finish the job right. Once I'm able to stand up without help."

"Joseph dispatched other warriors to search for more of those abominations. The daytime attacks on Dabyr have diminished substantially. They're finally making progress on the wall."

He offered her a weak smile. "Let's hope they save some for us. I have some payback coming their way after the scar those things gave me."

She didn't return his smile, but she did offer him something.

Serena held out her hand, and curled in her palm was his luceria. The rainbow of colors inside of it were still and lifeless, as if she'd never put it on. "This is yours. It fell off once you were out of stasis."

It would have only fallen off if he'd died, which he hadn't, or if she'd chosen to leave him.

Hot pain punched his heart as he realized what had happened.

"You're done with me?" he asked as he scanned her throat for signs of Link's luceria.

Had she chosen the other man after all? Had she gotten tired of Morgan or decided that he wasn't worth the effort?

She opened her mouth to speak, but he couldn't risk hearing the words that might come out of her now. He couldn't bear the idea of losing her.

"I won't let you go that easily," he said.

He sat up in the bed, though the effort left him panting and weak.

"I spoke to Femi."

Serena gasped. "What?"

"She was there, in that nowhere place you sent me."

"That's impossible."

Morgan knew it wasn't. He'd felt Femi, smelled her, seen her.

"She was there," he insisted.

Serena nodded as if she understood, but then she said. "You want me to send you back, don't you?"

"What? No." He hadn't even thought about that.

Though now that he did…. Was Serena right? Could she send him back there and let him live forever with Femi? And if it was possible, was that even what he wanted?

He knew after only a moment that it wasn't.

Morgan took Serena's hands in his. They were cold, trembling. Tears welled in her eyes, but her innate stubbornness kept them from falling.

"I loved Femi with everything I had in me. I devoted myself to her entirely. When she died, I died."

Serena's head fell in defeat. "I understand."

He lifted her chin with his finger. "No, you don't."

"I don't want to hear anymore. Please, Morgan. Just let me send you back."

"No."

Her luminous gaze hit his.

"I don't want to go back. I want to stay here with you. I want to bind myself to you so tightly you can never slip away. I want to be your partner, to raise our children together. I want to fight and laugh and live by your side for the rest of my days."

She frowned in confusion. "But—"

He laid a finger over her lips and enjoyed the silky softness of her mouth to the point of distraction. He wanted to kiss her so badly, his entire body ached.

The next time he took her, he was going to show her just how much he had to offer her, how good the two of them could be together. He was going to give her more pleasure than any man had ever given any woman. And then he was going to do it all over again, just to prove he could.

When he was done loving her body as much as he did the rest of her, she'd never again question whether or not she belonged by his side.

He levered himself up to sit on the edge of the bed,

because there were simply some things a man didn't do lying down.

Pledging his undying love to a woman was one of them.

He took her slender hand in his. "I love you, Serena. I didn't think it was possible to love again, and even if it was, I didn't want anything to do with loving another woman after Femi." He held her gaze, willing her to see inside of him the way she would if he convinced her to take his luceria again. "But I'm not afraid anymore. Whatever happens, you're worth the risk."

"Is this your way of thanking me for saving your life? Because if it is—"

He pulled her onto his lap. "When I thank you for that, I'll do it by giving you screaming orgasms until you're too hoarse to speak."

She blushed, which made her even more beautiful. "Oh. Well. I guess I can accept that currency."

"I think we've proven that." He opened her hand and took the slippery length of the luceria from her grip. "What do you say? Want to give this another go?"

"What would you promise?" she asked, her voice small and uncertain.

"I think I'd start with promising to love you forever and see where we go from there."

Tears made her eyes luminous. "I love you, too, Morgan. So much I don't think forever is going to be enough."

He smiled and kissed her lips. "I guess we'll just have to try it and see."

CHAPTER THIRTY-THREE

Days later, after Serena bound herself permanently to Morgan, after the colors of the luceria had settled into a rich, ruby red, and his lifemark had budded with a fresh batch of leaves, it was clear that her discovery of the source of the daylight demons had turned the tide of battle.

Teams had been dispatched in all directions to destroy the source of the demons, leaving daytime once again the domain of the Sentinels.

Serena didn't know how long the reprieve would last, but for now, they were safe again—at least when the sun burned high in the sky.

Another team was sent back to the cave where Link had seen the toddler. They scoured the system of caverns and tunnels, but there was no sign of either the child or the creature raising him, the one calling itself Vazel. Everyone had been put on alert to watch out for the boy, but the chances of finding him were slim.

The walls of Dabyr were swiftly going back up, though there were still nightly attacks that threatened the compound. But with time to rest and heal between battles, the Sentinels were once again holding their ground.

Soon, Dabyr would be restored.

The joy of new love filled Serena to bursting. Every day she felt a deep sense of gratitude and belonging, a deep sense of purpose. She was right where she belonged, doing what she'd been born to do.

She was still growing into her newfound power, but she could already see her future self as deadly and terrifying to their enemy as her mother had been.

It was strange how she could now think about Gertrude Brinn without anger. If not for her mother's overbearing nature, Serena might never have met Morgan. She might have taken an entirely different path.

Perhaps one less joyful.

There was no way to know for sure, but she found it was easy to forgive her mother now and wondered what things she might do to protect her own children that they would find horrible and unfair.

Serena smiled as she lifted Iain's newborn child from his arms.

The shelter was bustling, but the residents had all agreed that the infant deserved her own space to sleep. There were whispers that giving her one of the private offices had been as much about protecting the sleep of others from her tiny cries at all hours as it had been about helping the baby sleep.

Iain's daughter was perfect and tiny, barely any weight at all. She smelled like the color pink might, of hope and innocence.

Morgan was by Serena's side, though he gave her the space she needed right now to come to terms with her emotions.

Jackie was glowing with pride and joy. Iain was strutting around, all puffed up and overprotective.

Serena cradled the child she'd thought of as stolen from her—the one she thought she'd have with Iain. And yet, instead of jealousy or resentment, all she felt was happiness. This child represented their people's future, their hope. How could she not be happy to be holding such a wonder in her arms?

Once day soon she'd have a child of her own—Morgan's child—but for now, this little bundle of hope was enough to satisfy her. More than enough.

Her time would come, but not yet.

Serena still had work to do before she could become a mother. There were still abominations out there to destroy, still a stronghold to rebuild.

"She's beautiful," Serena told the proud parents.

They both beamed in agreement.

"And strong," Jackie added. "I never realized how strong something so tiny could be."

"We're sure as hell not sending her into battle anytime soon," Iain said. "Maybe never."

The women exchanged a look filled with rolled eyes and shared experience.

They'd both loved the same man, after all. If that didn't give them common ground, nothing would.

"She'll go into battle when she's ready," Jackie told her husband, "and there won't be a thing you can do to stop her."

Serena admired the woman even more in that moment. And surprisingly, she was relieved that Iain was no longer hers to deal with. That joy and that burden belonged to another.

She was free to be with Morgan, and that alone was more than she ever could have imagined for herself. She'd had no idea a person could hold so much joy without exploding, and yet every day, she swelled and grew to hold more.

"She'll grow up too fast like all children do," Serena said. She leaned low and whispered in a voice meant for the child's ears alone. "But not too fast, little one. If I have my way, there will be no enemy for you to fight by the time you're grown. I will have killed them all."

Morgan slid his arm around her shoulders. He was linked to her so tightly, there were no secrets between them, not even ones whispered to babies.

He grinned down at her. "A woman like you always gets her way."

She winked at him and said silently through their shared link, *You didn't mind last night when I had my way with you.*

She could hear laughter in his tone. *And I won't mind*

tonight, either, love. Do your worst. I'm man enough to take it.

Yes, she whispered across his mind, her tone filled with equal parts love and lust. *Yes, you are.*

We hope you have enjoyed this installment of *The Sentinel Wars*! Please take a moment to leave a review online. Your feedback makes a difference.

ABOUT THE AUTHOR

Bestselling author Shannon K. Butcher, who now writes as Anna Argent, has written more than thirty-five titles since launching her career in 2007. She has three award-winning series, including the paranormal romance series *The Sentinel Wars,* the action-romance series *The Edge,* and the romantic suspense *Delta Force Trilogy.* Her alter ego Anna Argent also writes several series with a fresh and interesting spin on paranormal romance (*The Lost Shards*, *The Taken* and *The Stone Men* series) as well as a contemporary romance series set in a small town in the Ozarks. As a former engineer and current nerd, she frequently uses charts, graphs and tables to aid her in the mechanics of story design, world building and to keep track of all those colorful characters, magical powers and alternate worlds. An avid bead and glass artist, she spends her free time turning small sparkly bits into larger sparkly bits. She's rarely on social media, so the best place to find out news about upcoming releases under either name is via her newsletter. You can sign up at AnnaArgent.com.

BOOKS BY ANNA ARGENT
(Also writing as Shannon K. Butcher)

THE LOST SHARDS
Shards of Blood and Shadow
Shards of Light (in The Secret She Keeps)
A Brush with Fate
Sing Me to Sleep

THE TAKEN
Taken by Storm
Taken by Surprise
Taken by Force

THE WHISPER LAKE SERIES
The Longest Fall
The Sweetest Temptation
The Biggest Risk

THE STONE MEN
Made Flesh
Heart of Stone

CPSIA information can be obtained
at www.ICGtesting.com
Printed in the USA
LVHW030903250222
711994LV00007B/182